THE UNTYING

The Untying

A Drunkard's Journey
Part III
The Conclusion

By Martin Gibbs

ISBN: 978-0-9887121-7-1

Cover art by Karri Klawiter (arbykarri.com)

Also By Martin Gibbs

The Spaces Between: A Drunkard's Journey Part I

Dead Spaces: A Drunkard's Journey Part II

We Three Kings

With Arthur Graham:

Voltaire's Adventures Before Candide (and Other Improbable Tales)

Voltaire's Excellent Adventure: The Broken Boarder

This one is for Mom.
Thank you for encouraging me to believe in myself, to stick it out for the long haul, and for sacrificing so much of yourself. And thanks for teaching me to clean up my own messes!

Contents

Map

After Zhy's visit to the Temple of M'Hzrut, Wrenflang collected the various charts, etchings, and other drawings and was able to create a revised representation of the world. Belden remained unchanged. New knowledge of the Spires and the Temple of M'Hzrut, however, required modification to the old map.

Prologue

"Why are we not in the final resting place?"

"Son, you've made a terrible mess."

I sighed. Inside the void, I had a decent view of the multitude of souls that wobbled between death and permanency. "I'm sorry, mother, I wish I had known..."

"You were blinded by him, blinded by power and allured into a false freedom from your simple mind."

Simple. Yes, simple. I had been that, once. A boy who could count the stars but not lace a boot, or saddle a horse; a toddler in a young man's body. All that mattered was a spicy hot drink and my sutan—I could play chords with six- or ten-string instruments that no man had ever heard. But I frequently soiled myself at night.

"Bimb?" she asked me.

In the void, I "shook" my head: "What can I do? How can I help...? You were able to reach Zhy, is there anything I can do to find him? Help him?"

A slight shake of an incorporeal head. "Possibly, but only you can do that. Think on it, son, but don't think too long. You can only spend so much time here." Her face blurred as if she were being stretched out into the blackness beyond. "I—I can't hold out much more myself, the pull is too strong. Zhy has done well, very well, you owe him a lot."

I wanted to tell her that I wished Zhy were dead, but the emotion was gone, somehow smothered by the atmosphere. It felt stale in here, wherever *here* was—I had spent such a short time here earlier that I hadn't noticed—I was too busy trying to... trying to—my thoughts stopped there. *I had tried to kill my own mother!* I should not be here, of all places, I should be down beneath the earth, boiling and festering with the demons!

"I am sorry..."

"You now have one chance to make it up, but as I said you must be fast. This place is stagnant and that is intended to get you to leave as soon as you can. And for your sake I hope you can find a better place."

"But Lyn..."

"What about him?"

"He was with me for years..."

"Only several—in the span of things that is not long. You don't have years, I'm afraid, and surely Belden doesn't. I'd hate to think of you going to the final peace when you have left behind a world in darkness. And with all of those demons... I fear to think of the sadness should they enter this world."

"But... I don't understand."

"Several weeks have passed already, Bimb, though it feels only minutes to you."

"Mother?"

"Yes?" Her face was only a thin mirage, the rest of her almost already vanished.

"I love you."

"I love you, too, son."

And she was gone.

I thought long and hard of what I should do, but nothing came to the fore. Perhaps the suddenness of death and his realization of my actions had dampened my brain functions.

Zhy. His face floated before me. A dead man had killed me. How? My willingness to fix everything was quickly clouded by an irrational hatred for a town drunk. I'd let Ar'Zoth kill him, hadn't I? Yes, but then he came back and killed *me!*

Sacuan blast it all, I need to get out of here. This place was stuffy. No temperature, no movement of air. It was clouding my mind. How I missed the snow, and the wind and the—

I jerked in the dead space, my body shimmered with an odd luminescence. That was it! The snow... the snow, the cold, and the wind.

The wind!

Chapter 1

A Final Swirling in the Inner Depths

There are knots and there are knots. Tied and bound, intersecting and intertwining. Cloth woven upon cloth, creating a binding that is only undone by death. Untie the knots that are known. But first know where to start, for an end is a beginning is an end is a middle is a beginning again.

Prophet Altyu-M'Zhkara, IV Age

*B*ump.

Zhy squirmed. *What is that?*

A shuffling of feet, followed by a girlish squeal, had broken into his dreams. Dreams of murder and bloodshed; of a mad Knight of the Black Dawn invading the Holy Temple of M'Hzrut. Zhy's nightmare played, over and over—Orfel, standing in the doorway, burned by the cold, and screaming of demons. Heayar, Wrenflang, Fanlas, Sorchal, Zhy... so many men, and yet so few. In the dream they were powerless. Orfel slaughtered them all.

But that dream *had* been reality!

In the nightmare of memories, Zhy watched Wrenflang unload twisted magical fires, Huyen swinging his steel deftly in attack. The old Protector of this holy temple had added his deadly lightning to the battle. Smoke filled the room.

Why was Zhy still alive?

Zhy relived each second of the horror:

A severed head burning in the fire. A corpse coming alive on the dusty floor of the Temple, attacking against all reason. A demon.

Demons!

His mind replayed the previous events:

A bolt of green lightning arced from Orfel's hands, but Wrenflang was quicker, and a searing knife of purple flame severed the energy. The room erupted in a deafening explosion. Heayar scampered across the small space and quickly doused the flaming altar with a wave of his arms. Orfel attempted another spell against the old mage, but Wrenflang thrust out his arm and a purple swirling ball shot out, exploding in Orfel's chest. The Knight howled in agony as the violet-colored sphere spun, grinding into his midsection, burrowing deep under the skin. Eyes popped wide, the Knight clutched at the orb that was grinding into him, clawed furiously as he screamed—the ball soon vanished beneath his skin and there was a sudden sharp pop as his insides exploded into the room. The Knight's head, released from its connection to the body, lolled forward and landed on the charred floor of the Temple with a thud.

But even as the head rolled across the sacred flags of the Temple, its mouth worked in a contorted grimace, and lips moved of their own accord, mouthing "demon, demon, demon." Heayar moved to kick the head into the fire, but Huyen stopped him with a hand, reached out and grasped the bloody head by its slimy hair and held it aloft.

"Orfel!"

Bump.

There it is again.

He tried to push his eyelids higher, but they were caked with sleep. He listened again, half blind in the dusty storeroom. The dream returned, this time ending in a flash of heat.

Darkness.

His bed rattled, but Zhy kept his focus on the horror that had visited the holy Temple of M'Hzrut:

Huyen, tossing the head into the fire, didn't notice the headless corpse move of its own accord and attack! Too-long fingernails reached up and gouged his legs, ripping, tearing. They punctured through a main artery and Huyen only lasted a few minutes. Huyen!

No!

Huyen had called him Zhyfrael. The name of a long-dead Welcferian queen. An inept woman who invited the enemy into her palace and wondered dumbly why they slaughtered every last living creature. Zhyfrael. Now Huyen. Both dead.

"Dead!" Zhy muttered in his sleep. His savior. Killed senselessly.

The bed rattled again, knocking his teeth together. He uttered an oath as he came awake.

"Oh, sorry."

Who is that?

Zhy wiped the gunk from his eyes and pushed himself up to his elbows. He lay on a rickety cot in the storeroom. A few moments of blank confusion passed before he realized he was at the Temple of M'Hzrut. *At the Temple, and not in Belden. Thank Sacuan for that—and Sacuan help us all, it means the dream was real... Huyen is dead.*

Once more he rubbed tired eyes and tried to focus on the strange form that slunk through the room.

"Just looking for—ah! Here it is, sorry Zhy."

Sorchal! Zhy realized, watching the young man. Sorchal was one of the so-called Protectors who guarded this holy Temple. Once this place was thought to be the guard-post atop the demonic underworld, a symbol for peace and security of both Belden and Welcfer. Now, however, it had been revealed that it was nothing more than a symbol. The true portal to Hell lay hundreds of miles to the west—where Ar'Zoth had been. Where *Bimb* had been.

Bimb. A boy who had been born simple-minded, corrupted by a dangerous warlock named Ar'Zoth, and who had been guided to Ar'Zoth's keep, only to kill the warlock and take control of the castle. Except the castle stood atop a portal to the demonic underworld, a fact that had escaped every high-ranking official and Holy Elder for centuries.

Because of a mix-up in paperwork, Zhy recalled. How can something like that slip past everyone?

Ar'Zoth had killed Zhy there, too. Only Bimb's mother, in death, had rescued Zhy (using a demonic bat, of all things, to carry him home). And in true epic-story fashion, Zhy had killed Bimb. With help. With help from Huyen, who's corpse was now stacked out by the firewood.

"Be seeing you." Sorchal's girlish voice was followed by a blast of frigid air as he opened the rear door and stepped out into the snow.

Now where in the name of Sacuan's scrotum is he going?

He didn't have any intention of following the man, but something tickled the back of his mind: There was something odd about Sorchal, his girlish laugh and those darting eyes. What if he was a demon? What if he returned, sword in hand, as Orfel had?

Just go see what he's doing, a voice—Zhy's voice—whispered. It couldn't hurt. Even if Sorchal were a demon, at least Zhy could be a bump in his path.

"What am I doing?"

Still fuzzy from the dream, he made a decision that went against all reason. He would follow Sorchal.

Zhy shrugged into his coat, stuck cold feet into colder boots and ventured outside. Though it was several degrees below reasonable, the snow depth and the lush evergreens added a strange warmth to the scene. Far ahead, on the small path that led away from the Temple, Zhy could see the strange Protector.

Sorchal stopped and spoke, but didn't turn. "Why are you following me?"

Zhy's stomach buzzed. "I—"

"Never mind!" the Protector replied in a sing-song, high pitched voice. "I'm picking wintergreen!"

"I—"

"Would you like to help me?" Sorchal asked. Not waiting for a reply, he bounded down the evergreen-lined pathway, every so often bending low and poking his nose in the snow. Zhy turned his body to leave, but watched him for another half-minute; at one point the Protector stuck his whole face in the snow and popped up, singing.

"What a strange little man," Zhy muttered, then returned up the trail. Where would anyone find wintergreen in the winter? At this he paused and laughed. Perhaps Sorchal had gone insane. He didn't seem to be possessed. Zhy's exhausted mind tried to work through the possibilities: Maybe the man just wanted to be alone, or he really thought he could find wintergreen, or he was drunk, or—

"Drunk, that's it!" he blurted out loud, pausing in front of the snow-covered branch of a white pine. The taste of minty schnapps floated on his tongue; memories of cool Belden mornings flickered past—memories of Zhy outside his home, sipping, gulping, drowning. *I'm not going back to* that, he thought, whacking the branch for good measure. Snow sprayed in his face and he spat it out in disgust.

The taste of pine reminded him of yet another liquor, and he swore in frustration, stomping cold feet as he walked back to the Temple.

φ

His mind filled with pictures of bottles, Zhy stomped blindly into the main living area. He looked first at the altar, then the fire. Everything looked clean. A glance at the floor told him otherwise. The dark stain remained.

"Zhy, eat." Fanlas said around a mouthful of food, then returned to pick at steaming lumps of—something—on his plate. Wrenflang sat across from Fanlas at the table. The other Protector, the one called Heayar, had apparently returned to his meditation room beneath the altar.

The last time I woke up in my bed, having been brought there by a demonic bat, he thought, staring at the dark stain on the floor. *Now I awake but the nightmare lives.*

"What was that?" Fanlas asked.

Zhy shook his head. "I'm tired."

"We all are. Eat."

"And I'm not mad," he added. "Am I?"

"Who said you were?" Bimb's father asked. Each time Zhy looked at Fanlas, he saw Bimb's face... that once-innocent face, dying. Dying. *I killed your son!*

"Never mind. Maybe the world has gone mad and we're the sane ones. Which reminds me—" his brain kept darting through thoughts. "Orfel."

"Mad *and* possessed," Wrenflang stated.

Zhy coughed again and rubbed his eyes. The constant film from wood smoke was impossible to wash away, and combined with the thick glaze of sleep, his eyes burned all the greater. He couldn't tell any more if any of this was happening, or he still dreamed. If he were dreaming, then there were no consequences for poor decisions. Unlike his namesake, he had an excuse. *I'm already dead.*

"What other groups can help us?" Zhy wondered aloud. "If the Knights of the Black Dawn can turn so easily..." he trailed off. The stain of blood still sullied the holy Temple's floor. He shifted his weight against the frame of the altar. "Who else is out there?"

Wrenflang spoke. When he did, his bulbous nose seemed to jiggle on his face. Zhy tried to focus on the words, but the huge nose kept filling his vision. *Ugly Nose, Fanlas told me you were called... Ugly Nose.* "There are very few, Zhy." *At least he calls me—wait!* A thought struck him and he nervously thumbed his earlobe while the mage talked—though he heard nothing, apart from the word Protector and Counsel Guard.

"What is it?" Fanlas asked, sensing Zhy's impatience.

Zhy looked at Bimb's father and felt a wave of sadness. The man looked so much like Bimb, so much like the man Zhy and Huyen had killed. How could he sit there so peacefully? Regarding Zhy as an equal, when he knew fully that his son had died at the hands of a drunk? "Fanlas, my name. Zhy..." he didn't finish the name, they knew. Zhyfrael. "It reminds me of Welcfer. Can we get help from Welcfer on this?"

"On what?"

What else, Wrenflang, what else? "Help with the demons. If we are going across Welcfer anyway to—to deal with—" here he looked at Fanlas again, but the man was unreadable. "Deal with the demons at their source."

"That is the best thing I have heard from your mouth yet, *Zhyfrael,*" Wrenflang said. He cleared his throat, scratched beneath his collar. "It's the best and the craziest."

Zhy could have squealed like Sorchal. Someone had finally taken him seriously. Well, at least not dismissed him out of hand. Perhaps squealing would have been a bit much.

We are all crazy, Wrenflang.

"If we can find Welcferians, and I'm sure we can," Wrenflang said slowly, pushing his plate away. "We will do just that. And then we will tell them who you are."

Zhy's throat burned.

"And we will all laugh and march into battle holding hands," the mage added with a crooked smile he couldn't repress. Zhy stared for a few moments before laughing himself. What could you do, anyway? The world was going to drown beneath a slithering horde of demons, and, like the stories of his youth, its fate seemed more and more to depend on a small collection of men eating rotten turnips.

The old mage cleared his throat. "You've got a point, an honest one. Maybe this bloodshed has unlocked a few dead secrets within you. Do you suggest we seek out the Welcferian army?"

Is he suggesting that I really am *Zhyfrael reborn?* "No." Zhy scratched his head, then ambled over to the table. It seemed strange to stand there, talking down to these men. When he sat, he caught a whiff of the meal, and wasn't sure if the dead bodies had smelled worse, or this. "No, if I remember right, they are usually out hunting these savage tribes, right?"

Wrenflang nodded.

"And we're going to be crossing the Icedown Plains. If they don't kill us first, we can try to get their help. It sounds too simple, doesn't it?" he added this last hastily and pinched his ear between his fingers.

"It no longer matters," Wrenflang replied sadly. "Simple, or complex, we have to do something. You're right. They won't kill *us*... they may wonder, but they shouldn't harm us. Now, if we could get the native tribes *and* the Welcferians on our side..."

Fanlas chuckled, but Zhy didn't laugh. If they were accepting crazy ideas, he had one more. But for now he let it go. Instead, he grabbed a full water goblet, and drained it.

He tasted ale.

Chapter 2

Stay Smart – Stay Strong

How quickly we forget avenues we have left. Do we think them closed forever? Can we not ask the stranger another question? What harm is it to return to paths we have crossed?

Cleric Huyen, Order of the Knot

As the sun set gloomily over the roofs of Belden City, Rhys wandered into an inn for a bite to eat. He fell dejectedly into a rickety pine chair in front of a table that had once been round; now deep gouges marred its surface and edges. A serving maid informed him that chicken was the main meal, served with smashed turnips and a small plate of smoked fish, caught only yesterday. Rhys nodded and sipped some lukewarm ale while he waited for his food.

The sound of a chair scraping across the dusty floor caught his attention and he looked up to see a small-man setting himself down in front of him. "Good evening," the man said in a gravelly voice. Feeling pretty down are ye?"

"Down and... yes," he answered flatly. He wanted to say *down and defeated*, but he didn't want to quite admit that he had lost.

"Yes, I can see that."

A chair leg dragged across the sagging floor as another patron rose to leave. "I—I'm not sure I have the honor..." Rhys said softly.

The man smiled with bright green eyes. "The name's Felyar."

"Rhys," he replied, extending his hand. The small-man's grip was exceptionally strong, and his round eyes twinkled in the firelight.

"I've been to Forshen," the man said, "or rather what is left of it." He shook his head. "By now the Holy Orders here must realize the pillars, or Temple, or whatever it is called, have fallen."

"If not, they are very close to falling," Rhys admitted, dropping his voice. Who knew what spies that puffy and pompous Gorand had skulking in corners.

"Aye. Well I hope that at least some of the army or Guard will continue to fight."

"Indeed." Rhys sipped his ale and grimaced. He had never cared for the stuff, and it was a terrible substance at room temperature.

"If it weren't the middle of winter, perhaps even our—Welcfer's, that is—army could help out. But the harbor is probably frozen, and the way north is snowed in."

Rhys stared down into his ale. The food arrived and he only picked at the meat. Seeing the steaming plate, Felyar ordered the same and leaned back in his chair.

"You look like you need to be eating that, Rhys," Felyar said after a long pull on his ale.

Rhys nodded glumly and mechanically dropped a bite of chicken into his mouth. After a moment, he took a drink of ale and regarded Felyar. "I'm glad I'm not the only one who sees this destruction. But by now it's probably too late."

"We are still here, so it isn't too late."

"But what can I do? What could *you* do?" After a pause, he added. "No offense."

The small-man shook his head and grinned. "None taken. But I am a mage, after all, and perhaps I could—"

Rhys waved him off. "Please do not take offense, but we are talking about an invasion, and I'm sure you are strong, but we need more of you. Hundreds of you. Thousands of you. Warlocks—" he glanced around quickly, but nobody noticed. "Besides..." he began, shifting in his chair. Suddenly he was unsure of what this man's intentions were. Had the Holy Elders seen Rhys enter the Guard headquarters? Had they seen him with Gheren, and set him up? "Why are you telling me this?"

Felyar seemed to read the concern on Rhys' face. "I saw you go into the Counsel headquarters."

"You did?"

"Aye. I was trying to build enough courage to do the same, but never got it—I walked up and down that street perhaps a hundred times. By now the guards know me and there is no chance."

"But why?"

Felyar ignored the question. "Why did *you* go in there?"

Rhys sighed. "Our village had fallen victim to a demon. And then another. Soon the townspeople were getting ready to arm themselves and go on a wild hunt for anything that even resembled a demon. I warned them, and then I came here to warn those in charge."

"I see. It seems we both had the same purpose then."

"I don't follow." He did understand, and all too well... this could easily be a setup. Or a common thief trying to take advantage of the stranger.

"I had arrived from Vronga, thankfully avoiding the snows in the north. I watched as ugly beasts flew overhead, and saw fire after fire break out all along my route. That was enough for me, too... I thought at least someone from Welcfer would be able to have a way into the headquarters. A voice of an outsider they might listen to. But, aye, I did not have the courage to do so."

"They did listen to me—Gheren that is. And now—" Rhys stopped, poking absently at his meat.

"I see."

"Well, what do you suppose we can do about now?" Rhys wondered, picking up the mug of ale. "They may have listened to me in the past, but I seem to have been forgotten. Maybe Gheren or Horesh will have work again, but I doubt it."

"Horesh? Gheren?"

Rhys described his meetings with the Counsel Guard and the somewhat successful outcome, the limited and ignorant view of the holy Elders excepting. Felyar was impressed with the village teacher's ability to chat with high-ranking Counsel officials, though he snorted audibly at mention of the Elders.

"Cursed fools, the church," Felyar said bitterly. "What do they know of the struggles of men?" He ripped apart a chicken thigh angrily. "Why you Beldeners listen to them is beyond me."

"I stopped listening a long time ago," Rhys said sadly. "I go to the temple only to be with my fellow citizens and to offer some sort of alternative view. But our Elder at least knew what was happening. It's too bad the man at the top won't listen."

Felyar took a bite of meat and chewed slowly. He drained his ale, wiped his chin and planet two fists on the table. "What were you planning to do, Rhys?"

Rhys looked up from his plate. Harsh blue eyes were staring at him. "Do? What can we do?"

"Think man, you have access to the Guard... you can go back in there, ask around. Maybe we can learn something, or they can—" he pounded the table. "I don't know! But it's better than sitting here!"

"Felyar, how many times can I go back in there?"

"As many as you need to! What are you, a common messenger? Let's go in there."

Both of us?

Felyar read his expression. "Why not? There must be archives or something there we can—""

Rhys leapt to his feet, the chair sliding across the floor. A leg caught an awkward plank and slammed to the floor. *Archives!* "Archives," he whispered.

The Welcferian eyed him with curiosity. "Are you...?"

Stay smart, stay strong. "Let's go."

φ

To his surprise, the guard waved Rhys through. Once the two men entered the main hallway, however, they stopped in awe of the constant bustle of activity. Rhys shrugged and started down corridor after corridor, but every last man and woman was so saddled with activity that they achieved no answers.

An elderly voice rasped behind them. "Are you gentlemen looking for something, or someone?"

They turned as one to face the Keeper who had just exited from the door to the warren that led to the Archives. "I—I yes, I was working with Gheren, and now I, well—" Rhys stammered. *Stay smart, stay strong.* "I—"

"What work did you do with—ah, you must be—" he stopped suddenly, looked around. "Come, through here." He ushered them through the nondescript door and closed it softly behind him. "And who are you?" he asked the small-man.

"My name is Felyar."

"I see. Are things as bad in Welcfer as they are here?"

The man nodded. "I had been sent out to look for any other mages, and near the border with Gray Gorge I saw at least three gherwza... I was able to handle them." He looked nervously at Rhys, then back to the Keeper.

Why would he be nervous? "So you are a mage, then?" The Keeper wondered.

Rhys raised an eyebrow but Felyar turned to him. "Please, I didn't want you to think—think anything of me, like I was, well... available," he stammered. "In that way I mean."

"What are you talking about?"

The Keeper cleared his throat. "He was concerned that you would think him available for certain—services. Would you have known that he was a Welcferian mage, perhaps you would have thought differently." A bony finger scratched nosily at silver hair. "Although I don't know why."

Felyar nodded. "Sometimes, in our country, mages get too full of their powers and are... put into a different type of service so they still can earn a living..." he trailed off, his oddly-shaped face blazing crimson.

"Oh," Rhys said softly. He clenched and unclenched his fists, and repeated dumbly, "Oh."

"I am not like that!"

"I did not think you were," Rhys said after a moment.

"Gentlemen," the Keeper interrupted. "If you seek knowledge, if you seek to help Gheren—" he pointed at Rhys. "Then follow me." He turned to walk down the dusty corridor; a set of precarious looking stairs stretched downward ahead of them.

"Where are we going?"

"To the Archives, Rhys."

He gasped audibly in the narrow chamber. *It's too good to be true... The Archives! A treasure of knowledge and history, that very few get to see... stay smart, stay—* but his mind darted like a child's, so full of excitement and anticipation. The Archives! *Imagine all of the wonderful—*

"And here we are," the old man said, pausing before the large door. His desk was piled with odd papers and the lamp near the door frame was half full of oil. The door opened easily and the Keeper motioned them in, explaining the complex numbering system.

Rhys's head spun. "How—how can we possibly remember all of that?"

"You can't," the man said gravely, "Instead, I'll tell you where to look, or I could just tell you what you need to know."

Felyar stared, open-mouthed. "Then why—"

"The Tunnels of Woe, gentlemen, they will lead you..."

Rhys and Felyar stood open-mouthed as the Keeper explained to them the Tunnels of Woe, rather the single tunnel that led from Vronga into Welcfer. He even gave them the not-so-secret words used to open them and gain entry

"Why are you telling us this?"

The Keeper smiled at Rhys. "The world is being strangled. Let's cut knots where we can."

"But how do you know the demons are coming from the Tunnels?" Rhys wondered. Felyar still stood, exchanging wide-eyed looks between the vast collection of scrolls and the Keeper.

"I don't know. It was an idea.... it is for you to find out if I'm right."

"Then why show us this place, if you know? Or, think you know, that is." Rhys gestured at the massive room.

"Now you know where it is," The Keeper replied with a wink.

Rhys sucked in the damp air. *Stay smart, stay smart...* Again his mind was giddy. "Yes, I'd like to read a little... Felyar is that all right?"

"Aye," the small-man replied absently.

Rhys returned to the table and sat down. The papers were old, yellowed, and musty with time, and disjointed in the material that was covered. Each was of some subject seemingly unconnected to the other, but upon further review, Rhys could see the entire picture clearly. Jafren had figured it out, and most likely the Keeper... and had anyone else?

"You said something about another person having access before..." Rhys said, looking up from a ragged piece of parchment. "Could they have been responsible for this?"

He shook his head slowly. "No, that person has never left this city as far as I know."

"But he could have told another how to—"

"No, Rhys."

"But—"

"No, you will have to trust me."

He thought of protesting again, but dropped it. The point was not worth belaboring any further—even if the person had relayed the information, it was too late now, they had to act.

"What does all of this say?" Felyar asked, peering at the collection of papers.

"It is a sad, sad story," Rhys replied. "On their own, these papers tell us nothing. But put together they tell a terrible story. Awful." He leaned back on the rickety chair. "See, the Tunnels were built as a fast route to the Temple of M'Hzrut, with one exit by Gray Gorge. However, the builders also noticed that there were disturbances in the rock they were digging through. Every so often a builder would vanish, or they would find his mangled corpse. Pressed by the Holy Orders, the continued their work, sealing any holes or openings with rock. So when I read about demons here—" he pointed to a scroll. "The entire truth comes out. Someone or something has opened these disturbances within the Tunnels... it makes the most sense. The only other means of summoning demons is complicated and involves a rune, of which only several exist. So, it makes sense..." he pointed at the table. "That something has happened within the tunnels."

"And what can we do?" Felyar asked.

Rhys smiled at him. "Stay strong, as mother used to say. Stay strong, and stay smart... and you... you are a mage."

The Welcferian's pale complexion reddened considerably, and he cracked his knuckles. "You can't mean—"

"Yes, I do," he replied standing.

The Keeper took a look at him and smiled. "Thank you," were his only words as he vanished down another narrow hallway.

Felyar turned to face Rhys, his face still flushed. "You cannot mean that I... no! I only wanted to—"

"You only wanted to help, I know."

"Yes, but—"

"But what, Felyar, but what?" His voice was strained. "Did you think you could help by sitting?"

Felyar bit his lower lip. "I did not expect to fight demons."

Nor did I. Hearing the words aloud set Rhys's heart fluttering. He did not expect to have to be in the field, either, but he had offered. He had come all the way to Belden City to warn people—what else should be expected of him? "Felyar, I didn't either," he said with a sigh. "But we must do something. We've been given the answer—the Tunnels of Woe. If the demons are coming from inside the tunnel, do you think you can help close off these 'disturbances?'"

Felyar scratched his head. "I can do many things, Rhys," he replied softly. "I don't want to die, but it's better than the alternative."

The double meaning was lost on Rhys. Darrell had spent his life avoiding a most unenviable "profession" as a Welcferian mage: That of male prostitute. "We just need to stay smart."

"Smart won't work against a thousand demons!"

"Felyar," Rhys said, his voice hoarse. "I am just as scared as you are, if not more so. You are the mage, you have skills in magic. I know nothing apart from the best way to cut up a large fruit!"

The mage laughed. "Well, we make a pair, don't we? Do you still know where your Counsel Guard friends are?"

Rhys took in a lungful of musty air. "I hope so. Good idea." He took a last longing look at the scrolls and papers. "Let's go see if we can find Gheren and Horesh— even if they don't help us, maybe they have some resources."

Felyar sighed. "How many demons do you think we'd have to kill?"

"As many as we can." Rhys smiled grimly. "we have to do what we can. They may be none, a dozen, or hundreds. We have to do something! We have to kill them." *You have to kill them, Felyar.* "Or die trying."

"Or die trying."

The oil lamp sputtered, sending a plume of rancid black smoke into the air.

"Come on, I think I can find Horesh and Gheren."

Felyar followed the teacher from a small town. He nervously cracked his knuckles again and padded along behind him.

Chapter 3

What Now?

Around, around, around I go. A hundred things that must be done, but which first, and where to go? My mind spins and whirls, lost. If I had not filled it with uselessness, it would function properly.

Prophet Z'Hara

"What are your plans?" Gheren asked Horesh. Rhys had long since left the Counsel headquarters, probably to some inn or tavern, Gheren thought. The well-educated man from a small village had been smart and had given them suggestions that were actually useful. Now he was gone—to Sacuan knew where, and Horesh and Gheren paced the map room.

"I'll rustle up what Guards I can and then we'll start out—not sure in which direction," Horesh replied, knowing well which direction he intended. It just had to sound like he was truly thinking about it. Looking at the map with a scowl, he pointed at the eastern edge of Belden. The table creaked when he leaned against it. "Possibly there... near Darvein. I've already sent men along the Crown Road up through Vronga, but not many to the east."

"That is where Rhys is from, isn't it?" Gheren said, crossing his arms and looking at Horesh.

The Counselor nodded. "I've had some reports from there, which are... disturbing. We at least owe the man a little effort." There had been only two reports. Horesh dared not reveal this; Gheren would have to trust him. Rhys's home town only played a small part in his plan— he had a strange gut feeling that Darvein was a major source of activity. It was on the ocean and not far from Welcfer, either. *They could come from anywhere, but something about Darvein seems odd.*

"I agree. And what about your warlocks?"

Horesh took his eyes from the map. "We've been able to deploy them, surprisingly without incident."

Gheren raised an eyebrow. "That's convenient."

"Very. It helps that we didn't advertise the fact. People probably won't notice until they start going mad and killing—" *No, I won't act like that.* "I meant to say, that they will take whatever help they can get."

"We've worried too much about nothing, it seems."

"Warlocks are dangerous, or can be." They were crazy, the lot of them. Over-educated wielders of the most dangerous power, allowed access to their crushing powers simply *because* they had all that education. No wonder they went mad! But Belden needed every last warlock who wasn't completely lost. They needed every last man or woman, period. "What must be done."

Gheren muttered a muted agreement.

"It's going to take me some days to get to Darvein. The weather is a mess, and so is everything else." *I'll kill ten horses to get there.* Horesh squeezed the edge of the map table until his knuckles whitened, then released and exhaled. "I shouldn't dally around here."

"I have as many Counsel Guards as I can, the new ones, and recently retired, too. We've recalled everyone we could, and we have at least twenty thousand troops total on the move. Many remain on the main roads." He pointed to the map. "While some have ventured to the smaller towns and villages, those numbers are kept small." Gheren spoke, not looking at Horesh.

"My friend, I must go." First Jafren and now himself. He hated to leave Gheren alone, but one couldn't sit here and stare at a map! Maybe his companion would give it one more go at talking to the High Cleric.

"Do you think we can beat this?" Gheren asked over his shoulder.

Horesh stopped and stared at the peeling gilt paint on the door frame. "Maybe if you talk to Gorand... Just... try to convince him. Be nice. He's touchy."

"Touchy, or touched?"

At that Horesh chuckled. "Both."

"He seems like a blind fool, but perhaps I can cut out an eye and make him see."

"What in Sacuan's name does that mean?" Horesh wondered, a half-grin etched into his scruff.

Gheren chuckled. "Oh, it's some old saying or other I heard from a holy man once... not really sure myself what it means." He walked to the meager fire, looked into the tiny orange flames, then addressed Horesh. "*Can* we beat this?"

Horesh opened his mouth to speak, when the door opened and Rhys entered, a small-man at his side. The Teacher panted. He took a quick look at Gheren and Horesh, then walked to the map table, jammed an ink-stained finger on Vronga, and cried:

"I've got it!"

Chapter 4

A Cold Front

We associate death with cold. Cold skin, cold ground, and a coldness in our hearts. But sometimes death can be a great relief, when we are rescued from our pain, and freed from our misery.

Prophet Haran

I stared dumbly at my space—my dead space, that is. Mother and Lyn were able to pull people into their spaces, in a way, in order to converse with them. Before she passed on to her final place, Mother mentioned that I could try to leave my box, but it would not be easy, and I couldn't be guaranteed a way back. Being stuck in a world of undeath was not a pleasant thought, but something had to be done, and the risk was worth it. For all the pain I had caused the world, perhaps my own sacrifice was necessary.

Cold, snow, wind, blizzards, flooding, and tornadoes: these were things I missed; this stale and stuffy space provided little comfort. With those thoughts in my mind (or what was left of it), I had a general idea of what I needed to do.

Sadly, there was so little time left for those still living. And for me, I guess, but for once it did not seem fair to think about myself, or whatever power I could somehow gain from an even more egotistical and selfish warlock. What a fool... no, what *fools* we were. It did not surprise me that Ar'Zoth was not here; he surely burned in a river of fire, somewhere. I hoped.

A part of me wished to see him in his lake of torment, wanted to see his face as it melted from his bones, hear his screams and smell the stench of scorching flesh. I was going to take the blame for the world's problems, but he shared a major part of this struggle—he should at least suffer. If I could only find him. But there was no time for that now, no time.

"You don't exist!" My own words flooded from my mouth. I'd looked at Zhy, a man who was supposed to have been dead, and told him he was a part of my imagination. He had been real. No, he still *was* real, and Mother had saved his body from death, brought him back to kill me.

Zhy.

Zhy.

Zhy and his drunken, dead self. A dead man had killed me, and I could not escape from that horrible memory. Though he might have freed me from Ar'Zoth's spell, he still killed me.

I hated him, if I could just...

No, no, I needed to get past this hatred, it was clouding my brain and there was no time left!

Time, time, time. It kept coming back to that tired old cliché about not having enough time. There were many tasks ahead of me, not counting my base desire for revenge, and, as usual in every man's life (or death), there were very few hours left. I had to make things right.

As I thought back on the hatred I had fostered, the grudges against mankind, and my desire to slaughter every last person in Belden, I felt sick. Well, as sick as a dead person could be, I guess. Still, I harbored a great many grudges against people, though I knew now that not all people of Belden hated *me*. Very few even knew I existed, and those few were my focus of frustration and loathing. Why should I wish the entire world dead because a few bullies in an inn harassed me?

Fa would never act in such a way. He would have saved a drowning man, even if that man had robbed him hours earlier. I had to be like Fa, and more so like Mother... could I reach into that world and talk to someone as she had?

When I looked down at the world and the countless spaces that stretched out—the spaces that were souls, some living, some dead, I thought with great wonder at how Mother had been so quick at finding Zhy. Perhaps she had been with Lyn the whole time, knowing her skill at keeping me in check.

So many questions.

In theory, a dead person should have ample time to answer those questions, but the world didn't have the time. Quite simply, I had to act before thinking, something at which the old Bimb had been a master.

I knew what I needed to do, but actually doing was going to be far more challenging. Stepping—rather, floating—from my space, I looked out upon a nearly dark landscape. She had said that was the world of the living, and as hard as I peered into it, my eyes could not penetrate the thick, violet fog that hung over everything. I needed to get down there, somehow, not to the living souls, but to the world that they inhabited. But how?

If she was able to pull her space into the world, and I had also been able to do so in the past (in my brief attempt at killing her), then it was possible to reach the living. My concern was that I did not have any specific person in mind to pull into my space, and so I decided instead to try to plunge headlong into that foggy canvas below.

My first attempt set me floating along a raging unseen current, which swept me from my downward descent and flung me higher into the atmosphere. I felt as if I floated on an invisible river, with a slight damp the only indication of moisture. But it was not water, it was air; it had to be air, perhaps a strong wind of some sort. There were threads and particles within this stream. I could see them as I whirled past, though I was being propelled at such a high rate that it was hard to grasp any of them.

At last I flung an incorporeal hand out and pulled in one of the threads within the river of air, desperately hoping that it would steer the entire current in a given direction, but the result was nauseating. Faster, ever faster the wind roared, catapulting me through space at a dizzying rate. The air warmed suddenly, and then just as suddenly, I was spun back out and found myself in the dead space, confused.

Once more I tried diving into the haze, and fell victim to the same result. Instead of pulling on anything, I let it carry me along. I whirled and spun through the current of icy cold air like a spider in a tube of running water. There were moments where I could see daylight below, but they were so fleeting and miniscule that any attempt at focusing on the world below induced severe vertigo (again, how could a dead man have such feelings?) and instead I closed my eyes as the current carried me along.

For what seemed like hours I was borne along on the cold air, and an icy rain slapped at my face and even icy snow flakes stung my cheeks. How far had I traveled? Where would I be deposited? Again, I attempted to grasp a particle, but instead of a single item, I corralled several together in my hands and pulled. Suddenly my topsy-turvy ride ended and I found myself riding the wave on my belly. A fragment of a memory passes:

"Fa, can I go to the ocean someday?"

"Sure, son, sure. There are people there that ride the waves, on little boards, or even on their bellies. It's quite a sight."

"I can't swim."

"I know, son, I know."

Now I could look down at the world. By using the group of particles I felt as if I was steering a horse cart; to my surprise, a tug to the left moved the current of air! Looking down I desperately sought landmarks that I knew, though I only rode over a wide spine of mountains—could this be the Spires? Far off to my right, it looked as if the land flattened, while to the left the mountains continued on ceaselessly. If I was guessing correctly, I could steer to the right, and would move south.

The white snow passed beneath me as I soared to the south, with forests soon coming into view. This must be Belden's northern region, it must be!

A horrible thought struck me—what if this wind would cause damage? It sure rode like a wild beast when I had no control, what if it was damaging living creatures? With a curse I steered further to the west, hoping to get clear of the coastline and test this out over safer waters. As I did so, the tiny brown dots of the northern villages came into view.

There were demons, and lots of them. I rode the wind down, down, faster toward the advancing horde. These were demons *I* had let into the world—either through my actions, inactions, or both, and it was my responsibility to stop them. My ears, or whatever counted for ears in this plane, filled with the roar of the airstream, the gust of air, the sad, terrified screams of a people I was trying to save.

Chapter 5

Plans

There is very little to prepare for, when dealing with the Dark. Find it, kill it. Smother it. Bury it deep, and erase it from your heart. Those who make plans to control it are fools.

High Cleric Gorand

Rhys explained his discoveries in the Archives, making sure not to mention the Keeper's revelations. It would be best not to implicate the old man. Gheren and Horesh listened, faces changing with every new revelation; how had they missed this? How had centuries of leaders looked over the obvious facts before them?

And who was the stranger with him?

Gheren had been so consumed with thoughts of Jafren, and his plans for meeting with Gorand, that the new information seemed like an overload. Rhys talked fast, gesturing at the map, words spitting out of his mouth like one of those belching swamp snakes near Moult.

"The Tunnels?" Horesh asked. "You believe the demons are coming from there?"

Gheren watched Rhys carefully when he answered. Though the Teacher looked to be mad, his answers were rational. It made sense, in a way, that an underground passage could provide holes to the demonic realms.

How many more of these portals were there?

And who was this small-man?

"Who is your friend?" Gheren blurted, not sure if he had interrupted something. Rhys didn't seem to mind. He smiled.

"He is—"

"Felyar," the man replied.

"Yes, and he's a mage."

Felyar cleared his throat and eyed Rhys strangely. Gheren clenched his fists and sucked in air. No, this man was not a mage. Those eyes, too dark, very little white; not just a Welcferian feature, but something else.

"N-no?" Rhys wondered, his enthusiasm faltering.

"I'm a warlock."

Gheren blew out the breath he was holding. A warlock? A Welcferian *warlock?* He chuckled inwardly as Rhys choked on whatever words he had lined up.

"Well, Horesh, weren't you just saying...?"

Horesh was too preoccupied, his mind churning. Over this new event, or his journey? Gheren wondered. His companion nodded absently. "Yes, Gheren, yes. Excellent. Be assured, Rhys, that whatever you have decided, the Guard backs you. Belden. And, um, Welcfer surely. I apologize, but I must go."

And the Counsel Guard dashed down the hall.

"Never mind him," Gheren said, smiling. "We are all busy now. He's off to Darvein. And you two? Off to the Tunnels?"

Rhys pulled his gaze from the spot Horesh had vacated, gave Felyar a look of amazement, then smiled respectfully at Gheren. "Yes, that is our plan. We will try to seal these entry points into the underworld."

Gheren had things on his mind, too. Like Gorand. Normally he would bristle at a common citizen and a warlock sprinting off to the Tunnels. It was so mixed up, backwards, crazy, and downright suicidal.

"It had better work," he said simply. "You have our blessing."

The two spun and flew from the room.

"The hallway must be a racetrack by now," Gheren muttered, returning his gaze to the map.

Chapter 6

Shattered Alliances

Should you ever break from the Holy Orders, or deviate from your intended purpose, every last one of your members will be sentenced to death. You are bound to the Knot, bound to Sacuan, and bound to mankind.

High Cleric Gorand, in a letter to the Knights of the Black Dawn

"Jafren, where are you?" Gheren questioned the map.

So far his questions about Jafren were only answered with further questions, inquiries that had little chance of being answered. Where had he gone? What were his intentions? What was he wearing when he left? How could Gheren know? Frustrated at the constant stream of inquiries he balled his fists and threw a log into the fire; orange sparks cascaded violently into the room. The Counselor waved away the shower of bright speckles and glared at the hearth.

A serving boy knocked and simultaneously entered. The Grand Counselor-in-charge sighed, holding back an urge to shout the man away. Instead he cracked his knuckles and bit his lip.

"I told them I was on my way," Gheren grumbled. The Counsel had called a special meeting an hour ago, yet Gheren still had a hundred missives to send and a thousand more questions to ask. *Must they be so impatient? In such a hurry to sit and talk for hours, while a nation burns!*

"Sir, a note!" the man clipped, and spun out of the room. No doubt he was sending notes back and forth throughout the building. Unlike the Counsel, the retinue of staff members were bustling, carrying out orders and trying in every way to staunch the demonic bleeding. It was an event that, as yet, was unacknowledged by the Counsel and the Holy Orders.

Gheren cursed and tore open the envelope, not bothering to check if the seal had already been broken. He expected another summons, a call for more papers, or even an execution order, but as his eyes scanned the paper, they glanced over the words carelessly, not registering a single word. Thinking it another order, he nearly tossed it aside, but the letter **J** popped out at his tired eyes, and as he carefully read each word, his hands started to shake. He fumbled for a chair and collapsed into it, his gaze faded and cloudy, the paper clutched with a dead grip. Tears welled in his eyes, he squeezed his lids shut, and salty streams flowed down his scruffy cheeks.

"At least you could have left a note, Jafren," Gheren sighed. His chest felt constricted and he struggled to breathe. He unclenched the note and read again, hoping the last words were not "there was no saving him." Instead, the horrid reality was scrawled on the parchment. Dead. Dead by his own hands.

The innkeeper in Vronga had found the body, after his guest had refused to come to breakfast. Blood covered the floor, and Jafren lay with his wrists slashed, a Counsel-issued knife on the floor. It seemed that the guest had been bragging that he was the Grand Counselor, but nobody believed him... just to be sure, the innkeeper sent the note to Belden City, describing the deceased in detail. Those who read it were made devastatingly aware that their Grand Counselor was dead.

Who has read this? He thought.

Reaching to the floor, he picked up the shattered seal and inspected it. He'd ripped open the envelope with such force, it was impossible now to tell if anyone else had opened the letter. There was no telling if it had been ripped before. But who else knew? Did it really matter at this point? Gheren leaned off his chair and tossed the wax seal into the fire.

As he sat down again and stared into the blaze, Gheren realized with a heavy heart that this would give him at least a small amount of authority. At least until the Counsel could bicker and argue about Jafren's replacement. The dreaded meeting with the full Counsel would offer him an opportunity to make his case and perhaps gain additional troops in the battle. "How can I be thinking like this?" he chastised himself.

He never wanted power, never sought Jafren's position, though others had clamored for it. Now that Jafren was gone, however, it was left to Gheren to be a decision maker, though the circumstances were pitiful, it was the reality. He disliked being in charge immensely, but there was a greater threat to deal with, and nobody else seemed to be moving.

"Wait a minute..." he whispered, rising unsteadily.

At that moment another boy crashed into the room, panting. "Sir! The Counsel does await your presence."

"Tell them I refuse to see them, that Grand Counselor Jafren is dead." The boy blinked, but betrayed no other emotion. Perhaps he'd already seen the note. "As acting Counselor, I have immediate business with the High Cleric." There, that should appease them. Never mind that he never intended to talk with them again until this was settled. Protocol could be resumed later. If ever.

He turned and walked out of the room.

"What message should I send?" the boy asked quickly as Gheren started down the hallway.

"Message?" he asked turning, his face contorted in a scowl. "No, no message. Jafren didn't leave one, and I won't either."

Gheren brushed past another messenger and stalked down the hallway. His left hand reached out to pull open the door to the map room when he realized he still held the scrap of paper—with a curse he balled it and smashed it into a pocket.

ɸ

Gheren could never get used to the opulence of the High Cleric's chambers—if the crenelated balconies of the Counsel Headquarters were considered lavish, the gilded railings, marble columns, and high peaked ceilings of this place were downright obscene. Gilt wainscoting lined the polished hallways, frilled with a silver and gold rope of some valuable metal, and endless paintings of prophets stretched along the corridor. Even the door to the anteroom was a polished oak monstrosity, holy symbols etched in each of its six massive panels, and gold trim encased it. The ceiling was likewise lined with a bright, glistening pattern, trimmed with silver and gold borders, and decked out with large holy symbols every six feet. And, as Gheren noted sourly, the very sconces on the walls were small, intricate works of metal, shined to a glow, the candles trimmed perfectly of any excess wax.

A curse nearly escaped Gheren's lips but he steeled himself and opened the door.

"Sir?" The secretary asked.

He sighed. This was merely the antechamber—the large door he had passed through was miniature in comparison to the one that led to the High Cleric's chambers; even inside this small room the paintings were lavish, the floor covered in a rich, gold-trimmed mosaic, and the walls glowed with a pompous piety. The vulgar opulence was sickening.

"Sir?" the man repeated.

"I'm here to see the High Cleric," Gheren finally uttered with as much formality as he could muster, though it sounded too close to a growl.

"Do you have a time scheduled to meet with the High Cleric?" the secretary wondered. Gheren's mood was souring at the egregious display of power and wealth—men were being devoured by demons, and a tray of olives sat next to the Cleric's errand boy. Olives!

"No, I have not set one up. Grand Counselor Jafren is dead," he said flatly. "Urgent matters are at hand and I need to speak to the High Cleric."

The young man sighed. An olive was halfway to his mustachioed mouth and he set it down. "Sir, Counselor Horesh has been here already. I believe he got what he needed." Gheren's fingernails bore into his palm at that—no, Horesh had *not* had any success! The puffy Cleric—"In any case," the man continued, cocking an eye at Gheren. "If you would like me to set up a time, I'm sure you can come back when High Cleric Gorand is not busy. You may ask—"

"It has come to the point where I refuse to ask." A pubescent chin raised but Gheren continued talking, as if the boy knew everything. "They will appoint a new Grand Counselor, but it may take them months or more. Meanwhile we are crawling with demons, towns are burning, and citizens are in a panic. And yet the Holy Elders and the Counselors sit and bicker. No, I refuse to ask, I refuse to go to them, I refuse to stay here." He paced frenetically, his fists clenching and unclenching. The young messenger merely stared as Gheren stalked around the room. Finally he stopped, staring the High Cleric's door.

The secretary bit hard on an olive, his teeth scraping along the jagged pit. Gheren sneered at him and ripped open the inner door.

φ

He'd read somewhere about islands that no living man
had ever seen—islands far off to the west, inaccessible
with any fishing boat or small caravel. It had been said
that these islands were overrun by sin and degradation,
and that demons rose up from the very earth and
swallowed humanity. No Temple to save them. Though
Belden was not overrun by demons, the leakage was
enough to confirm to High Cleric Gorand that Belden had
slipped into sloth, greed, and other perversities; it was a
land that needed cleansing.

With a grimace and a prayer, he tossed the request for
more Protectors into the fire.

Looking out of his double paned window with its hand-
carved trim, the High Cleric sneered at the frost-covered
trees and the small tufts of snow that lay in shaded areas.
It had been a very cold night in Belden City, yet by noon
the snow would be gone, and the trees only dripping with
moisture. From his vantage point he could see no
demons, no strange creatures that flew overhead. Gorand
sighed, and stepped away from the window as a brief chill
coursed through his body.

"I'm getting old," he whispered to his ornate cherry
desk. Joints popped as he eased himself into his chair.
Gorand leaned slowly forward on the desk, his hands
folded, propping up his wrinkled chin. Thoughts of
burning sinners and gherwza tearing mercilessly at the
throats of gluttons flittered through his mind's eye. He
allowed himself a crooked grin.

Suddenly his hands came away from his face and he
straightened. Outside, sounds of muffled argument
coursed through the thick oak door. He could hear the
voice of his secretary as he insisted that Gorand would
see no visitors, but a gruff voice continued to demand
entrance. The High Cleric swore he recognized the voice,
and was trying to place it when the door flew open and

Gheren burst in, his face crimson. Gorand's secretary stood behind him, arms outstretched, still trying to stop the Counselor.

"I'm not waiting until spring!" Gheren barked, not a second after hurling himself into the room. Gorand held his hands in the air, words of protestation starting from his thin lips. But Gheren continued. "Too much time has been wasted already! I demand that you activate your Protectors. We need every soldier for this fight."

High Cleric Gorand stood hastily, knocking the chair back with a thud. Gheren. Gheren... he'd heard the name before, yes, a pompous man, cloaked in the guise of hard-working servant of the people. A vile, pot-bellied clown.

"You demand?" the High Cleric's voice was dangerously soft. "You demand of your Holy Elders?"

He smiled briefly. "Can you not see that the world is being overtaken by demons? Whole villages have been pulled under, Forshen has burned to the ground, and now even Vronga reports that attacks have increased. The world—"

"I care little for your exaggerated claims, Gheren," Gorand replied quickly. "There is no flood, as is stated in the texts, the Temple stands, else you would be dead. No, this work is not of the demons, but of the actions of sinners."

The Cleric smiled at the Counsel Guard, enjoying the strange look his face had adopted.

Gheren had opened his mouth to protest the delay, but it clamped shut at the last words of the High Cleric. The Counselor's face turned a deep crimson and he balled his fists tightly at his sides; it took supreme effort not to draw his sword and cut the man where he stood. The work of sinners? Children were dying for Sacuan's sake! What evil did a child ever do?

"So you see Counselor Gheren, we must let the sin be purged, else it will return to us a thousand fold."

He had no words, only boiling fury. Let the children die, the women suffer, and men be torn apart by demons because of sin? What sin? What crime? Gheren believed that punishment was dealt on an individual level, that short-changing a merchant would result in a poor crop, not in wholesale slaughter of entire villages.

"I see you struggle. I have struggled myself, but have concluded that there needs to be a purging. To see it done at the hands of demons only furthers my anguish, but it is such—" he spread his hands out, palms up. "We must not question the acts of the Light."

"The Light does not kill children."

"Children sin, my friend, you are a fool to believe otherwise."

"Their 'sins', as small as they can be, do not warrant death!" Gheren snapped. "Certainly not the horrible deaths that we have been hearing about—mulargh, gherwza, twisted men who can tear flesh apart and seem immune to arrows and steel. Your Grace—" he spat the word, "this is not the work of the Light purging the Dark—this is the Dark trying to destroy the world!"

Gorand shook his head sadly. "It is indeed a pity that you believe so. But a secular man such as yourself would of course think first of the so-called innocents. When a man is killed, you immediately mourn for him. But what of the crimes *he* has committed, what of his sins?"

No wonder Horesh had wanted to tear every last hair from Gorand's head. How a man, especially a man of religion, could think such things was beyond Gheren. But this man had made it to High Cleric for some reason, and there were surely many in his flock who believed what he was teaching. If his beliefs were true, Gheren was not sure he wanted to walk in the Light in the first place. Why go on with good deeds if your single misstep lands you in the jaws of a gherwza? But such thinking was corrupt, Gheren reminded himself. Faced with a harsh reality, the Cleric was simply covering for his own insecurity, unwilling to commit a military force to deal with an issue, he hid behind his philosophy.

Gheren had had enough.

"I'm going to relieve you of your command of the Protectors, your Grace," Gheren said slowly, sure to place a hand on his sword. The look from the High Cleric was not one of fear (which Gheren had expected) but of mirth.

"What a horrible thing to say... you have no authority!" A small smile passed those puffy lips, then curled into a terrible grin. "You must be mad, or consumed by—" he leaned forward. "Consumed by demons?" With that small phrase, he easily could have condemned Gheren to death. But he let a glimmer of sympathy win out and let the opportunity pass by. "No, you have no such authority," he finished with a wave of his hands.

"I do. Jafren is dead."

Confusion, worry, and finally doubt splashed across the High Cleric's face. "You lie."

Gheren shook his head.

"What lies—?"

As an answer, Gheren extracted the paper from his left pocket and tossed it on the Cleric's desk.

Gorand gingerly unfolded the crumpled piece of paper. A look of disgust briefly crossed his face at having to unfold a crumpled scrap of parchment. However, as he read the note, the look changed to defeat; his puffy features sagged. Finally he looked up, a forced smile drawn across his face.

"You cannot do this. Jafren's death does not give you that power immediately. Only briefly."

"We don't have to wait for any formalities. I'm taking command."

"You cannot do this," Gorand repeated.

Gheren nodded. "I am doing it. As acting Grand Counselor, I am assuming control of the Protectors. Whatever sins men have committed, they shall be punished. But this punishment is beyond anything that any follower of the Light should accept."

"You cannot—"

"I *am*. Protocols are now worthless, past contracts can be burned. We are facing the end of our world if we do not act. You can relinquish your control peacefully or I can take it by force."

"You would not survive five minutes should you do that," Gorand whispered. His face paled slightly, but he forced himself to straighten.

Would you not enjoy that? Gheren thought. *Going out as a martyr?* "Perhaps not, but it would give me great satisfaction."

"You are letting your anger rule you, son. Even if you were correct about the flood of demons and their threat to the world, you have already given in to the Dark. You use the sword as a crutch, and you have given over to anger and lust for revenge."

Gheren bit back a reply. Sacuan damn him, the man was right. But even if Gheren had no emotion, if he were a simple carter or wheelwright, he would know that demons were threatening his existence. And he would want to know that the Guard and Protectors—and even the secret Knights of the Black Dawn—were taking action; such a man would not accept that his own sins had brought such destruction to the world.

Or would he?

The Counselor's hand fell away from his sword and he scowled.

"Am I not right, son?"

"Only partially, your Grace," Gheren admitted sheepishly. "Only partially. I am still relieving you of your command of the Protectors, that is unless you can send the order?"

The Cleric looked into the fire and Gheren nearly swore. "Alas, I cannot do that. I will not give an order to fuel a leader's revenge."

"Then I will give the order."

Gorand looked at him levelly. "You are creating a dangerous future for yourself."

"Not if I succeed."

"Should you succeed," the Cleric spoke with a scathing edge to his voice. "May I remind you that I could call for your head quite easily as soon as you step away from here?"

"You have no such authority. Besides, the demonic situation is grave enough that even the Counsel would table it until the threat was over. I do hope that you understand your position is not one of the majority."

"I don't need a majority, I am right."

There, he had said it. Admitted he felt himself the supreme moral leader, and as such a complete fool. "And could care less who is right or wrong. There are innocent people dying—regardless of what you claim their sins to be—and I must protect those people. The very word Protector carries with it that assumption that even the Holy Elders are doing their part. Your inaction is forsaking them."

"I tire of this continued argument, Gheren. If you are going to relieve me of my command, do so. If you are going to kill me, so be it; I will forever be remembered as the man who stood against the Dark. Do what you will. But know that I am right, and you have no authority by which to command Protectors to fight against something that must be let to run its course." He sucked in air.

Gheren was not listening. "You are hereby relieved of your command of the Protectors; I will send the order for Protectors to be sent out to—" he wanted to say, *to do their Sacuan-blasted jobs,* But caught himself. "Sent forth to cities and towns that are under attack."

"And what of my name? No one will accept your order."

"I'll take that chance." What he wanted was to put his steel to the throat of the pompous cleric and force his signature, or chop off the hand and do his best to fake the signature. Gheren expected fully that the Protectors were wondering why they were not marshaled—even the ones who bought fully into Gorand's caustic beliefs about sin and punishment. Surely they would expect to be called up to assist, but like good soldiers, sat there waiting for the orders. It thus fell to Gheren, as acting Grand Counselor, to give the order, High Cleric's blessing or not.

"Again, I tell you that you are starting down a very Dark path, Gheren. Very Dark. Be prepared for the consequences to be dire."

Not waiting for another word, Gheren turned and walked from the room.

Outside, Gheren ordered the boy to bar the door, putting his faith in the edge of his sword and the threat of action. The secretary protested with his reeking olive breath, but Gheren held firm, reminding him of his authority. Sputtering at the end of the acting Grand Counselor's sword, the young man agreed readily to keep the door locked and not to allow anyone out of the room.

Before he stalked out of the room, Gheren knocked the plate of olives to the floor.

ϕ

Gorand collapsed into his chair and folded his hands again. Soon, very soon, he hoped to hear of the death of Gheren, preferably at the hands or claws of a demon. The Counselor now had control over Protectors, but with any hope they would turn him away and wait for his orders, not the Counselor's

Gorand, after all, felt himself the ruler of Belden. The conqueror of the Dark.

As such, whatever deeds Gheren had planned, they would fail and crumble like puffballs in the spring. The man was a fool to attack the High Cleric's authority— surely it was nothing that Jafren would have done, no, this Gheren was mad; drunk with power, and *would* be reined in.

The Dark would fail, Gorand reminded himself. The Dark would fail and he would be hailed as the hero who saved the world. It did not matter how many so-called innocents had to die.

φ

Gheren thought of himself in much the same light, except he was taking action against the Dark. He feared more for the innocent than for his own gilded legacy, and so with a flurry of signatures and verbal orders, he set the wheels in motion for a larger army to address the demonic threat.

The cleric could sit and pray to his false god, puff up his ego, and remind himself he was doing good by the Light, but Gheren took pride an actually doing something.

Chapter 7

Action

The faith of the knots is a sound one, based upon years of confirmation and pious thought and scholarship. But time given to thought should be limited, for action is required even of those who are devout.

Cleric Archean, Order of the Knot

Gorand thought he had a hold on his Protectors, the vaunted warriors of Light, men who fought the dark. With any war, however, a strong man or woman can be inspired to pick up a weapon and fight, no matter the orders from above.

There were still Protectors who had heard screams of terror, pools of blood, and flying bats. These men had acted on their own; any orders or missives from the High Cleric were either not read or cast aside with the assumption that the information was no longer relevant. Surely, those in power could see that the demons were a real threat, and no longer a random occurrence.

Units of Protectors, joined by retired Counsel Guards and a stray warlock or two, set forth from Belden City, branching out in several directions. Forshen was a complete loss, and the unit of twenty-strong Protectors found only a few women and children huddling under a charred support beam—they were sent back to Belden City with a lone Protector as escort.

Battles still raged near the smaller villages as desperate townsfolk fought valiantly with pitchfork, bow and arrow, and the occasional sharp-edged steel. The small collection of Protectors or Counsel Guards quickly seized command of the vigilantes and battled furiously against the demons, though a few of the villagers were filled with a raging bloodlust and had to be silenced themselves. The world was turning red.

As each unit moved forward, they suffered minimal losses, while they sent back reports of their enemies' heavy losses. Yet each turn of the tide only brought more of the filthy creatures to the fore. For every village that was saved, two more were floundering under the weight of attack: gherwza and mulargh shredded through villages.

And Rhys had been right, allowing villagers free reign to fight demons was proving to be a greater challenge.

φ

They hadn't killed him, or his family. Yet. But the villagers still had them locked in the pig pen, throwing them tidbits of scraps now and again. Verell, Marease, and the little Nigel sat huddled in the cold, staring fearfully out of the thin slats of the cage. The only light came through the spaces between the beams; a heavy cloth tarp had been spread over the top of the prison cell.

"What do you say for yourself, Verell? You and your wife have been in collusion with demons, have you nothing to say for yourself?"

Verell strained to see, but the elder who spoke remained blocked by Thorsan, a giant of a man, who would rather do away with the alleged "demon scum" than care for his own family. "I am not a demon," Verell said flatly.

"You lie poorly, Verell, you lie while your own family suffers beside you. In that regard, you *must* be a demon! Perhaps we should starve you so that your true demonic self can come out."

"You may starve me, but you may not starve my family." He tried to sound strong, but three days in this pit, with little to eat or drink had nearly broken him. Nearly naked, he had made sure to give his warmer clothing to Marease and Nigel. If they survived this, he feared for Nigel—the poor boy would have nightmares of this for the rest of his life. *A boy can't have nightmares when he's dead*, he reminded himself grimly. He had to get them out of here.

"Fear not, they shall get what food they deserve. The question is whether you would dare try to consume them."

"Consume?"

"I believe you know what I mean, *demon*."

Thorsan grumbled something unintelligible and brandished his pitchfork, though Verell could only see the butt of the tool bounce on the frozen earth.

"I am not—"

"Yes, yes," the elder said impatiently. "How long will it take for you to show yourself? Days have now passed, and we expect—"

"Elder, pardon, but I want to kill them all. Why do we wait?" the brute wondered.

There was a spat of hushed muttering, a scuffle of boots, and then the elder spoke, with a voice that Verell thought only belonged to a man possessed. If the elder dared accuse his family of being demons, then the elder himself was a mulargh's bastard.

"You may kill them, Thorsan. I tire of this." And with a swoosh of a heavy cloak, a pounding of boots on frost, the elder was gone.

Verell watched in horror as the gate to the pen was wrenched violently open and two large leather-clad legs came into view. Shielding his eyes against a bright sun, he looked up into the cold, dead eyes of Thorsan, then shifted his gaze to the four-pronged pitchfork held aloft in calloused hands.

Tears started streaming on his face, but Verell wiped them away angrily and pushed himself to his feet. "Take me, take me only. If you take me, I will admit to being a demon."

"Ah, so he admits it!" the brute barked, looking back to the elder, but the holy man had already vanished. "Too late, man, too late!" His dumb smile enveloped his entire face.

"I do not—"

A massive, hairy hand reached out and gently tapped against Verell's chest. It took only a touch from Thorsan's heavy hand to send Verell flying backward into the straw. Marease and Nigel scurried to him and he put an arm around them both.

"No, you move away. The little one first."

No. "*You* are the demon," Verell spat, staring into those blank eyes.

"I will enjoy cutting you into small pieces, not so much as I will enjoy your face as I cut apart—"

"You will do nothing of the kind!" Verell's eyes went wide, and Thorsan jerked violently at the new voice. A deep, resonating voice. One of authority.

Or another elder...? Verell wondered in panic.

"Put down the pitchfork, now."

Thorsan turned slowly, still holding the weapon. Verell tried to peer around and get a look at the stranger, but he only saw leather.

When Thorsan's eyes fell on Horesh and three fully-armed Guards, he let his pitchfork dip only an inch before raising it again and gesturing at Verell's family. "These are demons and they are to be punished."

Horesh looked, but he only saw terror. Rhys had been right. A world gone drunk on bloodlust, seeing demons where only children played, finding blood and horror were cool waters ran. How common was this? *How do I save everyone?* "I do not see any demons in this village," he said simply.

"And just who are you?"

"I am Counselor Horesh. I've already asked you to put down your weapon. If you do not do so, the consequences will be fatal." He was supposed to say *you will face a night in the restraining house,* as he had said now a dozen times. But this situation was by far the bleakest he had encountered, and the grim words rolled off his tongue too easily.

The men regarded each other for a moment and in that brief period the elder came waddling from his hovel, arms crossed piously in his robe. "Gentlemen, gentlemen, what is the problem?"

Horesh turned. "Your—" be broke off, not willing to give this so-called holy man any respect. "You have falsely imprisoned the innocent. I am taking them into my care."

"You cannot do this," the elder spoke. He sounded as if he cheeks were filled with cotton. "These people are demons. If you aid or abet them, good Counselor, then you will be tried and found guilty. Thorsan," the elder added, dismissing Horesh with a sneer, and turning his greedy gaze languidly toward the village brute.

Horesh had never moved so fast in his life. Steel cleared leather at the same time he leapt from his horse— he bounded the short distance in a single leap, pushed the blade of the sword against the holy man's neck. "No," he rasped. "No, I will not be dismissed. *You* are dismissed." He only saw red. Red and a sobbing wife and terrified little boy—a boy who would probably never speak again. Years at headquarters had smoothed the struggle of life too much, had removed his perspective far from reality, and this injustice—as brutal and horrific as it was—shattered his frail grip on civility and decency. Why offer any lenience when none was given in return? What right did blind murderous fiends deserve? Crimson tears and a pulsating red rage filled Horesh's vision.

"In the name of the Light, I—"

The sword edge cut cleanly through flesh and windpipe. Men gasped behind him, a woman cried, and someone became ill, but Horesh only saw red. The holy man fell to the ground in a headless heap.

"Horesh, you don't know what you have done..." someone said. He still clutched his sword and turned slowly.

"I have done what needed to be done. Verell, is that your name?" he asked suddenly of the villager.

"A-aye." He cleared his throat nervously.

"Go to Yilbar here—the short one with the horse and cart. You and your family will have a ride to Belden City, where I hope you find a safer life."

The man began to prostrate himself and thank Horesh, but the guard had already turned to the burly Thorsan, who stood, staring dumbly at the headless corpse. "And you, waste of space that you are! You have a minute to leave this village and never return. I hope you can redeem yourself. If not, you will meet my steel as well."

Dumb, black eyes stared at him. The man roared defiantly, and brandished his pitchfork. Horesh calmly drew his sword, sliced off the arm holding the pitchfork, and severed his head as well.

The time for talk was over.

Turning, he addressed Yilbar. "Go." He then looked at his soldiers. "Come, we must ride... it is still far to Darvein!" The red was abating, now a hazy orange glow that hovered in his vision. How bad was the world? How many more heads would he cut off? *As many as it takes in this Sacuan-forsaken pit of Hell...*

He mounted his horse and trotted away, leaving a small village in stunned silence.

Chapter 8

Darvein Harbor

I have seen the top of the mountain called Death. From its heights I have learned a hundred lessons, each more powerful than the next. But before I can commit them to memory, I awake.

Prophet Vron'Za

Horesh felt as if they might actually be gaining ground. They had pushed northward successfully, with few losses, and his army had grown. Between the tiny villages of Garyyn and Goryyn (why would anyone name towns like this, he wondered), he had gained a rag-tag group of villagers, armed with swords, lances, spears and arrows. A few even carried sharpened farming tools. He had expected resistance, but the villagers quickly fell in behind his authority—he did not feel it, but he was still a Counsel Guard.

"Darvein's just up the road a piece, Horesh, sir," someone muttered as they dismounted for a rest.

Darvein. Finally.

The journey to Darvein was still a blur in Horesh's memory—riding hard from Belden, he and his thousand men raced almost recklessly along Crown Road, pausing only twice to offer assistance to other soldiers. Snow had slowed them down considerably at Vronga, but they had pushed through the muddy streets and continued westward, at one point killing several horses. From a small village still intact, they procured more and kept moving.

Of snow they had seen very little—at least not this far east, and not much more than a light flurry or dusting. Rain and mud were plentiful, and so too were the dangers of gangrene and other horrible skin conditions. Healers, the two he had thankfully brought along, raced from man to man, applying poultices, giving herbs, or administering final rights. Holy men and women were nowhere in sight—Horesh had long since abandoned any hope that the devout would see reality for what it was and offer aid.

As the army made camp, he noticed the lights of Darvein Harbor in the distance; smoke curled lazily from chimneys, ships bobbed slowly in the harbor, and a countless array of lights from inns, taverns, and homes twinkled in the twilight. From his vantage point he could see no sign of disaster or danger. It was as if the town were protected...

Or a sitting target, Horesh thought grimly.

Horesh sighed and turned to make is his way to the dining tent when he spun around in terror.

A horrible screech filled the air as a mulargh flew overhead, followed by a stream of gherwza. Horesh stood in horrified silence as he watched the demonic creatures race toward the large city. His men had been brave today, they had fought valiantly against a seemingly endless scourge of such beasts, and they were exhausted. Yet Horesh needed them to fight once more, he needed to protect Darvein Harbor from the hell on wings that approached it with fervor.

The number of demonic flying creatures seemed to be endless as they streamed northward.

"Attack!" he screamed, sprinting through the camp. "Form a line, form a line! NOW!"

Plates clattered and fell to the cold earth as men scrambled for their armor and weapons, and sprinted to the outskirts of camp. Horesh bolted to the field—someone tossed down a box atop which he could stand.

"There's not much time for us to act, but we need to kill those beasts. They are headed for Darvein—archers, to me! Soldiers, fall behind in a flank. And archers, be sure you shoot *up*! Get good angles. Where are our mages?" he barked to nobody.

Two tired hands went up among the throng.

Horesh cursed. At least a dozen mulargh and how many gherwza? Two mages. Two!

One did what one could... didn't all the stories have some great hero fighting off a hundred armed men with a shield and a hammer?

"Pace yourselves!" he ordered as some men sprinted forward. It would do no good to have them winded before they arrived in Darvein. The town was still a good mile away, but the unit covered the distance in under fifteen minutes, and some of the warriors were panting.

They are lost, he thought bitterly.

He had not dared look up at the sky—the screams from the city were enough to know that the demons had descended.

"Sir, Horesh, sir?" a soldier panted as he sprinted to him.

He waved the man off and get the mages in position; there was no time anymore. "Mages! Fire only in the air at these things, and be careful, for Sacuan's sake! The blasted mulargh—"

The grizzled mages wasted no time and soon blue lightning bolts began arcing into the black skies, igniting gherwza. Soldiers had run with all haste into the city and the sound of steel against bat flesh could be heard. Chaos had exploded in front of him and he hoped desperately for a successful outcome, though the battle raged with a boiling, gray, red-tinged mess of confusion.

So this is war.

Screams continued.

Horesh drew his own sword and started toward the main gate when the young soldier stopped him. "Sir?"

"There's no time, son! Get in the battle!"

"Sir, something is wrong, horribly wrong! The demons—they—"

"What, spit it out!" Horesh screamed.

"We've seen them before, they just wander into buildings or trees... at first. They seemed like they had no guide..."

That was enough to stop Horesh. He spun on the young man. "What did you just say?"

"It's like they had no guide, but now... now they—look, more bats! They fly as if they are being guided now. What is drawing them?"

Horesh thought on this. "Bats have some sort of special sense—after all, normal bats can fly in the dark, can they not?"

"Yes, but what are they flying after?"

The answer popped into his mind so quickly his eyes widened as he uttered the phrase, "Blood. Blood! Don't you see? The blood in our veins... blood being spilled. Blood, blood, everywhere! It must be!"

"Sir?" the young man asked, stepping back two feet. His eyebrows were raised in questioning, a disgusted look on his face. "Horesh, if I may be so bold, but you are suggesting that these creatures are... are..." he cracked his thumb knuckles and grimaced. "They are..."

Horesh raised a hand. "No, they are not blood-drinkers, those are from old, old children's stories. The worst ever written. I am only saying that they are drawn to the life—the life is the blood."

"You are in dangerous waters," the young man said darkly.

The tone of the boy's voice startled Horesh. "What do you mean?"

"I'm not sure. What if someone is guiding them?"

"Someone? It's possible there is a crazy warlock or a rogue mage out there. Let's not worry about this, we have a battle to fight."

"But, Sir, I—"

"No!" he barked. "Never mind, this conversation is useless. All that matters is that we have to attack them, we have to defeat them. I think they are being drawn to life. If they are not being guided by someone, they have to have some purpose or direction and it seems that they have found that on their own."

"The blood is life," the boy whispered. He sneered again. "I read that in a story."

"I wish this was just a story," Horesh replied, eyes blazing. "Then we could write the ending now, we could send all these demons back to Hell!"

Chapter 9

A Rush of Wind

Wind, rain, snow, sleet, and hail. All part of the world and the function of the seasons. As powerful as our magic can be, none of these phenomena can be controlled. Should the strong divine ways to manipulate the weather, beware, for the Dark shall win!

High Cleric Bertrand

Wave after bloody wave of the creatures rolled over the countryside and into the small towns and hamlets. Mulargh and gherwza screeched overhead, and the shambling elderly marched inexorably forward, moving as one mindless mass even as arrows and magic struck them. A small collection of men and women held feebly to a large hill, atop which a miniscule village sat. Inside the small huts, hundreds of refugees huddled against the cold and the fear of the oncoming storm.

Both the men and the women held swords, some in each hand, useless weapons against an army of horror that clawed its way up the hill. Even shambling and somewhat directionless, the approaching demons seemed of a purpose—to get to the top of the hill and slaughter everyone. For now the line of warriors stood its ground, the swords slashing at flesh that refused to lie down and die.

If only they could maintain their strength.

"Danya, get this one off of me!" a warrior named Lewa screeched. A half-dead man clawed at her leather leggings, coming dangerously close to pulling her garment down, while the other clawed hand scraped at leather, searching, searching for flesh that it could rend.

"I—I'm almost there—" the warrior named Danya growled, slicing a head clean from a demon, then swiping behind her at the arm of a gutted creature.

Lewa cursed and swung at the demon that hung to Danya's arm. As soon as the sword cleaved the second arm, something whispered behind her. She ducked instinctively to save herself, but she could do nothing to stop the demon that hurtled itself through the air.

Her throat erupted with a scream of anger and disgust as the oversized mulargh careened into Danya. The tiniest of howls rose from Danya, then the soldier was silent, as teeth gnashed and tore at flesh, bones crunched with sickening snaps and pops. For a brief moment the beast lay atop its prey, then raised its head to the sky, and dropped its massive jaw back down atop Danya's corpse. Lewa ran forward, slashing wildly at the beast with her sword, aimlessly swiping at anything that looked like fur or scales, though she could see only a foggy shape, nearly blanked out by tears of rage and frustration.

The mulargh merely stomped a hind leg and turned its massive head to face her, jaws wide. It flexed a leg muscle and made to pounce—

When a bolt of green lightning exploded in front of its face, followed by another that blew off its head completely. Lewa's sword swung wildly for two more passes at a dead body before the mage's soft voice stilled her.

"I—I—" she heaved, trying not to stare at the headless demon and the pile of mush that had been Danya. "I—"

"It's all right, Lewa, we need to—"

He was silenced as the flapping of leathery wings cracked the air between them and a gherwza swooped low, its giant fangs wide to the sky. Lewa had no strength left in her, and only had a passing thought of raising her sword, before the demonic bat clamped down on the neck of a small mage; the man's scream was snuffed quickly as the strong jaw slammed shut.

The gherwza flew away to the north.

"We're losing ground! Retreat!" Lewa screamed. *The bat is going to come back, with more, much more...*

"But what about the villagers?" a soldier wondered.

Her face twisted into a grimace and she traded alternating desperate glances at the oncoming horde—they had beaten only a handful of demons and ragged men, but the line of attackers seemed nearly endless. It was hopeless. *Poor Danya...* "Run. Tell them to run. Far away, anywhere but here."

"But the demons are everywhere! *Everywhere!*"

He turned in desperation, opened his mouth to speak—

The rush of wind was from nowhere. Or at least from a direction it should never have come; as if it was spun straight down from a cloudless sky, an angry ribbon of fury and rage from the very heavens. This region saw its fair share of storms and bad weather, but the intensity of this gust was beyond anything anyone had ever experienced. No clouds were visible on the horizon, yet the wind howled and raged. It flattened the approaching horde like archery targets in a cheap carnival game, shredded the thatched roofs of the village, and even tore the few slate coverings to shreds. Citizens, once terrified of demons, were now screaming in horror as the wind blasted away at everything.

Even strong clay tiles were torn violently from already strained roofs, windows smashed open in showers of shattered glass, lanterns and light posts were ripped from their moorings and were hurled violently into the air.

Even the mulargh and gherwza were shot from their courses and hurled into trees or hillsides—at one point a flying lamp post impaled a screeching mulargh and the creature spiraled to the ground.

The wind whipped angrily through the countryside, bending treetops down in right angles as it surged. Those able to escape its wrath found themselves in stinking crawl-spaces or beneath stone bridges, though even the loose masonry within these structures moaned against the onslaught.

"It is the end of the world!" a man screamed to a small group of villagers. They had thrown themselves hurriedly into the basement of the temple, shoulders hunched even now as the rough, ragged wind rocked the upper floors.

A few voices were raised in agreement.

"Sacuan has come to claim the world—we have not lived to our full potential, we have failed the Light, failed each other! The demons were only the start. Now the great wind has come to scatter us like the dust that we are, take us to our final deaths!" He ducked instinctively as something massive upstairs tore away from its footings and was slammed against a wall. The basement walls shook.

"I say to you, my friends, we must accept it! It is our fate as sinners, that we be punished!" Here he raised his hands. "Take us! Take us, we have been unfaithful, disloyal, and we have sinned!"

"Take us!" the villagers repeated as one voice.

And in a screaming, flailing mass of legs, arms, and heads, the wind took them. The floorboards were pulled up from their base, the six-by-ten planks slamming like hammers against the joists before being tossed up into the vortex. A roar louder than any coastal hurricane drowned the shouts and screams of the villager; the wind blew away the sprays of blood from severed body parts, or heads thrown violently against the joists.

Bimb tried desperately to pull the cyclone up and away from the village, but it squirmed in his grip and pushed along the landscape. Three more small towns were erased from the map before the storm blew out on its own power, leaving a jagged gash in the countryside; a dozen miles long by a mile wide.

Chapter 10

Stalking the Spires (Again)

Would you ever strike out unaided into a desert or a frozen wasteland? Would you ever jump into the ocean and swim blindly towards an illusion? Would you walk blindfolded into a moonless forest? Then why do we trust our teachers, leaders, and friends to guide us across the treacherous landscapes of our lives?

Prophet Zhera

By now Zhy had grown somewhat accustomed to the cold and the snow, as long as he kept himself moving. The motion and exercise, combined with the right outerwear, made the trek across a trackless wasteland a little more bearable. They had given up on their skis long ago. Given the prevalence of large outcropping slabs of granite, skirting the boulders would have taken more time than simply walking across them.

When Zhy looked out to the north, he saw nothing but snow, and a thin gray line that could have been either the edge of the Spires or a trick of the eye. It looked to be the edge of the world.

"It's the Spires, Zhy," Wrenflang assured him.

"What?" he wondered, then looked up; the mage was pointing to the grayish blur on the horizon. "Oh," Zhy finally said softly. "So we just walk until we run into them?"

The old mage nodded. "That is the general idea, yes. We'll continue northward for some time, but we will need to find the pass through the mountains, the one that Bimb was able to find."

"He had help from... from someone, though," Fanlas said softly.

"Yes... and we have a little help, too." The mage smiled crookedly.

Zhy returned the smile. "What do you have planned?"

"Oh, just a little box that was at the Temple of M'Hzrut."

Zhy scratched his nose. "What type of box?"

"It's a navigation box."

"Can I see it?" Zhy wondered, awe in his voice. He had heard of such a thing: Huyen and Yulchar had talked about boxes that could tell a man which way was north.

Wrenflang shook his head. "Let's keep going for some time—it's buried in the pack. But yes, soon, very soon, we will test it out. We need to take advantage of the sun while we can; the guiding box will come in handy should we lose our light."

Zhy looked out at the thin gray line far in the horizon. How his own dead father had guided Bimb over those very hills, through a narrow path, and to Ar'Zoth seemed amazing and impossible at the same time. And to think the goal had been to save Zhy... but Bimb had—

"Something's coming," Wrenflang rasped, breaking Zhy's thoughts. He pulled the group to a stop. "Sorchal, try that looking glass thing again, I think I see someone far ahead."

The young Protector squinted, shook his head, but retrieved the cylindrical device anyway. Sorchal peered through the eyepiece, then stuck the rod back in his pocket with a shake of his head. "Fogged up." Nobody noticed when he tossed it casually in the snow.

The men squinted into the distance, and as they edged ever northward, the shape of a person or persons seemed to coalesce in front of them. Fanlas quietly drew his sword, with a strange, flat look from Wrenflang. However, as they neared the stranger, they quickly realized that they were approaching an object, not a person.

"Trees!" Wrenflang blurted suddenly.

"What?"

"Look, Fanlas. Zhy! Trees!" he gestured wildly. The men quickened their pace along the crusty ground, bounding through the snow, careless of what worked its way into their boots.

Two small pine trees rose out of the cold ground, giving the appearance of a man waiting with his arms akimbo. Yet as they neared the apparition, and it resolved itself into a forest (where no forest should be), the phenomenon only grew stranger.

Thick green grass grew at the base of the trees!

The men stepped into the strange oasis and at once the weather warmed; coats were doffed hurriedly and faces turned up to the warm sun with broad smiles. Zhy stared in wonder at the large area. It was perhaps as large as a village inn, with tall green grass and a clump of maple trees—*maple*, of all trees, and green as the first spring day! Beside the trees was a very small wet area, filled with mossy rocks and a familiar green plan.

"Labrador tea!" he exclaimed, waddling over to the small bush.

"What is that?" Fanlas wondered. "Tea? What are—"

"No, no, it's not really tea, but a plant. Darrell, he made a tea with it, but that is just the name of the leaf." Zhy muttered this last as he bent down. Melancholy filled his heart as he stared at the strange plant growing in the middle of the arctic. Darrell, with all of his faults, had been a good man, a true companion, and now gone.

As Zhy reached to pluck a leaf from the bunch, Wrenflang's stern warning stilled his hand.

"Don't touch it, Zhy! Don't touch anything here... this is a very bad place."

As soon as Zhy heard those words, his brain clicked with a past memory and he leapt backward, jumping away from the small bog.

"What is the matter?" Fanlas wondered.

The old mage barked something and Zhy realized quickly what it was: "This is a reversal." *A place where day is night, and summer is winter!* He remembered his last reversal, a demon racing from a temple; an inert Darrell and a raging Bruce.

Wrenflang stared.

"I've seen one before," Zhy explained. "Back in Belden. A place where it was cold outside, but warm inside the reversal. There was even a temple there. And then..." he trailed off, making his way for the frozen edge of the oasis.

"What in Sacuan's name is a reversal?" Fanlas wondered.

Again, Zhy answered, while Wrenflang looked on with slight bemusement. "Quite frankly, it is evil."

"Evil?"

Zhy heard himself rattle Darrell's words: "Where night is day and light is dark, and winter is summer."

"Summer," Wrenflang whispered. He opened his mouth to add more, but his eyes filled with a wild look and he hollered: "Go, go now!"

Zhy had already stepped outside of the green field. He bundled himself into his coat, the cold biting his warmed skin severely. Hands were thrust into gloves, then deep into fur-lined pockets as he watched his companions standing in the lush sanctuary. Wrenflang barked another order, but Sorchal and Fanlas stood, staring dumbly.

"Please," Zhy barked. His voice was swallowed by the cold. He exhaled a cloud of frustrated steam, and with a shock of dismay, noticed that it *rippled* as it *collided* with an invisible barrier and flowed out like the pattern of waves around an obstruction in a pond. He yelled louder, but his words died again. Wrenflang was agitated, screaming, and barking. Outside the reversal, Zhy could hear the words clearly, but Wrenflang and Sorchal acted deaf.

He thought about stepping inside the oasis, had a foot forward in that direction, but stopped himself short. No, it was safer to stay outside, wasn't it?

"Out, Sacuan blast you all, come on!" the old mage finally pushed Fanlas, and the large giant shifted uneasily, finally emerging from his trance, though his expression was still blank.

"What?" Bimb's father asked dumbly.

"Out! And you too Sorchal, move!"

"The buzzing..." was all Sorchal said clearly. His eyes never moved from the tall pine trees, and his fingers flicked at his ears, mimicking Zhy's nervous habit.

"Go, *now!*" Wrenflang swore, threw up his hands, swore again. He opened his grizzled mouth to speak but slammed it shut, and raised his left hand. A bolt of white fire, tinged with blue, shot out from his outstretched palm. It *cracked* with a deafening retort.

Zhy leapt backward.

The roar of the spell finally got the attention of the travelers and they stumbled out of the green area. It took a deal of convincing for them to don their coats, even in the howling icy wind; wide eyes still stared at the reversal.

Mesmerized, as I was, Zhy thought. *They think they are close to comfort and safety, but they sit at the gates of Hell!*

"What... what happened?" Sorchal asked in his quiet voice. He had not spoken much the entire journey and his high-pitched tone rang oddly in the cold air. Its sound still rankled Zhy, though he could not quite figure out—the man had been sheltered in the Temple of M'Hzrut his entire life, true, but he *had* traveled through the Tunnels of Woe to retrieve Bimb's father and Wrenflang. *Strange little man.*

Wrenflang broke his thoughts: "This is a reversal, as we have established. A very dangerous place, I'm not surprised a demon didn't pop up from that bog, or the trees didn't attack you."

"Trees? Attack us?" Fanlas sneered, then laughed.

"Who knows what could happen in a reversal. It's time it was destroyed."

"Destroyed, how?" Zhy wondered. Darrell had given no intimation that a reversal could be destroyed: After Bruce and Darrell had killed the old man back in Belden, they had bolted from the vile place with haste, assembling next to Zhy, and shivering with the sudden cold. Here, the cold was even more bone-numbing.

"Why... excuse me?" came the soft voice of Sorchal. "Excuse me, but how can you destroy something like this? Look, my breath!" he repeated Zhy's earlier experiment in blowing steam on the invisible barrier. For a little man, Sorchal's cloud was huge; it plumed forward, hit the barrier and tendrils of steam split, coating it like broth over an over-boiling kettle.

Before Wrenflang could reply, Zhy piped in with his own question: "And just how does something like this even get here? The one we saw was right off the main road—at least I think it was—surely skilled mages would go by it and try to get rid of it..."

Wrenflang sighed. "I doubt you saw something on the main road, Zhy. The danger in these things is their allure, and their pull; you surely were drawn to it, but I cannot believe it would be right next to the road."

"But it..." he shook his head, then nodded at the old mage. *But it was close to the road.* "Perhaps you are right," he whispered. He remembered running fast though the bright opening in the forest had seemed so close to Crown Road. So close. And so far.

"I think we've spent too much time talking," Wrenflang said. "Let's move back a few paces."

The group shifted, eyes still on the strange green parcel of land. Eyebrows rose in curiosity as the mage extracted wrinkled hands from his gloves, and blew on them furiously as he rubbed them together. He let out a final sigh and extended his hands toward the bubble.

A bolt of yellow lightning materialized in his right hand, and in his left, a streak of blue fire. He loosed both strands simultaneously, and they raced along the small space parallel to each other; a split second before they reached the invisible barrier, Wrenflang swung his arms together and the beams touched, creating a single glowing orb of sparkling green fire. For a moment it sizzled, crackled, and hissed as it bobbed in place along the barrier, before it exploded into the space with an earsplitting roar. Zhy stumbled and recovered himself before sprawling into the snow. He watched in awe as the orb broke through the barrier, and split into countless tiny green filaments. These branched into an ever-expanding network of tiny, swirling, cascading threads of energy and light, most dropping down onto the green grass; nearly blending in save for the pulsating glow. Other threads floated out along the barrier and clung to its inside edge.

The old mage barked some strange word to himself, his arms still extended, but hands empty. He grimaced as a violet ball flared out between his wrinkled appendages and raced through the air, into the hole the green ball had created. As soon as the purple orb left his hands, Wrenflang covered his ears, but none of the other travelers had any time to react before the shockwave knocked the men into the snow.

An explosion louder than any clap of thunder rent the lush green field, its sound reverberating through Zhy's ears, setting them to ringing immediately. He sat in the deep snow and stared as the once-green paradise vanished in a cloud of dirt and ash.

The reversal didn't so much explode as implode; sand, dirt, grass, trees, and the various plants collapsed downward into oblivion. Wrenflang's magic had somehow torn apart the connection the place had to the demonic underworld and it fell in upon itself, defeated. To Zhy's surprise, the mage still stood, and his hands extended for yet another spell—this time beams of pure white arced from his hands, the white light only visible when it clashed against the falling avalanche of brown. When the beams entered the void, snow began to fall.

"Snow!" Sorchal screeched. "Snow!"

Never mind the explosion, Zhy thought, glancing at the Protector. *What a strange person* you *are...*

"I was hoping for ice," Wrenflang replied. He grunted and shifted his weight. Again, he rubbed his hands together and blew on them, then tried another spell. This time it worked, and the snow turned to large chunks of ice. Chunks falling from a cloudless sky.

Soon Wrenflang was on his knees, his face drawn and exhausted, though he refused to lower his hands as he kept working on creating ice chunks. The particles slowly grew in size, and though they mostly fell through into the dark void, but some caught on the edges of the pit and held... larger, larger, Wrenflang groaned with the exertion as table-sized pieces fell. He raised his hands higher, giving him more room in the sky with which to work—and even larger blocks of ice merged with the smaller ones, until pieces as wide as the chasm descended. For several more minutes he worked until the pit was covered with a sheet of ice. The mage warmed his hands again quickly, then created more snow—it snowed until the cold white powder was a yard deep.

At last, Wrenflang rolled on his side and panted. "I think that should do it."

Chapter 11

Dark Help

We cannot do this alone. Life is not spent tying one's own thread into a knot, focused only on the self. Rather, we help and are helped by others, and must ensure that we aid even those whom we despise. As well we should welcome their help when given.

Prophet Vron'Za

Horesh's eyes fluttered and he popped one open to assess his surroundings. Half-expecting to be lying in the street of Darvein, or atop a pile of corpses, his hand drifted to his side seeking his sword. The scabbard was empty. Panicked, he opened his other eye and sat bolt upright when a hand pushed him gently back down.

"Horesh, you have been through an ordeal. You must rest."

The voice belonged to one of the commanders he'd run into. A man who had been slopping stables only last week. Gulven was his name. *Gulven? Galven? No, Gulven, or...* He rubbed his head. *Gulven, I'm sure.*

"Gul-Gulven," he rasped. "No, I need to—I need to get back. How many? How many are—"

The hand pushed him back down. "Rest. We can discuss when you have recovered."

"I *am* recovered!" he snapped, but before he could say more, he descended into a fit of coughing.

"No you are not, you must—"

Horesh rolled on his side, cleared his throat violently, and spat out a thick wad of green phlegm, tinged with pink strands. The effort it took to empty his lungs was enough to set the world spinning in a black and red whirl of spots, lines, circles, and swirly shapes—he was thankful he still reclined, else he would have collapsed. He spat out another small dot of fluid, muttered a litany of curse words, and forced himself to his feet, willing away the descending darkness.

"Where am I?" he asked. He could smell wood smoke drifting from somewhere; heavy boots trod on a wooden floor. Was he in a hospital?

"Darvein is lost, but so are the demons," the man was saying.

He knew Darvein was lost—it had been so before he arrived. It's moment of false peace lasted all but three minutes. "Lost? How can you lose an entire army of demons?"

Gulven scratched his head. "Sir... sir, the demons, they attacked, and then they scattered, some north, some west, others south."

"That makes no sense." He had heard reports of coordinated efforts. Gherwza and the dreaded mulargh working in concentrated efforts, but this was new.

This was worse.

"We can't..." Horesh trailed off. Beldeners had never faced a war of any magnitude, ever, as far as he knew. But even soldiers knew the basic concepts—they were *supposed* to be to be fought with armies, organized teams of men setting up lines, trenches, bunkers, archery support, and magic. A scattering army of demons, loose in a hundred directions, an army of individual combatants;

this was an impossible situation in which to mount a defense. "Give me a map... er, please, set one up here, Gulven." Though the world spun slightly and his head screamed, he didn't want to lose his respectability as an official of the Counsel.

Gulven nodded and brought over a large box, atop which he unfolded a map.

Horesh stared while Gulven pointed out the locations of the demons relative to Darvein Harbor. It all appeared completely random, and the numbers of demons, the types, did not match a single pattern that Horesh could think of. He chewed his lip and stared at the map, thinking of Gheren, of Jafren, and of Rhys. Hopefully the teacher was making headway in the Tunnels. If not— "It makes little sense from what we have been seeing, doesn't it?"

"Excuse me? Sir, this is the first we have heard—"

Horesh waved him off respectfully. "I know, I know, but the rest of Belden has been suffering under this threat for quite some time. After hearing reports from Counsel headquarters, and talking to villagers, the pattern here is completely wrong."

"Demons are wrong. Sir." The man added hastily.

At that he could only laugh. "Gulven, you are right. But we can't fight these things individually... we were prepared to face a demonic army, not a thousand demons on their own!"

"No, but *we* are." The new voice belonged to nobody Horesh recognized.

Horesh turned. A man had slipped into the tent, dressed in black—rather, an outfit that had once been black; now it was coated with dust, streaked with dirty brown stains. His face was pale where a mask had covered it, but already fresh stubble was growing there.

"We?"

The man nodded and extended his hand. His calloused hand engulfed Horesh's. "My name is Narand, I am a Knight of the Black Dawn."

Someone coughed. "So that answers that question," Horesh clipped, nodding to the man.

"What question, Sir?" Galvan wondered.

"Whether you—excuse me," Horesh coughed again. "Whether the Knights of the Black Dawn were real. Jafren kept his mouth closed on that subject; Gheren never said anything, either." He peered at Narand.

Narand shrugged and extended his arms, palms up.

"So what can you do for us?"

"My men are outside the camp, still waiting to see if I come out alive." He laughed. "So many of us are too paranoid. Anyway, we saw the smoke from Darvein and traveled by night to get here. I'm sorry we were not in time."

"Could not be helped," Horesh said sadly, "by the time we got to town, the—"

Narand nodded. "I understand. Things have become bad very quickly. We have not slept at all in days." The pitch-black ovals beneath his blue eyes testified to that fact. "We have been lucky to find them only in pairs, or maybe a lone gherwza here and there, but this—"

"Is beyond anything we've trained for, either... I don't think I have an army any more."

The Healer coughed. *I don't, do I?*

Narand was already speaking. "We fight them like this normally, even without, the—issues we've been having. That is, we are used to working with demons as lone fighters—the demons, that is." His stumbling speech contrasted with is smooth voice of authority. "Perhaps each of us could take some of your men and hunt them down; it is all we do."

Horesh nodded, but then looked up. "Three of you— and how many of my men? We don't want an army stomping through the woods!"

The look from Narand was one of pity and anguish. "It would only be a total of twenty or so," he whispered.

"Twenty..." Horesh repeated. "Twenty?"

The Knight nodded.

"We had *two thousand* to start! Two thousand!" At that he collapsed back on the cot, sitting down with a loud sigh. *Two thousand...*

Within the tent there was a long silence and the soft sound of shuffling feet. At last one of his soldiers spoke. "Commander Horesh, we will fight with you until there are no more."

"No more what, Poru? Men? Demons?" he asked with a bitter smile.

The man shrugged. "Either."

He wanted to sob, wanted to plunge a knife into his heart and die. Two thousand men! No, he could not give in. The demons had scattered, but what would it take for them to regroup? How long would it be before an organized horde descended upon the land?

Horesh's head throbbed and the room wobbled. He dismissed everyone, including the Healer, and fell back and closed his eyes.

He slept for a few hours, or was it days? People came and went, each person cloaked in a swirling haze, and he muttered incoherent words as they visited him and left the building.

After a long rest, he lifted his head from the pillow and noticed the room was in one place. Tentatively he set his feet to the ground and pushed himself upright—glad for once that he didn't topple over from dizziness.

Outside a horrifying screech stilled his heart. He glanced around desperately for his sword, but the room was empty. With a curse and a prayer, he snatched a poker from the fireplace and stumbled outside.

As soon as he stepped into the cold air, a gherwza leapt at his throat.

Chapter 12

Not Much to Go On

Did you douse the campfire? Are you sure? Embers burn underground, flames can be kissed by the wind, and quickly erupt into a raging inferno. Beware the fires you left burning.

Prophet Vron'Za

"No word? None?"

The Keeper shook his head sadly.

Gheren paced the Keeper's small apartment, then collapsed into a chair. The cushion was surprisingly soft, given the ancient look of the furniture that littered the small room. Even the carpet was plush... Gheren's gaze tottered around the room and locked briefly on the window casement. *Is that gilt?* He turned his focus back to the Keeper. "There must be some word by now, unless... no, we sent a large enough force."

"Perhaps the snow, or—"

"No, they were to send their reports as soon as they got to Forshen, and there are villages south of that place where there is no snow. Something has gone wrong. I fear they are being completely overrun."

They sat in silence for a while. The Keeper sighed and reached for his small tea cup, took a tiny sip and set it back in its saucer. Gheren's attention was riveted on a speck of dust on the arm of the chair, and the light clinking of the pottery shook him from his reverie.

"Perhaps I'm being too impatient," he said softly.

A few more quiet minutes went by before the thin door nearly buckled from an onslaught of pounding. Who could be here? Gheren shot to his feet, looking for a bolt-hole, but already the door was open and an armed guard stood there. Behind him was a man dressed in the garb of the Holy Orders.

Damn you Gorand. And damn your boy, I should have blocked you in myself and cut the man's throat.

"Counselor Gheren?" the guard asked. He didn't wait for a response. "You are under arrest for treason."

φ

The trial was a sham, as he had expected. High Cleric Gorand had made up his mind and done his job of convincing his puppet of a judge that Gheren was a treasonous monster and deserved to die. Citizens muttered among themselves, and Gheren heard one person hush another who dared use the word "demon." Would no one step up and admit to reality? Was everyone blind?

"Gheren Trayfel, you have been tried and found guilty of usurping the authority of the Counsel and of the Holy Elders, and thus the Light. As such, you are to condemned to death by hanging. Have you any last words to say to your defense?"

His jaw set, he offered Gorand a glare of loathing. He had heard the High Clerics could be a cunning and conniving group, but Gorand's actions bespoke of an evil nearly as dangerous as the one that Belden faced. An evil the man denied, and had gone to great lengths to cover up. With a sick feeling, he realized that the cleric was now a conspirator to the entire situation; by doing nothing he was enabling the catastrophe. "I do. I want the High Cleric to remember this day. To remember, as his face is being eaten by a gherwza—"

"Counselor, please!" the judge interrupted. "If you have nothing else to say, I—"

"No, you will listen!" Gheren snapped. "Everyone in this room knows the evil that is swarming over this land! We are being overrun by demons and the High Cleric instead sets out in a personal vendetta against me. Jafren knew the truth and killed himself. I did something. That is, I *tried* to do something. I have served the Light, your Grace," he said, staring at Gorand. The man refused to look him in the eye. "I have served the Light, and by that same Light I have been damned. Well... damn you too."

There were a few gasps in the room and Gorand stiffened at those words, but still refused to acknowledge them. A heavy hand pulled Gheren upright and he was hauled away. His execution would be done in private and in silence; Beldeners did not like to watch men die, even if they were labeled traitors.

The world was going to end, and very badly, and those in charge were letting it happen.

Chapter 13

A Simple Trick

We have devised so many tools, to solve a wide range of problems. But if you hold only a paintbrush, everything is a canvas.

Prophet Z'Hara

Horesh screamed and darted sideways as the creature bounded forward. The frame crunched under the weight of his shoulder and his head swam. The Counsel Guard slipped sideways and the bat screeched through the open door of the house, talons clicking across the wooden floor.

He should have slammed the door and walked away, looked for Narand. But his instinct as a commander took over and he gripped the poker as he fell back into the room.

The demonic bat continued its slide across the rotting floor, knocking Horesh's sick bed to the far wall. Unable to stop its forward momentum, it crashed into the hearth; the gherwza roared with irritation as its fur was singed by the hot fire. Quickly adjusting, it spun and jumped again and Horesh tried to sprint away, but stumbled. Poorly.

He still clung to the rusty poker and swung it wildly at the beast. The implement clanged against the floor, the shock numbing his arm. Again the beast jumped, but he wisely ran toward the fire and stood in front of it. The gherwza growled, snorted, and spat a vile substance from its mouth. Horesh ducked and the green slime boiled against the stone hearth with the stench of the dead.

Though the heat from the fire burned her backside, Horesh stood firm, daring the creature to attack him. Not nearly as mindless as he had hoped it to be, it waited, growling low in its throat.

"Come on then," he said. "Come on demon, have at me... try to take what you want!" He waited for the beast to attack, planning a feint.

This time, however, the gherwza outsmarted him. By now it expected him to leap to the left and timed his jump perfectly—a claw swiped at his arm, ripping open the flesh in a ragged, red-streaming wound. Horesh bellowed with anger and swung the poker again.

It struck something hard, a jaw bone perhaps, and again the shock set his arm quivering. The gherwza growled again and leapt—by now Horesh stood near the upturned bed.

As the beast lifted its talons from the ground Horesh held the poker firm, crouched low, and forced the weapon up, towards the belly of the beast. He expected the poker to strike through soft flesh, but the underside of the gherwza was coated in a thick, leather-like scale, which the weapon could not penetrate.

But still he put his weight behind the thrust, pushing against an impenetrable substance... impenetrable, except that as he pushed upward, the small barb on the poker caught against that joining of the leathery plates, twisting the tool in his hand. With a final curse, Horesh squeezed tighter against the poker and pushed again, but the barb slipped.

"No," he groaned as the poker came free from the belly.

But his groan quickly turned into a roar of triumph.

Curiously, as the barb struck the beast, the forward momentum of bat and weapon created an almost wondrous situation. As the beast careened forward, it rotated slightly in mid-air; and when the barb flipped against the underbelly, it increased the speed of the beast's rolling motion—when Horesh finally lost control of the poker, he had given it one last, imperceptible twist. This was enough to push the gherwza completely over and flip it on its back. It landed with a thud, feet spinning in the air, leather-scaled belly heaving.

Horesh gripped the weapon tightly, staring.

The gherwza did not move, it only spun its legs, the fur-covered appendages whirling helplessly in the air. It turned slightly on its back, but quickly went still.

"What...?" he wondered. Raising the poker, Horesh drove the poker through the neck of the demon. Once, twice... a hundred times, the poker rose and fell, cracking bones and severing arteries... he stood in a thick pool of blood, tears of frustration and rage covering his face. All of the death, destruction, and blood! The world suffered beneath the flood of these horrific creatures, and he had completed a simple trick to kill one. Too simple. He could have prevented so much! "No time, no time, no time," he repeated. One more thrust. "No. Time!"

Horesh took a tentative step closer to the creature. One last nerve impulse shook the demonic bat, and Horesh tried to dart back, but fatigue had rooted him in place. A talon lashed out, its final attack a deadly one; the sharp claw pierced Horesh's belly, pushed through stomach, liver, kidney before poking out through his jerkin. The Counsel Guard gurgled, stumbled backward and fell against the dusty floor, eyes wide.

Narand stood in the doorway, sword in hand, torso covered in blood.

Chapter 14

Harnessing A Hurricane?

⌘

Can you corral the raging currents within yourself? Will you be able to channel the power and energy that lies within to benefit mankind? Or will you destroy yourself?

Prophet Vron'Za

I had caused too much trouble and had learned nothing. By trouble, I mean mass destruction and the loss of too many innocent lives.

Was there any way that I could do what Mother had done? How had she so tightly controlled my body and my internal organs such that I writhed in pain at every turn? I needed to do that, in a decent and effective manner, with the rest of the world; instead I was simply causing destruction and devastation.

Perhaps my goal was not within the confines of Belden and Welcfer—the lands far beyond the oceans were unknown to everyone, even many of the dead. Why had they not decided to travel out there, instead of bumbling around an old land that had forgotten them? I sighed inwardly. At least I could try to venture out into the great beyond and look for something.

As I started floating out and away from Belden, the ocean looked infinite. Miles and miles of rolling blue ripples and waves stretched into a indigo line in the far distance, with no indication of other land. But as I turned my gaze north east, a strange white fleck caught my eye.

Far out to sea, I could see a giant white cloud that encircled a section of ocean; a piece of deep gray water that was nearly double the size of Belden. Free from my land-locked world, I ventured out to it.

The ocean was deceptive in its length and breadth—the giant storm looked close, the farther I traveled, the farther it seemed to be. I came within reach of its swirling vortices after several hours.

"What are you doing here?"

I started at the voice. If I were not dead, I would have left a large puddle in the ocean... I could not imagine another person out here. "Who—where?" I croaked.

The light voice answered. "My name is... well, I think my name is perhaps forgotten. I don't remember much for some reason, my head it—it was beaten badly and I only remember white, like this. But this is not snow, is it?" the voice was trembling and disjointed, a man's voice struggling to find volume, unsure of its surroundings.

As yet I could not see anything, could hear only his voice. Where was he? *Who* was he? "Where are you?"

"I'm, well, I'm over here. But sometimes I can be over there—I've been watching this for quite some time. Years, maybe, or possibly just weeks." I thought I heard something pop. Knuckles? "But I like to watch from here."

He spoke as if I could see him, but trying to scan the entire swirling mass was nearly impossible, for it even as it spun as a whole, tendrils of white clouds cycled off of it many directions. For a brief moment, I thought I saw a wisp of something that vaguely resembled a man's face, but it could have been the massive hole that gaped at me from the center of the storm.

"It's called the eye—and the storm, it's a hurricane or orkan."

"Orkan?" The name sounded familiar. Was I thinking of orca? Perhaps.

"Someone up here—a man passed by—he called it that."

"I—I see... thank you."

"Yes, I do remember some things, and these were very scary where I grew up out east."

"Would this storm cause a lot of damage if it hit land?"

A gruff laugh in the ether. "Aye, it would. I think it could destroy half of Belden." Maybe I didn't need to do anything, after all. If this huge storm could kill as many or more people than the demons, what then would the point be of trying to atone for my crimes?

"But nothing like this could ever reach Belden," he answered my unasked question. "No..." he paused, taking in a lungful of invisible air. "My head hurts so much, I want it to stop! Anyway, this has been here for a very long time, growing and growing and growing. I don't know when it started, but it has not moved much along the ocean—very strange."

I thought back on my experiment with the water and how the resulting explosion blew me across the room. For several moments after, the ground seemed to rumble and shake beneath my feet; I attributed it to my shock at what I had done. Could I have caused something like this? Even if it was thousands of miles away? I asked as much.

The stranger laughed. "No, I don't think you could have done this, even if you say you can use all of that magical power."

"Hmm," I wondered, taking another long look at the slowly twirling monstrosity. Why was it unable to move?

"There's no wind," he answered flatly. "At least, no wind that is strong enough to push it toward land. Say... I know you." There was another rush of wind, which struck me as strange. No wind, yet—it must have been his figure bobbing about, I just could not see it. His sudden question startled me, but I was slowly adjusting to his personality.

After all, I had once been like him—my mind racing from subject to subject.

"You know me?"

"Yes, you called me by name."

"I did?" I wondered.

"You did."

"But I don't know if..." I trailed off. For a moment I thought I heard a soft cry, or perhaps a light sigh.

"Oh. My head... I don't know why it still hurts here. It shouldn't, should it? Maybe I just keep letting it hurt and need to stop thinking about it. Yes, now, I remember..." Another quiet pop of something. "I saw you there, you know, at the last minute."

At that I knew exactly who this person was. "Your name is—"

"Why were you just hiding there behind the table?" he interrupted. "You let my friends die—or were you a slave of... of the warlock? What was his name?"

"Ar'Zoth," I whispered.

"I see."

"Do you know where the other man went, the small-man, I mean?" he wondered.

"No."

I could sense a sad shake of a head, but as hard as I looked I saw nothing of the man's persona. He was either slipping away into the final place, or he was clever at hiding himself. Knowing now who he truly was, I knew it must be the former. "He left shortly after. I wanted to see some things and my head hurt so bad I just wanted to rest, if a dead man can rest! Someone back in Belden told me that I didn't have long here, and it's probably why you can't see me... I feel like I'm being pulled away."

"That is a feeling I can understand. There is not much time left—I get so tired of hearing that."

"So what were you doing there?" he repeated his earlier question. There was a rustle of wind and I could sense he had shifted to somewhere else nearby.

"I was hiding—waiting for Ar'Zoth to finish before I killed him."

"You watched us die?" A sadness filled his voice and a red vein of anger lined its edges. He had every right to be upset—by doing nothing, I had let his friends die, and I had betrayed Lyn. Now Zhy and Fa worked their way across a frozen landscape, trying to fix a mess I had created—a mess that was seeming impossible to mend.

"I—I made a very big mistake," I admitted. "I thought that Ar'Zoth could grant me power, I thought I could get revenge on the world for treating me so poorly."

"How could the world treat you poorly?"

I sighed. "I was, well, a very simple person. Mother drank when I was still inside her stomach, and well, it turned me into a sad, pathetic creature. I used to be able to talk to the dead—when I played my sutan or sang songs, they would come visit me between the notes." My incorporeal throat caught. Why was it so hard to talk about this? And why couldn't I stop talking about it? A hurricane spun below us and time was slipping away from Belden and Welcfer.

"And...?"

"I-I'm sorry, it is a very sad story. One day Ar'Zoth visited me. You shudder at that, and I do too... it was wonderful, at the time. Now, I realize how horrible it was. He took it all away from me, yet still kept some veil of the idiot I had been—those around me could not see through it, not even Fa. Not even Zhy's... not even Zhy's father."

"Zhy's father visited you too?"

"Very much so—he led me to the north, to Ar'Zoth!"

"What?" When he blurted the word, I could definitely see the dim, fading outline of a large head shaking.

"Yes, he wanted me to keep an eye on Zhy, he wanted me to kill Ar'Zoth before the warlock killed all of you."

"I don't..." the man trailed off and I could feel the depth of despair that floated in this place. Below, the white cloud of the hurricane spun slowly, almost peacefully, though far below the waters raged and waves taller than mountains roared on its surface.

"I am so very sorry, to you, to Zhy, to Darrell."

"You could have saved us."

"I—" Yes, I could have. So much I could have done. I could have played the sutan and ignored Lyn, ignored the quieter, deeper voice of Ar'Zoth as he beckoned me northward. I could have killed Ar'Zoth with the poisoned sword. No, I waited. "I killed you all."

There was a brief movement of air and I thought he nodded. "No, you did not. I did. It was my idea, or was it? Was it—I don't know, my head hurts. Someone told me to, no, that isn't right, I—well, in any case, I wanted to learn magic. Yes, and someone sent me, I just can't remember..."

"Is everything all right?" I asked. "Are you being pulled back?"

"No, my head... just hurts a little. I'm sorry, too. Sorry for everything."

"Well," I sighed. "We can sit here watching this storm and lament our bad decisions, or we can do something... someone wise once told me that... someone who is now working with Zhy to fix this mess we are in."

Thoughts of Zhy set my emotions to boiling again. The man had killed me, more or less. I should let go, but I couldn't. Maybe if I somehow talked to Fa?

"The mess that I—"

"No, the mess. Period. The mess. The time for blame and pity is over. What can we do?"

"I wish I could help, I just can't seem to hold on any longer, I am being pulled to the final place." His voice was quieter now; I strained to hear.

"You must be, since I can't see you at all."

"Aye."

"Before you go, Bruce, tell me, this—this hurricane, do you think somebody could control it?"

"Why in Sacuan's name would you want to do that?"

"It's the only way I know how to help Zhy and Fa. I can't stop the demons, but I need some way to help. Right now the weather is the most powerful thing that I can possibly use, but so far I've only caused destruction!"

"What do you mean?"

I told him about the windstorms.

"Oh," he said. "You still have a lot of magical power, it seems, if you can control the weather! But this thing... I don't know how you would move it; you'd need more wind. A lot more wind."

I stared at the hurricane despondently.

"What is your name?" Bruce asked softly.

"My name is Bimb," I replied sadly.

"Bimb? Bimb," he repeated. "Bimb, I have to—"

And he was gone.

The hurricane spun and I watched. I tried to pull at it, but it was too massive—not large or heavy, but wide, broad; it covered countless miles. As I had discovered earlier, the clouds were just water vapor—and the wind was spiraling them into the strange bird-wing pattern, it would not move. But how could the wind move it? And why was it just *sitting here?*

If I could not move the giant storm, perhaps I could at least learn a lesson from it. For several hours I watched each section of the beast, moving from its lower levels up to the top, then dove down through the eye-hole in the center, where the winds were surprisingly calm. In that moment an idea launched itself into my undead—was that even a word?—consciousness... though this monster was uncontrollable, could I perhaps move the wind in a circular pattern, carve out a hole in the middle, and then direct it from the relative calm within?

"Calm within," I whispered. Could I ratchet back my hatred of Zhy? Could I push his face away each time I grabbed control of the weather? If that was possible (but by Sacuan it was hard; the man had killed me! Killed me!

A dead man... ach, but the time was over for that), then I could do this.

"Fa..." I called out. "Ma...? I'm sorry."

I took a last look at the storm and floated back to the east, wishing Bruce a peaceful eternity.

Chapter 15

The Tunnels of Woe – Once More

It will be hard to keep the Tunnels a secret. Too many now know of their existence for it to remain closely-guarded. We must do our best to repress knowledge of their existence, and to deny entrance to those unworthy.

High Cleric Gorand

"Unbelievable. Unbelievable." Rhys repeated as he gazed down the seemingly endless chain of blue lights.

Felyar breathed out a cloud of damp steam.

"Stay smart, stay strong."

The companions found it hard not to be mesmerized by the dull glow of the blue lights. Miles whirred by underfoot before Rhys shook himself and stopped. "How far have do you think we gone?"

"I don't know."

"Feels like a lot," Rhys said.

"Those lights are strange. What kind of magic runs them, I wonder?"

Rhys shrugged and inspected one up close. The smoky haze around the fixture caught his attention. "These are definitely magic, though it appears they burn... there's no smoke, but it appears to be consuming something very slowly, it seems. Look!"

Felyar leaned closer and peered at the glowing blue orb. "Yes, it does, but how does it not use up all the fuel?"

"I'm not—say, look!" he pointed up a head, perhaps a thousand paces. One of the blue lights had gone out.

He went up to investigate, for the moment forgetting the task that lay ahead of them.

Rhys howled a warning, though it came from his throat like a gurgle: Two black eyes peered back at him and nail-like claws scratched stone. Rhys leapt backward, tried to sprint, but his feet slipped on the slick damp, and he crunched to the floor. Felyar turned at Rhys' yell, opened his mouth, and froze—

From an infinitesimally small opening in the rock, an inch above the dead light, the eyes moved forward, followed slowly by the small skull that they lived in. A rat's skull. The creature oozed from the wall, screeching and chirping as it wriggled free from its confinement.

Felyar shook himself and thrust his arms outward. The blue bolt of fire seared the creature in mid-air and it fell hissing to the ground. To their horror, the animal bulged as the miniature rats inside scratched for the surface— Felyar, however, kept firing... the air filled with the sickening stench of burning fur and the deep rotten foulness of a sewer.

Rhys stepped back and away from the melee, though soon he ran out of ground and his back thudded into the stone on the far wall. His foot stepped in the freezing spring water, filling his boots, and he took one step forward before a skittering stilled his heart.

"Fel—" he uttered, but the black rat had already leapt out from behind him and launched itself at the mage.

Felyar raised both arms and the rat burned quickly, though stray tendrils of energy skittered along the space between the men and struck Rhys on his shoulder. He screamed and rolled, falling into the water.

The mage tried to step forward to offer aid, but exhaustion claimed him as well, and he fell to first his knees, then his entire frame flopped to the floor in a heap.

"Felyar... Felyar, are you all right?" Rhys asked, his lips bubbling against the shallow pool.

Only heavy breathing echoed in the chamber. Rhys repeated his question and finally the mage responded. "Y-yes, I think so, it makes me so tired..."

"My arm is burning."

A sigh. "Is it in the water?"

"Yes... cold, so cold, but it burns."

"Keep it in the water, the pain will go away. I'm so very sorry, but the rat... the rat." *I hope there are no more,* he thought with desperation. If anything—*else*—should come from the bowels of hell, they would die. "I'm so sorry..."

Rhys tried to sigh, but his lips only fluttered against the surface of the puddle, creating a spray of bubbles and ice cold water. "You did what you had to do..."

"I hope it is enough. I can't keep this up much longer..."

"You are doing well."

Felyar grunted. He *was* doing well. The spells he used were devastating, they completely destroyed the poor—no, he would not call them poor—creatures upon impact, but such spells were the most demanding of his energy. These were surely demons and he did not want to risk a lesser spell in case such magic did not succeed at first. Rhys would be no help, a man with more brains that sword skills, and Felyar felt he must take most of the burden. It was painful to think that he could not keep up with the physical demands of his magic... perhaps if he could reduce his efforts with some effect, they would have success.

"Thank Sacuan nothing else has come out," Rhys said softly to the water.

"Yeah."

The men lay there for some time before rising slowly, and with exhausted groans and a creak of joints. Water dripped from Rhys's outerwear and he shook his head to clear his soaked scalp.

"Well..." Rhys began.

Felyar nodded to the unasked question. "I suppose. I'm as ready as I can be, I guess."

The teacher from the tiny village steeled himself and padded further into the dull blue void.

Chapter 16

A Guiding Box

The sun can be a guide, a guide which leads you to your damnation. Trust only in the true Light, not a false one.

High Cleric Bertrand

The sun had only been above the horizon for a couple of hours when Wrenflang pulled the group to a halt. As soon as the boots stopped crunching in the brittle snow, the air became painfully still.

"What is it?" Zhy asked.

"I think it is time we tested our tool," the old mage said, un-shouldering his pack and letting it fall to the ground. He pulled off his gloves, reached inside for the map and the strange box. It was about the size of a large hitching post, constructed of cedar slats, with one at the top extending slightly outward. Wrenflang pulled out the longer piece to reveal a sheet of glass. The glass fogged quickly in the air, but the mage wiped it clean frequently, allowing the men to observe the rotating ball nestled inside.

"See, the ball is attached to an outer rim of metal, here, which is then pinned to the inside of the box—that lets it rotate freely. Inside the glass you can see the black needle with the red tip, that will always point north."

"Always?"

"Yes, almost. When you get too far north, it will spin wildly—for every mile north it points another degree to the west."

"Why is that?" Fanlas wondered.

"There is a big metal rock beneath the earth, another magnet such as this box uses."

"How do you know that?"

"Fanlas," Wrenflang sighed. "Always the doubter. We don't know, really, but it is written in the old books."

Bimb's father nodded, not quite accepting the answer.

The old mage directed his attention elsewhere. "Zhy, come look." The mage turned and walked east, and upon wiping the glass clean again, they noted that the needle pointed north. He stomped to the south and the needle spun to point behind him.

"Amazing."

"I could have used this in the Tunnels of Woe," Sorchal said suddenly. Zhy jumped at the sound of his voice—their companion had been so silent on their journey, so averse to talking, that each time he opened his mouth, it surprised Zhy.

"Excuse me, but why?" Wrenflang wondered. He turned to look at the young Protector, and his look set Zhy's heart fluttering. *Something is wrong with Sorchal,* Zhy thought, *something very, very wrong, and Wrenflang sees it...*

"Why not?" the young Protector asked.

"All you had to do was follow the path... there was no need for such a device in the Tunnels." The old mage's voice was soft and soothing, though he stared hard at Sorchal, his gaze a harsh contrast to his quiet voice.

"The path?" Sorchal wondered; his body jerked as he turned his attention to Wrenflang. "The—oh, the path, yes, the path. It only went one way, but how was I to be sure? Be *sure,*" he added with a hissed emphasis.

Zhy stepped back from the group.

"Did you fear getting lost in the Tunnels of Woe?" Wrenflang wondered. "I did not see any diversions or pathways that led anywhere else. The Tunnels end near Fanlas's farm, do they not?"

"I like the box," Sorchal replied quietly.

Wrenflang nodded.

With a soft clearing of his throat, Fanlas spoke up: "Sorchal perhaps you would like to rest a little while? Shall we make our camp and just rest?"

The Protector shook his head violently, leering at the guiding box. "I don't want to get lost," he muttered.

A silence fell over the group. Zhy kept a wary eye on Sorchal, but the Protector's eyes were cast to the ground.

Suddenly, Sorchal fidgeted, then burst out in a wild, screeching panic; his voice was again far too high-pitched for a man. "We should have taken the edible food from the reversal, we need more food. Give me the box! I want the box, it's my box!" Clumsy, frozen hands reached for the wooden box, clawing, clawing with fingernails that were too long, too long and black.

Fanlas drew his sword.

"No!" Wrenflang barked, stepping between the two. He raised a hand, but Sorchal grabbed at his leg, pulling him down. "No!" the mage screeched, even as he fell. "No, he's... the snow, the cold..." and he trailed off—

Sorchal had pulled him all the way into the snow, and was clawing at his legs, tearing, pulling, reaching for the box. "The box, my box!" the Protector howled, reaching for it. The guiding box had slipped from Wrenflang's grasp and fell into the deep snow. "My box!" he yelled, letting go of Wrenflang. Sorchal dove into the snow, hands furiously searching the cold powder for the box.

"Sorchal, what is the matter with you?" Wrenflang demanded.

For an answer, the Protector leapt to his feet. "You are all crazy," he sneered, his voice dangerously soft. "That was my box!"

With that, he bounded away, to the east, squealing and swearing.

The travelers stared, Fanlas clutching his sword hilt. He took a step to the east, but Wrenflang set a hand on his arm. "No, no, he is lost... the snow and the sun, it can sometimes make a man go mad."

Zhy cursed. "That was my fault. We should have left him at the Temple."

"Your fault, why?" Fanlas wondered.

He told them of the trail, and Sorchal's search for wintergreen. Wrenflang sighed and Fanlas shook his head sadly.

"He would have gone insane anyway, I suppose. Such an ordeal—so much bloodshed that he has seen." The old mage picked up the box, wiped the glass free of steam, and motioned them to follow.

"Does that really work?" Zhy wondered.

Wrenflang stopped and smiled. "Yes. Would you like to try it?"

Zhy thought a moment, then nodded.

The old mage fingered his beard, releasing a spray of frozen flakes of sweat. "All right, we will follow you... for now ignore the box and start walking north."

"W-what?" Zhy wondered. For Zhy, the box was his connection to men and the cities in which they lived. But he still found it difficult to trust a needle in a wooden crate.

"Go ahead, just for a little bit."

Zhy thumbed his earlobe, then pulled his hood back down as a gust of air ripped at the exposed flesh. He quickly replaced it, and started northward.

Or in a direction he thought was north.

After several hundred paces, Wrenflang called a stop and Zhy examined the box; after wiping the glass clean, he cursed. "The needle is pointing that way!" he exclaimed, his left arm extended straight out. Zhy felt a clamp on his stomach. He felt as if they were going north, could have sworn to that fact.

Wrenflang laughed. "Trust the box, Zhy, trust the box!"

Chapter 17

Recall?

If, in order that you must do right, you must ignore orders and defy authority, you are absolved in such action. Perhaps not by man, but at least by the Light.

Prophet Yoz'Hru

"We refuse to go."

The Guard bristled. "Refuse? You cannot refuse orders!"

"Who gave the orders, and why?"

"The High Cleric, acting as Grand Counselor, until such time as—"

"We take orders from the Grand Counselor now," the Protector rasped. His voice was strained and tired, and his eyes were wide green pools, full of terror. He had seen more blood and destruction in the last two days than he had ever seen his full thirty years as a Protector.

"The Counselor is dead, and the High Cleric—"

"Dead?" He scratched his chin, scowled briefly. "I'm sorry to hear that, but my orders are quite clear."

"Your orders are to—"

The Protector growled. "The orders I now follow are mine. The innocent people of this country need our help. I have seen more demons than this land should see in a thousand years, I have seen the weak and the strong die horribly. These demons are killing everybody. Whatever orders you possess are void. Is that clear?"

"The High Cleric himself *demands*—"

Steel whispered from a sheath and was leveled at the Guard's neck. "We are fighting a war. We will return when that war is over."

"The Orders—"

"I said to Sacuan's scrotum with the orders!" the Protector barked. "We are fighting a war. A *war*."

The Guard swallowed, his enormous Adam's apple bobbing. "The... the order—I mean, the High Cleric has stated that this war should not be fought."

"Not be fought?" The sword edged closer.

"No." A very slight shake of the head. "The High Cleric has stated that this is a result of the wages of sin, a result of misdeeds against the Light."

Suddenly the tip of the blade was at his neck, only a hair away from his jugular. The Protector pressed lightly and there was a sharp sting as the honed edge pierced the skin. A small rivulet of blood trickled down his throat, and pooled on the point of the sword. "Turn around and walk over to that barn over there," he growled.

"What?"

The Protector pushed slightly on the sword. "You heard me."

"What are you—what are you going to do?" He sputtered. "Why? I never—"

"Shut up and walk over there."

The Guard's lips moved silently, but he slowly turned and walked to where the Protector had indicated; when they had arrived at a pile of rotting fence posts, he poked the tip of the sword against the spine of the Counsel Guard. "Tell me, Guard," he spat, "tell me if that—" he bobbed his head to indicate a shredded corpse on the ground. It was only a foot long. "Tell me if that is from *wages of sin!* Tell me! What evil can any child do such that it deserves to be torn asunder by a mulargh? No, don't tell me, you can tell your High Cleric. Leave. Leave now before I kill you."

Wide-eyed, the Guard backed away. Upon seeing the small corpse, his hackles rose, and his knees buckled. The Protector only grunted as the burly man collapsed to the ground and retched.

Chapter 18

That Which Is (Now) Known

The enemy of my enemy could be called an ally, it has been said. Said by fools! A man who wishes another man ill remains an enemy to the greater good. You cannot make peace when you are dead.

Unknown, IV age

Drunplug stretched in his saddle and sighed heavily; his breath plumed out from his small mouth in a cloud nearly twice his own size. He balled his rough fists inside the woolen gloves, trying to work some warmth into them. Around him, his soldiers hunched in their saddles, backs against the howling wind that tore across the Icedown Plains. At the same time, furtive glances darted in all directions, looking for the hordes of savages each man knew was hiding... though how they hid in such a flat and desolate terrain was beyond Drunplug. Often they seemed to appear from the rocks and snow of the ill-named "Plain" and strike with an unfettered brutality. He clenched his fists again and cursed.

The Welcferian soldiers had ridden for several days, lucky to have seen none of the vicious horde. However, each day farther from their base camp reduced the food supplies all the greater, and they risked much in this freezing clime. The land was unforgiving and without any nourishment, which made it all the more baffling: how did these savages survive?

Soon Drunplug would have to make the call to retreat—he only hoped that they would not be attacked on their return to camp. Such would be the standard way of these naked tribes. *Retreat from what?* He thought. *There is nothing here!*

As he clenched his cold fists in his gloves, he wondered how the savages could keep themselves so warm, dressed in only thin hides and various leather outfits. *They aren't men at all,* he thought. Merely primitive beasts with human faces. *No wonder Beldeners think we're the birthplace of demons...*

A cold sun dipped further in the sky and the men rode their horses slowly over the terrain. Tonight would be the last night in the wild, Drunplug decided. There was a little extra food left, and he wanted to have enough to return, should they run into resistance. Once they returned, they would uproot the base camp and move it another day ahead—further into the heartless and barren wasteland. And closer to the Spires of Solitude. If they could find the savages quickly, they could push them back into the mountains, back, back, and ever back, until every last one was dead. For generations, these natives had lived on the flat and barren ground, and by moving them into the rugged mountains, Drunplug could create perfect ambush points. Mostly, however, he hoped the mountains would pose a greater challenge for them to survive. Then again, he'd seen these tribes survive battles in which they surely should have been obliterated... they were tough, if not shabbily-clothed, and primal.

"Darrell, where in Sacuan's name are you?" he whispered to his saddle.

He was lost in thought and did not notice the young soldier approach, his cheeks red and breath steaming. "Sir? Sir?" Finally, after a third, "Sir", this time a little louder, Drunplug shook himself out of his reverie and acknowledged the young man.

"Yes?"

"Sir, our scouts have noticed three men approaching. They don't look like the Hjor."

He shuddered at the word, for the moment ignoring the young man's first statement. Hjor. Drunplug would rather that name had never surfaced—it gave these thugs an identity, something to cling to; he only wanted them to cling to the hard ground with lifeless fingers. "Why do you use that word?" he asked. "And further, how do you know it?"

"I've—I've heard the men talking, sir. One of their fathers used to serve and he said he heard that was the name of these beasts."

"They are men—well, they are very closely related to men, I should say." Drunplug sucked in the cold air. "And they are not called Hjor, they have no name... Hjor is just one of the tribes... he must have talked to one of—*them*."

"Aye, sir, said the man was dying and asked to be killed. The man's father... he asked first his name, and the beast actually spoke, and said Hjor. Not sure how you even spell that gibberish."

"You can't." He supposed that more of his men knew the names of the tribes. And there most likely was no harm in it—but putting a name to these brutish fiends seemed strange in his ears. "Now," he said, sighing again with a cloud of steam, "what was this about people approaching? Where? And how far off? Are they armed?"

"They are two miles away, according to the scout, and they surely see us. We cannot tell if they are armed. There are only three."

"Don't our scouts have those new glasses...?"

"Aye, but it's too Sacuan-blasted cold! All you see is fog!"

Drunplug clenched his fists again. "Keep an eye on them. Three, you say? Hardly an army, but they could be anything. I suspect a feint from—from Hjor, or whatever tribe is out here."

"I doubt that it is a trap, sir."

"Why is that?"

"They are heavily clothed, from we could see—fur coats, hats, thick gloves I'd imagine. No, they are not of the Hjor or any tribe."

"What in..." he wondered, but dismissed the soldier. There was no need for this young man to hear him try to work it out. The only things he needed to hear from Drunplug were orders. They would have to come soon.

Who in their right mind comes this far? He thought. "Wait, boy!" he barked over his shoulder.

"Yes?" the soldier said, turning quickly back.

"Were any of these strangers... small?" It was more than he could hope for, but it was a faint possibility.

"No... no, sir." The young man dipped his head. "I'm sorry," he added sadly.

"Thank you."

Darrell, where are you? He wondered again, then tried to force his thoughts back to the situation. *Who would be this far west? And why?*

After fifteen minutes the soldier returned. "Looks like one has a sword, but otherwise they are unarmed. They surely see us and are approaching our line... I had the scout circle around, but one of them saw the horse, and simply waved. I'm not sure they mean any harm."

"Thank you. Still, send out a rider—no, two. Approach them and be ready for anything... they could be mages, or worse. This is no climate to be in for anyone but ourselves and these blasted Hjor." *Unless they are trying to get to the Spires.* He'd heard of men trying to climb those forbidding peaks, but they usually started from just north of Foltrag; the so-called adventurers never returned. And if these men were from Belden, why did they not start from near Gray Gorge? It didn't make sense. There was nothing—*nothing*—out here, and nothing between them and the Spires.

"Stupid Beldeners," he muttered under his breath.

φ

"They're sending men out to us," Wrenflang said. "I'm sure they wonder why we are out here and what were about."

"I don't blame them for that," Fanlas replied. "Wrenflang," he said, balling his massive fists. "Are you sure of your plan?"

The old mage shook his head briefly, then nodded. "Of course I'm sure," he said, trying to laugh. His white-capped head swung pendulously back and forth and he frowned. "Those are Welcferian soldiers—focused on the savages, and pushing them farther back. They must wonder what we are doing. I am sure of the plan, at least for now."

He looked at Zhy and Zhy pointedly ignored his gaze. Wasn't this his idea? To try to gain the support of the Welcferian army? Wrenflang had added a wrinkle or two, but it had been Zhy's idea. Now that that same army had appeared before them, however, his stomach felt like a liquid ball of nervousness.

"Great Sacuan's scrotum..." he whispered.

Two soldiers arrived, geared for battle, their horses seemingly unaffected by a hard run in the brutal cold. Both men were small in stature, Zhy noted; and the maces and chain mail added an even sinister look to their craggy features. "What is your business here?" one asked. His voice sounded frozen.

Wrenflang stepped forward, his arms at his sides. Fanlas wisely shifted his sword around to his back so he could not reach it easily. The old mage spoke. "We are travelers from the Temple of M'Hzrut, and we are passing soon into the Spires."

"The Temple of what?"

"M'Hzrut," Wrenflang replied softly. "It is far back to the south, in a valley," he pointed back along the trail. "It is a holy temple, designed to—"

"I know what it is," the second soldier snapped, looking at his companion. The other scowled behind his thick hood but was silent, small tendrils of steam floated from his nostrils. "But why have you come this far northwest? Should you not be heading south?"

Then why did you ask? Zhy wondered. *Pompous ass—*

"We are trying to get to a path through the Spires," Wrenflang answered softly, his voice smooth. "There is something dangerous, we feel, on the other side. Something that concerns the Protectors of the Temple."

"And are you all Protectors then?" the soldier asked, ignoring his first statement for the moment.

Each man nodded. As Zhy's head bobbed, a strange feeling trickled over him, and his cheeks flushed as if he were telling a lie in school. He had to remind himself that this was no lie, that now, even defenseless and unarmed as he was (save for his trusty fruit knife), he *was* a Protector, however temporary the assignment.

"What's so dangerous behind the Spires?" The other soldier spoke so suddenly that Zhy jumped slightly. He made an effort of stomping his boots to cover the action.

His feet were cold from standing still... he had been hiking for so long that his appendages had sweat freely, but now they froze in the cold. He remembered another time, which seemed so long ago, where his sweat froze to his skin, then shattered on rocks, much as he had splintered himself.

Only to be rescued by a gherwza.

Wrenflang sighed. "It doesn't hurt to be honest, I guess." Fanlas gave him a worried look, but the old mage ignored it. He stood there, staring at the two soldiers, his face blank. "Demons."

That was not in the script, Zhy thought with a rush of panic.

At that both soldiers laughed. The first spoke after a few seconds. "Aye, we fight them too! Though we just call them savages, you call them demons!"

Zhy started. The savages as demons? He remembered Darrell talking about the Welcferian fight against the native tribes, and their vicious nature. But he had never painted them as demons... what had he left out? Or was this soldier just hot-headed?

"I understand your fight," Wrenflang said, glossing over the statement. Zhy still bristled over it; a little more since the mage ignored it. "But we fight real demons... beyond the Spires is an entire horde!"

"We fight real ones, too, although Commander Drunplug doesn't want us to call them that—they truly are."

Drunplug? The name echoed in his mind. Drunplug? Could he possibly be any relation to his companion...? The names were too much alike, in fact he *had* to be some relation or other. He thought back on Darrell: His friend and companion, a mage with a quick trigger finger but a great deal of knowledge. Drunplug. Darrell. Who else could it be?

"You are lucky you have not gotten lost," the first soldier said. "Unless you already *are* lost." He still wore a slight grin, but it faded as he tried to think of the myriad of reasons a group of three men would try trudging across an inhospitable wasteland.

"I could say the same of you," Fanlas put in. The soldier eyed him warily, with a long glance at the sword hilt. The muscular farmer never moved. "How do you keep from getting lost?"

Smart, Zhy thought. *Stick in a compliment before he guts you.*

"Old Drunplug helps us out. And our scouts. Been all over this country, fighting these beasts, time and again.

Magic doesn't hurt either, does it?" At that he cocked an eyebrow at Wrenflang, who nodded slightly.

Drunplug and magic? Drunplug is a mage? "Drunplug is a mage?" Zhy blurted.

The soldier turned to Zhy, almost startled. "No, not as such. He just seems to know where he is all the time, plus he has some box that must be magic. Commander Drunplug says it always shows him where north is."

"We have one of those, too," Zhy said quietly.

"Aye, and where is it?"

"I have it safe and warm," Wrenflang answered.

"Too bad it doesn't point out the Hjor!" He glanced quickly behind, making sure Drunplug was out of earshot.

The second soldier chuckled. "We're trying to find them and push them back into Spires for good. Out to the frozen seas if we can."

Zhy wanted to ask the reasons, but Wrenflang glanced at him, and his look was warning enough. Darrell had told him the story of Zhyfrael, and how the savages decimated an entire city. The female leader of Welcfer had invited these (Hjor, were they called?) into her castle, unarmed, but they still slaughtered nearly every living creature.

Zhyfrael.

Zhyfrael! He lurched forward slightly.

At that thought, his stomach tingled. Zhyfrael! Were they to meet any more of these soldiers, and Drunplug himself, he would have to give his name, and then the questions would start, and he'd have to reveal his *full* name, and then... and then—

Everything whirled abruptly as the scuffed point of a giant spear suddenly stuck out from the second soldier's chest. The young man's eyes went wide, he clutched briefly at the wooden bolt with gloved hands, then toppled over on his horse. Something heavy shoved Zhy and he fell face-first into the shallow snow. He jerked his head off of the cold surface in time to see Fanlas fall to the ground. Wrenflang stood. His grizzled frames was lined in the dull light, and fire arched from his wrinkled hands.

φ

With a roar of "Hjor! Hjor!", fifty shabbily-clan men rose from hiding places so shallow a sardine wouldn't cover itself. One threw another ragged, overlarge spear from leather-gauntleted hands. From his vantage point, Drunplug screamed at his soldiers, but they were too far away to hear. He grimaced as the second one took the spear straight through his chest. The first solder kicked his horse and retreated at a dead run toward Drunplug, but a half-naked man sprinted faster, and slashed at the horse's hind legs with a curved scimitar. The animal reared and topped its rider before collapsing in a screaming heap of animal. As the soldier tried to roll away and draw his sword, the naked man was already slashing downward—the scimitar sliced the man cleanly in half and dark blood poured out onto the once clean snow.

Drunplug screamed orders and the line quickly formed, more out of directed panic than coordinated effort. His son's face floated before him for a moment but he pushed it away.

"Trap! They set a trap for us, the bastards!" his second-in-command was screaming, indicating Zhy and his companions. "Kill them!"

"No!" Drunplug bellowed. "No, look, they fight!"

The half-naked warriors of the Hjor clan came as one toward Drunplug's line, covering the short distance at an impossible speed. But even as his men fell into stance, readying for the onslaught of the Hjor, white-hot explosions erupted among the throng of charging men.

φ

Wrenflang's arms were a blur.

Fire and lightning arched out in a single wave from his right hand, and eventually split into twenty different ropes of energy, while from his left a purple ball rocketed up and out in a perfect elliptical pattern. The threads of fire exploded precisely against their targets: The chests of the storming warriors. Now aflame, the brutish men screamed in agony, thrashed among the snow in an effort to douse the flames, but Wrenflang did not reduce the intensity of the spells. While the fire burned, the purple ball floated down softly just paces in front the charging multitude, and exploded in a towering cloud of snow, rock, dirt, and body parts of the leading Hjor.

Drunplug's men took several paces backward, but at his bellowing did not break their line. They stood still to a man, each posed to engage the warriors of the Hjor tribe as they approached.

A gruff, guttural cry rose over the churning battle. Another line of the Hjor popped from their hiding place, each wild soldier carrying a long spear. Drunplug's men held and the Hjor raced forward, spears level. Steam clouded the scene: the breath of two dozen men screaming for blood.

Drunplug's soldiers only had a moment to level their own weapons.

Another purple ball arced forward and fell inches before the feet of the advancing Hjor. The men paused only a second, regarding the strange light with wide eyes. They would only have that second.

The ball exploded. Many of Drunplug's men fell from the concussion, and others dropped spears, and threw hands in front of faces. For the spray of body parts and blood was like a summer's downpour in Moult. No more Hjor advanced.

Drunplug turned to stare first at the mess that had once been the Hjor (if indeed these were Hjor men), and the white-bearded old man who panted in the cold.

Wrenflang had wrought utter devastation. Any living creature that still approached the line of Welcferian soldiers had been completely decimated. A few of the half-naked men retreated, Hjor included, but a single mage had wiped out nearly everything that remained of this unit.

Drunplug stared, dumfounded. *Darrell, could you have done that?*

φ

As they approached the Welcferian soldiers, Zhy noticed that the man atop his horse was strikingly familiar. And as he shook hands with him, a shudder shot up his spine, and he had been right: *This is Darrell's father...* crushing sadness and towering guilt raced through his stomach, to his back, across his chest and in his throat. He swallowed hard.

"You are lucky we did not attack you," Drunplug said, addressing Wrenflang. "It is very odd to have men travel here, this far north." He forced a smile. "And I for one am glad that we did *not* attack you! I don't know how we can repay you for your efforts."

Wrenflang gave him a look that said *you will pay*, but he smiled over it quickly. "It had to be done."

"What brings you here?"

They explained their situation, sparing no detail. A mulargh had flown over the night before, and even the Welcferian soldiers had wondered what type of creature would survive in this wasteland. It was clear that the demonic threat was not limited to Belden.

Zhy only heard fragments of sentences. His gaze was locked on Drunplug.

"What is it, son?"

"I—you look—I think I—" Zhy stammered.

"What is it?" He sounded patient, a trait that most definitely had not belonged to Darrell. Was he merely seeing Darrell in this rough-looking small-man? *The name, the face.*

"You look familiar, that is all, like someone I knew."

At that Drunplug's face seemed to light up. A name jumped to the tip of his tongue and he blurted it out, uncaring as to whether he sounded like a child or not. "Darrell?"

Zhy swallowed another lump and nodded.

"Do you know my son? Where is he?"

Zhy lied. "I—er, I apologize, no, I don't." He tried to look at the snow, at Wrenflang, at anything else but Drunplug. If he admitted to knowing Darrell, he would have to admit he had been there when he died, that he was powerless to stop Bruce, that Darrell had attacked first, that—

"Son, I asked you a question."

"Er, was Darrell your son?" he heard himself ask. *What a stupid question.*

"Yes, he is my—" He broke off and his face fell. There was a catch in his throat. "*Was?* What do you mean?"

Zhy shook his head quickly, and tried to change the subject. "I traveled with your son on a long journey, if he was indeed—"

Zhy closed his mouth and looked at the small-man with what he hoped was kindness and sympathy. He'd said *was* too many times.

The look was enough. Drunplug wheeled his horse around and buried his head in his hands. Zhy and the Welcferians stepped back a respectable distance and muttered in quiet, idle chat. When at last Drunplug turned, his eyes were heavy and drawn.

"I—perhaps we can discuss this at a later time," Drunplug said softly to Zhy. "There is no time right now. We have an enemy to fight."

"Indeed we do," Wrenflang answered.

Drunplug continued as if the two were discussing the same enemy. "We have the small problem of the tribe we just destroyed. I saw their leader retreat. Again."

Wrenflang thought on that. "Let them retreat."

"Let them?"

"Yes."

"You are mad."

Wrenflang forced a smile, but moving his lips made his cheeks feel like ancient sheets of parchment; as if moving them would cause them to shatter. "I think it best if we let them go, then follow behind."

"Why?" he growled.

"We will need their help in all of this."

"We *what?*" Drunplug spat in the snow. "The cold has frozen your brain. These savages—do you not know the story of Zhyfrael?" Zhy instinctively took a step back and dropped his gaze. If they ever asked his name, he'd be murdered...

"I do, but that is centuries past. We need their help, Drunplug, we need their skills... if we can arm these men and train them, we will be able to provide a force big enough to fight the demons. If we are seeing mulargh this far north, think of the hell that is rolling over Belden!"

"My son went to Belden and it got him killed—no offense, mind you," he said, looking at Zhy. "But I could care nothing what happens to that land."

Zhy bristled at that remark. How could the man simply disregard an entire nation? Did he not know that people in Belden would often say the same words in discussing Welcfer? Though Wrenflang was dipping his entire body into a raging current of madness, the old mage still had a point: the world would soon be overrun by demons, and such arguments would be moot.

Wrenflang aired Zhy's thoughts. "It will come here, it will come here and you will no longer have any land or home. This fighting serves little purpose."

Drunplug spat and waited for the tinkle of shattering ice. No, it was not yet that cold, but such cold was fast approaching. "You have no proof of anything," he said flatly.

Zhy found it difficult to disagree with Wrenflang. The senseless slaughter and destruction Beldeners tugged at his heart, but yet he no longer felt any attachment to his home—a place that had boiled him alive in spirits. No, a place where he had put his head willingly into the bottle. He sighed softly.

"This battle must be fought," Drunplug snapped. "We fight these Hjor, or whatever they call themselves. We must fight them. They are more of a threat than any demon."

"We have been—"

"No, they are not," Zhy heard himself say. *So much for keeping my mouth shut.* "Torp—Drun—Commander," he stammered. Drunplug didn't seem to care how he was addressed; he stared at Zhy with the same contempt that he had shown Wrenflang. "We have killed a man, a warlock, who was supposed to be in charge of guarding a portal to the underworld. And *not* at the Temple of—"

"Who are you?" Drunplug clipped.

Zhy stammered and coughed. His knees tingled and his stomach churned—a sudden warmth crept into his face. "I—"

The old mage saw the look of terror in Zhy's face and swiftly tried to divert attention from him. "He is with us, and what he says is true. Demons are pouring out into the world, even though the Temple is guarded."

"I know about your Temple," Drunplug said. "I never thought it truly guarded anything. Why should I rely on the word of two strangers, that demons are pouring out. Did you actually see them?"

"I heard them," Wrenflang lied. It was Huyen who had said he could hear buzzing—even Zhy's companion Bruce had mentioned the buzzing at one point, if Zhy's recollection was to be believed. "Like a swarm of bees, buzzing beneath the earth. We need to get through the Spires and put an end to this. And if you want to help save your country, you need to—"

The commander raised his gauntleted fist and spat again. "I need, I need. No, what *I* need is an explanation. You cannot expect that I will give up centuries of fighting a sworn enemy just because a mage tells me to?"

"No, but we need to stop the fighting... for now."

"We? You make it sound as if we are working together. I don't know you, you don't—"

"Pardon me, Commander," Wrenflang politely interrupted, "but we are now forced together, I'm afraid."

Drunplug scowled. The old man was right... he'd done well against the Hjor, too well, and now that he wanted to stop and suddenly make peace—the idea was insane. "After what you have done to the Hjor," he said slowly, "I would wonder why you would now wish to end the fighting?"

"Self-defense demanded action, Commander, there was no other option, or you were going to lose many more men."

"Do you question my ability?"

"Of course not, but casualties were unavoidable..." Wrenflang trailed off. Now was not the time to call Drunplug's resilience or battle acumen into question; he was a very skilled commander and leader, but he was going to be overrun, and it would have cost him his entire unit.

Drunplug looked up suddenly. "I will accompany you, since I have an idea where they have gone. That is all... if they choose to fight, we will fight, but if you are somehow able—"

"I will be able."

How ridiculous. Zhy thought. *Men would honestly stop to fight the demons and then quickly slash at each other's' throats? What kind of "peace" would there be?*

Honestly... He thumbed his frozen earlobe and looked out beyond Drunplug, at the bare, scrubby wasteland. *I need to get out of here.*

Drunplug echoed his thoughts. "And then we can resume killing each other?" Another wad of spit splattered in the snow.

The old mage smiled wanly.

Drunplug chuckled mirthlessly, then abruptly glanced at Zhy, then at Wrenflang, eyes curious. "All right, you have not answered one question... one of many, I should say. So," he snapped, "who are you?" He pointed at Zhy.

Zhy grimaced. "I—my name... is... Zhy." The last was only a whisper.

"What?"

"I said Zhy." With effort, he raised his head to look at Drunplug. The Welcferian had started to crack his lips open in reply, but Zhy charged forward, hoping again to avoid focus on his name. "And I have seen the demons. Not only the giant bats, but men transformed. I have killed," he started with a catch in his voice. He had killed a man. An evil, possessed, deranged warlock hiding in the shell of an idiot, but yes, he had killed. Putting voice to the words only seemed to sink his spirits all the greater. "I have killed the warlock who would release enough of those damned creatures to drown all of Belden. *And* Welcfer. But it did no good. Now they are pushing to the surface, surely, without restraint!" *If I just talk fast, maybe he will forget my name is—*

"Zhy? *Zhy?* As in Zhyfrael...? What is a Beldener doing with *that* name?"

To that question, there was no answer.

For a brief second, Drunplug sneered. He thought better of a scathing comment and instead grunted. "I see. Come, let's talk on the way—to wherever it is."

There was a flurry of activity as Drunplug corralled his troops and gave a few orders, namely to start moving north and east. They would walk the horses across this stretch, for the rocky outcrops were more jagged, and there were depressions where a man could hide. One could not be too careful.

It was several thousand paces later when Drunplug finally spat again and grumbled. "So far you've not done a good job of convincing me of the value of this plan, but what can I do? We would be worse for wear without—" he looked back at Wrenflang and stopped for a moment. "Ach, I keep repeating myself... must be the cold. Unless *you* can convince me of your ill-thought plan," he said, jabbing a frozen finger at Zhy.

"Perhaps if I..." Zhy began, looking nervously at Drunplug.

"If you what?"

"If I told you about—about Darrell."

"I don't want to know any more," he barked, voice trembling.

"If I tell you why he—why he sacrificed himself, perhaps—"

The small-man shook his head violently. "I don't want to know."

"Your son was a very strong man," Zhy continued as if Drunplug had not spoken. "He was a powerful mage who could cast *Bolt of Sacuan* as if it were breathing." He could feel Wrenflang's burning look—no mage could use that spell with ease, and surely not Darrell. But they needed the support of the Welcferians and the Hjor... a small lie would not hurt. Would it? "He had a way, of..." Zhy thumbed his earlobe nervously. *Sacuan's scrotum! What did he say? What?* "... a way of talking, like a teacher, and he said, he said 'such savagery' often." He repressed a loud sigh—that detail could be very important.

Drunplug's eyes filled with wet liquid. When they affixed themselves on Zhy, they were soft; all hardness had vanished. "That's because I say it—I used to say it quite often. Not any more. He picked that up that from me. So," the man said, sighing, "you obviously tell the truth. Tell me, did he ever tell you why he had not returned home in so long?"

At that Zhy squirmed in his freezing garments. "He did not want to be put to work. *That* kind of work, not yours."

At first Drunplug's face was splashed with confusion, his eyes thin slits. Then suddenly the orbs filled with more liquid and his mouth split open. Steam rolled into the air as he laughed. "He *what?* Oh, such the bull-head he could be. A word here, a word there, and he thinks you're going to skin him alive! Oh, Darrell, you were always the most..." The smile remained on his face. He wiped his eyes, but they quickly pooled again and his focus faded.

The most what? Zhy wondered. "Darrell was very quick," he offered.

"Too quick," the grizzled small-man replied. "I worried it would get him—" he spun his head around, looking at the far horizon. "Tell me," he asked in a deadly soft whisper. "How... how did he—?"

Zhy shook his head briskly. "No, no you do not want—"

"I want to know," Drunplug answered. "I need to know. I've gone this far."

The cloud of frigid air froze his lungs as he inhaled. Freezing moisture was forming in his own eyes as he let his mind drift back to the castle and his companions' final moments on the ledge. And so, with a voice quivering from arctic air and misery, he slowly explained their trek to Ar'Zoth, careful to point out Darrell's heroics and magical ability, not his quick trigger finger. But quickly the story wound up to its final, brutal conclusion, and Zhy was forced to acknowledge that Darrell had struck first. As he relayed the tale, his mind pictured the scene as if it was occurring once again before him:

Defying all reason, Darrell began casting again. Zhy's focus shifted, and suddenly, he felt as if he were watching from above as the tiny man furiously tried to cast a spell against the massive warlock who grinned at him maniacally. The image quickly faded and he found himself turning his attention to the seith.

"ENOUGH!" Ar'Zoth bellowed, his voice echoing across the valley. "You killed my gherwza, you little fool, but you cannot kill me!" Green light danced on his fingers, and Zhy almost wet himself.

Darrell was unable to finish his spell. Purple light had only begun to dance on his fingertips when a swirling green finger of lightning leaped off the seith's hand and skittered across the short distance between him and the mage. For Zhy, the event unfolded in slow motion—the green light arced forward, dripping tiny tendrils of a paler green light. Darrell tried to unleash Bolt of Sacuan.

The bolt was half-formed when the green tendrils sliced through—darting between the mage's fingers. Bolt of Sacuan splintered, and the green bolt suddenly split into a hundred different tentacles of light. Zhy and Bruce watched in horror as the tentacles crawled over the small-man, covering him in a net of bright light. Then there was a crack, and a small white ball of light flew out from the seith's other hand, suddenly plowing into the small-man's chest. He had no chance on the slippery stairs. His body stumbled. He tried to move his legs, but the magical spell kept him upright and in place. The combination of spells lifted him up and out, then sideways, and he dangled over the cavern, and then—

Zhy looked up at Drunplug through a waterfall of tears, wiped them away, expecting the same of the small-man. But the Welcferian's face was flat, his eyes bright and clean. After a second, a thin smile broke across his lips, which stretched and expanded into wide grin.

"Wh...?"

"I would expect nothing less of him. He was trying to save you."

"Save us?"

Drunplug nodded. "The second that that warlock stepped out to see you, Darrell would have known. Would have seen. And when this... Ar'Zoth... mentioned the demon-bat, the vile gherwza, Darrell had every right to fire first. There were no other options. We likewise strike first at these... Hjor."

Yes, but that has to stop, Zhy thought, but said instead: "Not all warlocks are evil..."

"He would have felt the magic like ice in his veins."

"But he said he felt—no, wait, he did say he felt something. Or was that Bruce?" Zhy muttered to himself.

"Hmm," Drunplug bit his lip. "The warlock was going to kill you all anyway, surely, else Darrell would never have fired first. I know it. I know him." He sounded as if he were convincing himself of the fact, though he was correct: Ar'Zoth had never had any intention of teaching Bruce a dribble of magic; he had been bent on killing them all. And Bimb, the simple-minded man, had waited. Waited! But Drunplug continued, "As a leader, there are times when you have to let your arrows loose even though you don't see the enemy clearly—you just know. And if you are not willing or able to make that split-quick decision, it could be your neck on the pike."

Zhy shivered at that thought. Who was to say when the instinct would be wrong?

"He—I thought he had just gone mad!" his chuckle was forced.

"No, never. I'm sorry he did not succeed." Drunplug opened his mouth to speak, but closed it again. The overwhelming sadness over the loss of his son finally overtook pride and his eyes clouded over; he turned away.

Zhy stomped his feet to warm them. His toes tingled as we walked and his heels felt like solid blocks of ice. *I'm going to lose my feet*, he thought glumly, stomping again to try to increase the circulation; he received no strange looks for his action, and was mildly surprised when others followed suit. Drunplug ambled over to his soldiers and Zhy eased alongside the old mage—if stomping ones feet against the frozen earth could be considered leisurely.

They walked for some time, focusing only on the next step.

"Wrenflang?" he asked.

The grizzled mage's gray beard was coated with a thick layer of ice, and tiny icicles hung from his hug nostrils. "What is it, Zhy?"

"How do these men survive out here?" Zhy wondered.

The mage chuckled. He brought his hands to his beard, and finding the block of ice, cleared his facial hair with a grimace. The small ice particles tinkled to the ground. "They are used to it—grew up with icicles in their cradles and snow in their bottles," Wrenflang said, rubbing his hands together. "A cold spring day in Belden City would be enough melt them, surely!"

Zhy cracked a small smile.

"Well, let's catch up, then," the mage said softly. "Drunplug has already moved on ahead and I need to make sure I'm nearby for when we find the Hjor."

"Will we find them?"

"I hope so... well, no," he said, scowling. "Yes and no, that is. By Sacuan it is cold here! My brain is frozen... if we find them, we may have more work up front, but if we don't we risk attack from them later on."

"What will stop them from attacking us anyway?"

"Honestly, Zhy, I don't know, we just have to try. There are two very powerful armies here in Welcfer, and while Drunplug, and even Darrell, have painted them in a very dark and demeaning way, the Hjor are most likely just as skilled as the Welcferians. They fight because it is the way of things, not because of anything else."

"I thought it was for food, resources..."

Wrenflang nodded. "Yes, that is part of it, but to have survived out here for millennia?" he looked around, shook his head slowly. "They survive because there *are* resources here, we just don't know where to look. And if there aren't resources, their survival against all reason makes them even more formidable."

"As enemies or allies?"

"Both."

Chapter 19

From Within

To succeed against the Dark, we must battle the Darkness within ourselves. Deep within our souls are great festering boils of madness and murderous thoughts—sever them, slice them, behead them first, before you venture out to tackle the Darkness in the rest of the world.

Cleric Archean

After the Knight of the Black Dawn had left—Orfel, his name was. *Orfel.* The stranger had never said his name, but he could see it on his mind and in his heart; a conniving, vicious member of a ragtag group of demon-hunters; shadowy villains who claimed to keep the world safe. Orfel had been with them, surely... those days ago he had come to find food. So he had claimed. How long before he would be back?

The man, who had been called Yarel long before escaping to this remote village near Gray Gorge, sat at his cluttered and dusty table and stared at the pile of miscellany that covered its surface. Beneath the pile was an object he had covered with a purposeful fury; had the ground not been frozen, he would have buried it. Still, hidden beneath the rubble of various papers, utensils, cookware, and foodstuffs, it called to him. It sang. It howled his name in the night. And as he began to slowly remove articles with a shaking hand, he paused, holding his breath.

The rod sat there, barely beneath enough papers with which it could be covered, or hidden. Orfel had likely seen this. And if he had, it meant he would soon be bringing back other members of his disgusting Order of the Black Knights, or Knights of the Order of the Dawn—or whatever it was called—and they would quickly dispose of him and torch his hut. And none of the villagers would pay any notice. No, for they had already cast him out of their ranks many years before; now they only tolerated his existence.

But what was he to do about this rod? Orfel had seen it, it was too late to deny. With a frustrated hand, Yarel picked it up.

It was hot, burning, like grasping a poker set in a fire!

Yarel let it drop to the table and cursed, grabbing the seared palm of his hand with the other, and winced. He had not used the amber wand in several years, though its presence was a constant comfort to him, a reminder that he could summon up a demon and make a chatty neighbor, a loud dog, or impetuous child disappear. They always blamed him for such events, though they had no proof—nobody had yet seen the wand, until Orfel, the hated—

He cursed again and stomped to the fire, threw a log into the already roiling flames. Turning back to stare at the table he stopped.

It glowed.

The ancient wand glowed with a deep, purple hue, of burning blood and roasting flesh. This, he had never seen, even when he summoned the demons. Putting his hand tentatively atop the object, he pulled back, for he swore he felt a radiant heat.

It's in your mind.

He jumped backward. "What? Who's there? Who said that?" he bleated. Eyes darted to every corner of the dimly-lit cabin, but there was nobody there.

A log rolled off the stack in the hearth and he leapt backward, heart hammering. Yarel cursed loudly, spat into the fire and stomped his foot. "I'm going crazy," he muttered to himself.

Pick me up.

He jumped again. The voice had come from the rod.

"Wh..." he whispered, mouth tensed, ready to spit, curse or shout at the voice.

Pick... me... up!

Tentatively, he reached out, yet held his arm short, remembering the heat. The searing fire, the pain! The agony of life that burned inside the wand.

Pick me up, the fire has ended.

"Sacuan curse you!" He retorted.

You have nothing to fear.

He was going mad. The villagers had planned this, hadn't they? Surely, they must have. No, they didn't know, but—what if one of them were a warlock or mage? No, not here. Orfel? Perhaps. But the rod, and rod alone had been talking to him; in his mind, deep inside. And the small runes were stashed away in a small drawer. How could this be happening?

Oh, it is. Pick me up.

"Did the villagers do this?"

Villagers, what are villagers? Pick me up.

"I want everyone dead!" he heard himself scream. The world was evil, Orfel was evil, his village was but a tiny speck on the landscape of nothing. He'd summoned demons before, now he could summon hundreds, even thousands?

Couldn't he?

"Couldn't I?" He asked. The pupils of his eyes were huge black circles.

The voice was quick to reply. *You can do anything.*

"Anything?" he wondered. A thousand vile thoughts coursed through his mind, a hundred burning pyres flashed before his eyes, and he could smell the stench from the piles of corpses.

Pick me up.

"Do you lie?"

Why would I lie?

He heard the lie, heard the stench of depravity in that voice; at its very core was a rotted, hollow promise, a hope made of dead leaves, and wasted youth. Yarel *knew* the voice lied, that whatever creature behind it only wished for freedom, extrication from its underworld prison. He knew. But his overriding hatred for living creatures boiled over, stilled the tongues of the warning bells, and set his tongue racing.

"I want everyone to die. Die, die, die," he whispered.

Pick. Me. Up.

Yarel roared in the back of this throat, reached to the table, and whipped the wand off of the table. As soon as his gnarled fingers curled around the amber rod, a shock coursed through his body. As old men had been transformed into gherwza, so too was Yarel's shivering body being wrenched apart. His skull expanded forward and razor fangs pierced forth from his gums, dripping blood and saliva.

With a brief cry of horror, he realized he had no feeling. Yarel was numb. His mind could do nothing to move his body, there was no pain when the demon entered his mind, and wrenched his flesh. Blood poured onto the rotted floorboards but he could feel nothing.

Only hatred. Hatred and disgust.

Another entity had been added to his list of beings he wanted destroyed.

"You—" his throat rasped, rented and ragged from the transformation. "Lied."

I always lie.

"No—"

Yarel reached a hand forward, desperately trying to cling to anything before his arm was twisted back behind his shoulder blades and slowly transformed into the wing of a bat. The flesh of his arms was stretched down and outward, his elbow joint torn and tugged against its natural swing; his fingers stretched together as webbing formed between them. And yet he had a brief, desperate thought.

The rod was still clutched in his left hand, though barely, for the webbing was thickening. He pulled his hand back, back, groaning in pain as his arm felt it was being jerked from its socket. His control over motor functions was slipping fast as the wing was forming, but he was able to bring the rod forward, forward, ever forward—

NO, the creature hissed.

He wanted to scream "Yes! Yes, you demon," but the wand had already begun its forward trajectory and it smacked loudly against his forehead. Where before it would have slapped against flesh it cracked dully against a fur-covered mass, and instead of pain, Yarel felt an intense release, as the demon inside seemed to be knocked "backward", further into his mind.

There was a very faint cry from within his brain, but it faded quickly.

With a yelp of frustration, Yarel realized he was in no better shape than before. His skull felt too long and too narrow, his legs were starting to web together, and his arms were nearly useless. Something furry tickled his backside and he realized he was probably sporting the tiny tuft of a tail... he was gherwza, only not yet fully formed!

But he still held the rod.

He was in control.

"Aright, then..." he said softly. "How do you complete the process?" if he could beat out the demon, he would win.

Even if he were a bat.

A bat!

Sacuan curse everyone, he was turning into a gherwza. His mind turned constantly over the phenomenon; stunned, amazed, elated, terrified. Ha! The demon hadn't lied had, it? He could still kill everyone. Everyone! Only this time, *he* would be in control. And it was so simple, too, so easy to smack the rod against his head. He smacked it again, once, to be sure... he could be a demon himself!

Imagine the faces of the Knights of the Black Dawn! If they walked here now, and came face to face with a gherwza.

Silence.

He took a shambling step forward. He'd won this battle, somehow, hadn't he? If only he could complete the process, under his terms, and control his own body.

He could sense a gurgling in his mind.

"That is not an answer! Tell me how to do it!"

Nothing.

"If you want any control over me, tell me." There, that had done it. With that slight offering, an offering that wasn't an offering—an half promise rolled into a threat, he had triggered something. Deep down in his mind a slight hush sounded. Was it a sigh?

You...

"Yes, tell me how to complete this and you will have the opportunity." Yarel was quick on his feet, quick to adjust to others' words and actions. True, the demon would have the opportunity to regain its foothold, but it would be narrower than a strand of baby's hair.

I, it began, sighing. *I need control now before I tell you.*

A-ha! So that was how it was going to go, was it? "Try again. You can stay like this, or you can tell me how to complete the process. I will wait."

A shifting, squirming. Frustration built within the demon, he could sense it; as if he could smell the emotions of the demon. Was that part of becoming such a vile creature? *You win, this time...* the *s* slithered through his brain, down his spine, and stung the backs of his heels.

"Tell me."

Another shift. But the demon had been cornered. Nearly successfully, it had assumed it would have a clear path to destruction, but now it was forced to comply with Yarel's demands. It was silent for several moments, before hissing the commands into Yarel's head, and in a matter of minutes he was soaring out into the cold winter air.

Yarel's stomach lurched into his throat with a simultaneous wave of adrenaline as he soared through the air, his bat form screaming over the tops of the leafless birch trees. Branches swayed violently, waving angrily at him. They had no idea of what he was planning, the stupid trees.

Seeing through the small beady eyes took a deal of adjusting; he kept squinting his eyes shut, trying to put the two separate images together, but everything looked as if he were viewing it with a wall between his eyes. With a shake of a furry head, the distinct worlds coalesced, but the image also shifted outward in a narrowing cone pattern—trees in front were huge monstrosities, while objects in the far distance were thousands of times smaller than they should be.

Then sight disappeared entirely.

Yarel panicked. But then another strange sensation filled his mind—he could "see" the trees, the hills, lakes, etc., but within his mind! Obstructions were now a *reflection* of what he had known as a human. The reverse image of a birch swam before his new vision and he could picture each branch, frozen bud, and ragged piece of bark.

Now, give me back control. The demon broke his thoughts.

Yarel's gaze drifted away from the forest and stared blankly at the empty dull sky before him. He had offered an empty promise, hadn't he? Well, now what was he going to do? There was a tugging in the back of his mind, but he simply ignored it.

Hundreds of mulargh and gherwza flew in a pack ahead of him, like a horrific squadron of geese, except these were hairy, dripping, slimy demons. Again, his image of them was an image with colors reversed, but he filled in the details with his mind.

"And I'm one of them!"

Now, give me back control!

Again, he brushed aside the tugging and thought he felt a thud. Was it that easy? If all he had to do was simply push the voice aside and continue, his journey would be that much easier.

Give me—

"No," his bat's mouth spat, though the utterance came out as a high-pitched screech. "Never, go away!"

You promised...

With a mental shove, he pushed the creature back. The demon had promised much, the lying, conniving creature that it was! Yarel could make empty promises, too. Another squadron of gherwza whizzed by him and he smiled inwardly—they were on a path of their own destruction, flying on their own, no leader, no direction, free; as free as a pack of like-minded creatures could be. The demon had thought it could have its own chokehold on Yarel, but Yarel was stronger. He was in control!

Chapter 20

Lights and Dreams

Our minds are fertile and pliable, often so much so that we create realities that may not exist. The Dark and its demonic hosts surely enjoy such a playground for their heathen perversions.

High Cleric Gorand

Fanlas somewhat enjoyed the bracing cold of the north. They had made excellent progress westward, thanks to the guiding box and the determined pace that Wrenflang had set. The nights were brutal; without any wood for a fire, they did as best they could with the snow, their tents, and blankets, in creating windbreaks. Wrenflang splurged on some nights and set a magical fire for an hour or two, but it was not the same.

Drunplug's troops kept to themselves for the most part, though the leader himself would chat with Wrenflang, often trying to talk him out of any non-violent meetings with the Hjor. But the old mage stuck to his position and Drunplug invariably returned to his unit.

Fanlas enjoyed the small company of Zhy and the mage. They had become fast friends, if only out of necessity.

But it was still Sacuan-blasted cold, as much as he tried to tell himself he enjoyed it.

Though bundled in thick clothing, Fanlas felt it impossible to shake the digging fingers of icy cold that found every last inch of warmth and froze it; it was impossible to keep any appendage warm for more than a few minutes, and the damnable wind was relentless. Shivering, exhausted, and wanting only to sleep, he tried to close his eyes, but the racking chill kept forcing his eyes open.

"What was that?" he whispered, watching as his breath flowed out in a heavy cloud that stuck in front of his face for several minutes. "What was that?" he repeated loudly to himself. The sound of his voice was strange in this utter cold, sounding too loud, too brash. Yet at the same time it was comforting to converse with himself.

"Bimb?" The face of his son, smiling as he worked out complex chords on the sutan, haunted him. It was too cold to cry.

A light flickered, but not from the east. Looking up, he noticed that it was not a single point of light, but a wide, flowing ribbon of deep green. It bent and bobbed, dipped and surged, rolling across the sky in eerie and disconnected patterns. "What sort of magic...?" Fanlas wondered. The light would dim, brighten, and finally dim as it flickered, covering nearly the entire sky before retreating back over the Spires. The knight heard a loud crackling sound within the light, as if it was burning the air through which it flowed.

"Bimb?"

Wide-eyed, he watched as green turned to yellow, to blue, then back to a deep emerald green, swirling and flowing continuously.

"Sorcery, that is not," he spoke, trying to comfort himself. "No, those are the Boreal Lights, the Northern Glow, the Lights in the Spires! I have read about these, many years ago." The cold caught his words and froze them in the air. A cloud of steam, reflecting the green light, hung in the air. *I have always wanted to see them,* he thought.

He let himself relax as he watched the display of color and the occasional crackle of sound. Fanlas dug in his coat and extracted a stick of dried meat, frozen solid. Grumbling, he stuck it under his arm to thaw it, then chewed with considerable effort, for it tasted of smoked meat and old sweat.

As the lights danced, his eyes fluttered; swaying on the edge of sleep, he was nearly over the precipice, or perhaps just over, when a man's voice sounded in the air. Fanlas roused himself and looked out across the barren land.

"I'm over here."

Fanlas turned his attention to his right, and started when he saw Bimb sitting there. He squeezed his eyes shut, opened them again, then smiled. This was probably a dream. His little boy, now grown, facial hair covering his face, looked very much alive. His eyes danced with an intelligence, one that Fanlas knew was there, but always stifled by his condition. Now, in Fanlas's dream (it *was* a dream, wasn't it?) Bimb looked like a wizened scholar.

Funny, that, Fanlas thought, taking a second look.

Bimb sat atop a large birch log, with tufts of wintergreen plants growing in the snow at his feet.

"I'm dreaming aren't I?"

"Hello, Fa," his son replied. "Yes, you probably are, but can you be sure?"

Fanlas stared.

"Fa, you need to help me. I have made a big mess." The birch logs changed to maple. "I've tried to control the weather—from here, wherever *here* is. I just wind up killing people!"

A sutan appeared in his hands, he played a chord, then tossed it aside. Tears were frozen on his cheeks.

Fanlas choked back his own sobs, but forced himself to remember that he dreamed. "I wish I could help you. I—"

"I keep thinking of Zhy."

"Zhy?" Fanlas glanced over to where Zhy would be sleeping, but nobody was there. Just a slab of ice. *Just a part of the dream.*

"He killed me, you know?"

At that the knot in his throat grew. "Y-yes, he has said that. But he had to, Bimb, he had to. You completed an evil deed."

The sutan appeared again and Bimb slammed out a minor chord. "I don't want to be evil! I want to sit by the fire and sip the spicy drink. With Ma! And I want you to come in and muss my hair and call me out to help count turnips! I want... I want..." he descended into heaving sobs.

Above their campsite, the bobbing lights turned red, swirling violently. A crackling sound skittered across the bleak landscape.

Fanlas cried freely. *I want that boy back, too. I want you back, Bimb. As you were.* But he had to remain strong. "You can't go back to that Bimb. Even if you can fix your mess, control the weather..."

"I know!" Bimb replied, lifting his head. Now he held a small cat; it purred contentedly. "Zhy put me here!"

"No, son, you put yourself there."

For that, Bimb had no response. "The weather," he whispered and the lights crackled again. "It can fix this, maybe give you a gateway, clear away the dust. Show you what to do."

"What do you mean?"

Bimb vanished.

φ

I left Fa and went back to my dead space. As much as my hatred for Zhy fogged up my work at redemption, I still felt a deep sadness at having caused all of this. Fa was right. I put myself in this position. The first call from Ar'Zoth was the death knell to nights sipping spicy drink and counting turnips.

Sacuan bless it all!

Was my dislike of Lyn's son interfering with the control of the weather? Possibly. No, *certainly*. I needed to suppress it, forget it; ignore the fact that the man with a fruit knife sent me to Hell!

"No, Bimb, no," I aped my mother's voice. "You must believe it in your heart." She would probably say something like that, I'm sure she told me that once or twice. But now I could only see the cozy fire in our small home, and the face of Zhy as he stalked me to my death.

Sacuan bless it all... I needed to get over this!

Chapter 21

The Enemy of My Enemy

Your foe's foe should not be considered a compatriot. He would turn and slaughter you if given the opportunity, he would raze your fields, and steal your bread. It is best to reconcile than to trade with the Dark.

Prophet Z'Hara

"Do you have any men in your group who you could consider natural leaders?" Wrenflang wondered of Drunplug. The two sat apart from the group, their breath filling the air.

"No, there's—well, there is one back on the supply line. He's still learning some things.

"Good. I'd like you to send a unit and a few Hjor back to Foltrag."

Drunplug laughed.

"I am quite serious."

The Welcferian's mouth opened for another laugh, but when he saw the set face of Wrenflang, he stopped cold. "What is this?" he asked softly, steam emerging from his mouth in sharp bursts.

"We need to stop this fighting. Let's forget our history, if we can. The time for war is over; I need the help of your army in doing that. Or a small part of it." Wrenflang was growing tired of the same argument, but he gave it one more attempt. He knew that asking a man to forget his entire mode of existence was worse than futile, but time had long since run out, and he was becoming infuriated that they still dallied.

"The role of 'my' army," Drunplug replied coldly, "is to keep the hands of the savages away from the people of our cities. Away from our leaders, and our children alike. Not bring them down to Zhyfrael's Folly for a drink!"

Zhy sucked in the cold air. *They even named a tavern after me... or, her?* "The Hjor had kids, too," he said instead.

"Listen, Beldener," Drunplug snapped, "these Hjor don't care! They don't care. Yes, they have children, but they breed them differently. Breed them to kill."

The hypocrisy was almost too much—no, it *was* too much. Zhy muttered something and wandered off, leaving the two to their discussions. Wrenflang watched him go with a pang of sadness. *Such a young man, with so much to offer and so little inside his head!*

Wrenflang was struggling with the obvious. That the Welcferian commander could not *see* the obvious was maddening, it was what he had feared the most, that neither army could realize their missions were mutually destructive and self-defeating. The battles had continued for centuries, and would continue to rage until every last person lay dead.

"Why do you fight?" the mage asked softly.

"I have already told you that," Drunplug replied, the steam of his voice curling out from his mouth like a venomous snake.

"We don't have time for this anymore, do you understand?" The mage could take it no more; it was getting ridiculous. "Fix this Sacuan-blasted mess NOW." He coughed briefly, violently.

"I'm—but—" Drunplug stopped and rubbed his fur gloves together. "This is madness! How am I to tell my men to put aside hundreds of—no *thousands*—of years of fighting?"

"Yes."

"Sacuan be damned!" Drunplug cried, voice hoarse. His face was screwed into a wrinkled mass and he stared ahead. He looked up at Wrenflang, scowling. "You forget that they will attack us at once, the minute we enter their territory. Do you not realize that?"

He *had* thought of that. It was the biggest flaw in his entire plan, even a child could see it. "Not if we go unarmed," he muttered.

"*What!*" Drunplug stood suddenly and kicked at the snow. "Sacuan damn you. But..."

But I'm right.

Wrenflang smiled. "I think I can guess your thoughts." He ran a finger through his beard. "I'm not asking you to put down a thousand or more years of fighting because of a grand plan. It's a simple one. End the fighting, kill demons and get on with things. If you don't we all lose."

"And if they kill us all when we go in there?"

"Then they kill us all. We would have at least tried."

Drunplug coughed. "Damn. Damn! I wish Darrell were here."

"What good would that do?"

The commander sat with a huff. "I don't know," he veritably whined. "I don't know, but at least I'd feel better." He chewed on his lower lip until it bled. "Sacuan damn all of this! Fine. *Fine.*" He stood again, then sat down. Stood once more and glowered at Wrenflang. "Damn you old man. This all rests on your shoulders."

Drunplug stalked away, leaving Wrenflang alone.

"I know," the mage whispered.

φ

Wrenflang expected bloodshed within the first few minutes, but perhaps the presence of Zhy and himself persuaded the Hjor that violence was not necessarily a predetermined outcome. He had been confident he could talk to both the Hjor and the Welcferians, and broker some sort of an agreement, but as they trudged through the unforgiving terrain, doubts mounted. *We might not get out of this alive... what in Sacuan's name have I done?*

When they crested a small rise, a collection of snow houses and dead campfires came into view. The "village", if it could be called that, was littered with a rag-tag collection of human-like creatures. Drunplug was smart and left his army behind, though he still insisted on carrying a sword. Grudgingly he let Wrenflang and Zhy take the lead and start first down the hill, and unarmed.

The reaction of the Hjor was unexpected. Rather, their *inaction.* Drunplug had also anticipated a violent outburst, but for a long moment none of the villagers seemed to notice the approaching strangers, instead they moved slowly about their business.

They ignore us on purpose, Zhy thought. *Or they don't see us. Impossible. They hide in—*

Zhy and Wrenflang lurched as a cloud of snow exploded into the air behind them. Turning on their frozen boots they watched as a Hjor tribesman emerged from the snow, all but his nose and mouth covered with cold white powder; absently he wiped his eyes clean, while producing a long, rusting sword.

He grunted something unintelligible.

Oh, no, Zhy thought. *This is not going to go well if they don't speak our language.*

Again the man grunted. For the moment he dismissed Zhy and Wrenflang, and looked back up the hill at Drunplug. Another grunt and the sword went into its tattered sheath and a leather-clad arm waved Drunplug forward. The bulky Welcferian nodded curtly, set his lips in a line and trudged forward.

The Hjor gurgled again, coughed and spat a wad of green phlegm onto the snow.

"I—" Wrenflang started.

A wave of a massive hand stilled his voice. "I apologize, I tend to have a flair for the dramatic. And a cold."

"You-you speak our language?" Drunplug wondered.

The burly man laughed. "Would you rather I grunt and make noises like I am supposed to?" He shook his head. "Can't a man clear his throat?" At that he chuckled to himself. "Or should I talk in halting, broken speech, so I sound more like the so-called Wights of your past—" he poked a finger at Zhy and smiled.

"What...?"

"Come, come, not all of us are mute savages. We fight only for a small scrap of food, a warm tent, or a stable place to stay. Some of us—other tribes that is—may not be as advanced as we are." He gestured to the collection of huts. "By your open mouths and stunned looks, you assume we were *all* mindless."

"I—" Drunplug began.

"Never mind, never mind. You never bothered to understand us, to learn. Since Zhyfrael's disaster you have been on a mission to destroy us utterly. It's quite sad, really, but since the only ones you have been able to wipe out were those truly backward, inbred peoples. But they *were* people... something you have forgotten."

The man wiped his nose, and at last Zhy took a long hard look at him. While he expected the man to have some inhuman features, there were no fangs or horns. He *was* taller, wider, and had a larger nose, but apart from his ragged clothing and wild hair, the man looked like any other Beldener. Beldener... thoughts raced through his head, a memory of a discussion he had had with his companions—where had the Wights gone to? As he recalled, or at least tried to recall, they had discussed how the Wights had perhaps migrated *back* up from Belden to Welcfer... or was it the other way around? In any case, if they had gone north, was it possible that they had become the Hjor? No, that could not be—he remembered seeing a Wight—a Wight that Bruce had killed. Or was it? Everything was a blurry image now, so it couldn't be true...

The Hjor's response was enough for Zhy to cough loudly. "Ah, at least one of you has not forgotten. We *are* descendants of the Wights, or so it is said—that they left Belden and migrated here. Once the inbreeding started in some of the tribes, it was over for them, and it signaled an endless battle for us. Now—now we fight you, much to our dismay." The man exchanged glances with Drunplug and Zhy.

"I don't know what to say," Drunplug said softly.

"Not much to say, it is what it is."

"What—what may I ask is your name?" Wrenflang asked. The conversation was awkward and stilted, Zhy thought. *But what else can we say to each other? Drunplug looks like he lost all of his blood.*

"Ah, the mage! I saw you earlier in your wild attacks. I'm sure you only know us by one name, but in fact we have many. You call us Hjor, I believe, and that, strangely enough, is my name. Many of my ancestors have names that are completely unpronounceable, including my father's father... I won't try to utter the name. I simply call myself Hjor Hjor, and you may call me Hjor."

Zhy glanced at Drunplug, who was mouthing the name to himself—the way Hjor spoke his name was slightly different than the Welcferian's interpretation. Drunplug had heretofore pronounced it *Ho-jer,* with a hard *J,* while the man himself put only a bare emphasis on the H, saying *H-jor,* the space between the H and J a tiny exhalation of frosty air.

"So," Hjor breathed heavily. "What do you need?"

"Why would you—"

"My dear general, you need something, else you would not have risked the lives to two unarmed... well, one unarmed man, to get it. You wish perhaps to use us as arrow fodder for something?"

Drunplug and Wrenflang shared a quick nervous look.

"I thought as much. You will fail there, if you wish to do so. Men!" he barked, and suddenly ten more soldiers appeared behind Zhy and his companions. "I would hope you came here for a better reason."

"We need help," Zhy heard himself say. Drunplug nervously counted the men and glanced at their weapons. The Welcferian looked at Wrenflang with a questioning glare, but the mage shook his head sadly and scratched his throat. When Zhy looked, he noticed that each soldier wore a spell-shatterer around their neck. *Now, where did they get those? And, if they did, how was Wrenflang so successful at attacking them before?* He stared at the snow, then at Wrenflang. *Just who are you, old man?*

"Yes, but why?" the Hjor leader rumbled.

Wrenflang nodded and Zhy explained as quickly as he could, making sure to describe the absence of any type of control over the demons. Hjor watched with interest, his soldiers stepping a few feet closer to hear Zhy's story.

"I see. That sounds like it could be a problem for all of us. But I'd like to know a little more. What is your name, son?"

Zhy's throat caught at that. If he was nervous about revealing his name to Drunplug, his heart hammered enough to fly over the Spires. Hjor leaned back on his heels and crossed his arms. "M-my name, sir, is Zhy."

Hjor let out a chuckle. "Funny."

"No, sir, it is my name. My name is Zhyfrael Lynnheard."

Zhy's knees nearly buckled as the sound of swords leaving leather scabbards filled his ears. Blood rushed to his head. He slammed his eyes closed.

Boots crunched in the hard snow and Hjor Hjor barked a few unintelligible commands. His voice was strained, but he quickly brought it back under control. "And are you a relative...?" He took a deep breath. "Or was that a joke on your father's behalf?" Hjor asked, his voice dangerous.

"I'm not sure either way."

A crunch of leather feet on snow and ice indicated that Hjor's soldiers stepped closer. "Why would you not know?"

Zhy finally opened his eyes and they stung at the onslaught of cold. "Because I was a—because I was a drunken fool my entire life, and I never asked."

Hjor snorted. "You warm-weather folks are too soft. Much too soft. How long have you been in this climate? A day? Two?" he asked derisively.

"A few months," Wrenflang answered. "He has been through the Spires, to the Temple of M'Hzrut, and back. And we have further to travel yet."

The native nodded. "I see. This changes things. Perhaps we can work something out, but right now we need to know why this man is named Zhyfrael."

"My name is Zhy."

"Zhyfrael," Hjor repeated through clenched teeth.

"Battle-master, Hjor, sir?" came a shaking voice from the line of soldiers.

"Yes?"

"She has returned. She has returned for forgiveness. Sir."

"Forgiveness," a voice echoed.

"Forgiveness," came another.

"Forgiveness!"

The word rippled through the soldiers, and each one knelt down upon the frozen ground, swords point first in the snow. Hjor turned slowly to stare at his men, his face set in a scowl, which slowly bent back into a flat line as the men bowed their heads.

What in...? Zhy wondered.

Wrenflang leaned over and whispered, "They think you are Zhyfrael reborn."

Hjor Hjor turned back to Zhy, his face unreadable. "So they think you have come back, that you are she, that you come to ask for forgiveness."

"Forgiveness, for what?" Zhy asked.

Anger flared on the man's face in bright red flashes. "You do not know, how can you be expected to know?"

The words triggered a memory and Zhy remembered vividly the story that Darrell had told about Zhyfrael, a leader of Welcfer several millennia ago. She had invited the tribes of the region into the castle, disarmed them. But the brutes attached with bare hands, feet, and teeth, wreaking havoc before Welcferian soldiers could quell the violent rebellion. That *Zhy* had come back as this woman to ask forgiveness was absurd.

"If anything, you should ask forgiveness of Zhyfrael," he said, trying to keep his voice steady. "Unarmed, your ancestors were still able to kill hundreds before they were stopped."

"You—you *do* know the story?" Hjor's eyes widened slightly, then narrowed to slits. "At least, you know *a* story, a version of that story. It is the false version, I'm afraid."

"But," Drunplug wondered, "back in Foltrag, that is we all know it to be. It is told over and over. Zhyfrael was sent off to exile for her folly."

"It was a folly, indeed," Hjor Hjor replied. "But we remember it differently. Zhyfrael invited the tribes in for her 'Speaks' as she called them, and then she ordered every last man killed. She was exiled because she started a war that would not end—and has not ended still."

Drunplug reeled, looking as if he would fall over. "I—"

"And so my men, apparently they see Zhyfrael here as the woman reincarnated, brought back to ask for forgiveness. Do you ask for forgiveness?"

"Yes." The word flew out of his mouth and he wished it back. Drunplug and Wrenflang stared at him, horror and confusion on their faces—the Welcferian soldier looked ready to kill; had Zhy betrayed some ancient pact? Already he was struggling to understand up from down, back from front. Why had he said the word? His mouth had opened of its own accord and he could not pull back what he had said.

Blood roared in his ears.

"Forgiveness," the men repeated.

Hjor Hjor drew his sword and quickly raised it to the sky. "Forgiveness! Forgiveness! Forgiveness!" The metal caught the muted light of the sun. Soon the small space was filled with a dozen twinkling lights as the Hjor soldiers raised their swords, and the word forgiveness exploded into the air.

Zhy felt as if his brain would drown in blood. The world seemed to spin around him, the chorus of words, the glinting swords, the stunned visage of Wrenflang and Drunplug; they floated away, spun off into another dimension while he stood in the middle.

A drunk man was being praised like a returning hero.

A failure to the world and himself—he stood in the light, honored as a...

Hero. No, I am not a hero, will never be!

"Come, warm yourselves by our fires!" Hjor exclaimed, pushing his sword back into its sheath. His voice was suddenly full of excitement. The change was so abrupt that the very atmosphere seemed to snap with the shift in direction.

Zhy and his companions stumbled as they neared the once-black fire pits that had roared to life; bright flames billowed into the cold air, consuming nothing.

Nothing! "How does a fire burn without wood—" Zhy stopped, knowing the answer to his own question.

For an answer, Hjor merely winked at Wrenflang. "Come, sit!" He gestured to some traveling crates that the soldiers used as chairs.

Zhy sat and stared into the flames. For several moments, the others did likewise, their gazes lost in the strangely burning fire. *How can this be happening? I'm sure Father had no idea about Zhyfrael, he just named me Zhy because he like the name. This cannot be possible—I cannot be a—no, it is too insane. It is too... cliché.*

"So. Zhyfrael," Hjor Hjor chirped. A murmur went through his men.

"Please, call me—" He paused. *I am very tired of saying that. So very tired.* "Er, never mind. Yes?"

"You have caused quite a stir."

"I did not mean to."

Wrenflang shifted on his crate and opened his mouth, but Hjor Hjor spoke first. "I realize that, but for us, your presence here is something we will not attribute to coincidence."

"This is not coincidence," the mage said slowly. "I have deliberately sought you out. Sought both you and the Welcferian soldiers."

The admission was said with as much as enthusiasm as a bar maid states she plans on retrieving more ale from the cellar. Hjor Hjor, however, looked stunned, as stunned as his normally placid visage could muster. "Excuse me, did I mis-hear you?" He asked, quietly; then, not waiting for a reply, barked. "Just who are you?"

"I am a simple mage from Belden," Wrenflang replied coolly.

"No, you do not answer my question. I see what you are, I see your actions. How does a 'simple mage', as you so describe yourself, suddenly appear within our tribe? Here, on the very edge of the Icedown Plains. So close to the Spires. Here, you arrive with a man named Zhyfrael and your burly companions? A *man* named Zhyfrael!" Hjor Hjor pounded his fist on his pallet. "You are no simple mage!"

"No, I am not," he said. He cleared his throat and changed the direction of the conversation. "It is a long story of how we arrived here, a very long one."

"I would like to hear it."

Another sigh. "The story is long, and for most of it, I had no idea what was unfolding. But suddenly, violently, I became aware of the danger that this world finds itself in."

"I would like to hear it," the Hjor leader repeated.

Wrenflang detailed his version of events, starting with Fanlas visiting him in the inn. Why would a strong man like Fanlas have sought out an aging, decrepit mage such as himself? Well, as the events had unfolded, Wrenflang had become aware of Bimb following them—the poor boy had just wanted to follow his Fa. But whenever Wrenflang dared to look back, he sensed a dark, swirling violence within the young man, though he had always held his tongue. Who knew what was really happening? Was the father involved? What plans were being brewed...? He had kept his thoughts to himself until Bimb suddenly left, cutting off any further inquiry. At that point, he had wished he had mentioned something to Fanlas and Sorchal.

"Why didn't you?" Hjor Hjor asked.

"I wish I knew," Wrenflang said sadly. "Something seemed to stop me, hold my tongue. We kept on to the Temple, but it was finally there when I talked to Fanlas. The poor man acted as if Bimb had already died... which, he did in a way." Wrenflang pieced together the final events as Zhy had told them, then explained the most recent encounter with Bimb. When Zhy returned to the Temple with Huyen, it was clear that the situation had spun wildly out of control.

"I'm sorry."

The mage scratched his big nose. "If I had stopped Bimb. If I had confronted him in the tunnel, this could have been prevented."

"But what about this Arzith... Ar'Zoth, as you call him? The demons would still be loose, would they not?"

"That is true, I guess. Either way, a man had to lose his son. It's too much to think about at times."

Hjor Hjor leaned over. "You cannot blame yourself for things that are past. You did what was correct at the time. I think I now understand why you have come here. Like me, you can see a larger field of battle than the one you fight."

But what keeps you fighting Welcfer? He wanted to ask, but they were on mostly amicable terms now; no sense in disrupting the balance. "We need help. I don't know what the situation is like in Belden, but if this Yulchar had let demons out of the Tunnels of Woe, the land could very well be drowning."

Hjor Hjor sucked in air. "It will not take long for them to move north, once they have used up... I mean, once they have, well..."

"I understand, Hjor, I understand. And I thank you."

Hjor nodded. "In the morning, we will need to strike out."

"Together," Wrenflang whispered.

"Together," Hjor Hjor repeated.

Drunplug went back and brought the news to his troops. He told them they were invited to the village, but not a man moved; instead they made camp just outside the Hjor settlement.

φ

Morning came quickly, but the soldiers awoke slowly. The events of yesterday had not been a dream: many of the Hjor soldiers and Welcferians alike stared at each other with tired eyes and resigned looks. Change had come with the strangers.

Hjor Hjor and Wrenflang walked out among the soldiers and chatted idly, softly in the crisp air. Zhy and Fanlas were packing their gear, discussing turnips of all things, when the two men approached; warm greetings were shared around.

"Wrenflang and I were discussing our plans," Hjor Hjor said quietly. "I've agreed fully to lend aid to fight the demons."

The mage nodded.

"But we have pressing matters... first we must try to deal with the other tribes, but they will surely be of no use—all they understand is violence... ha," he said suddenly. "You bring with you many coincidences, Wrenflang."

"How is that?"

The Hjor leader simply cocked an ear. A great ululating call, hard-edged but bellowing, echoed across the valley. Zhy thought he heard Hjor mouth something about "the devil", but the camp was suddenly a flurry of churning snow, creaking leather and clanking of swords.

"Attack. Here." Hjor Hjor clipped.

There was no time to react—the camp soon exploded into chaos. As the half-naked warriors cleared the rise, Drunplug grimaced and drew steel. *These* were the savages that the Welcferian army had fought those many years, at least in their dress and their action.

Wrenflang wasted no time in unleashing a bolt of lightning down upon the center of the advancing collection of warriors; snow, blood and limbs erupted into the cold air. Hjor Hjor's forces followed into the fray.

Zhy's father had used the word chaos several times, often to describe situations over which he had little control. Vronga and its bustling, maddening clogged streets could be called chaotic—or extremely disorganized. But as Zhy watched the battle unfold, the word grossly underestimated the display of bedlam that ensued on the frozen landscape.

Standing there, huddled in his coat, he felt the fool. Watching as swords flashed, spears thrashed, and arrows flew. Wrenflang's bolts were devastating, but yet the more primitive Hjor were unrelenting. All Zhy could do was watch—powerless. His knife felt like a dead weight in his pocket. It was now useless, pointless.

He yelled at one of the Welcferians, but the roar of battle was overpowering and the spear struck his stomach before sliding up through his mouth. Zhy's stomach tingled, but he swallowed, turning to shout a warning to another man, this time one of the allied Hjor—the man heard and spun in time to avoid a spear, then thrust with his sword.

At least I can do some good.

An hour passed, rather an hour in Zhy's mind, as the snow churned and the screams of the dying pierced the air. Zhy shouted a few more warning calls, careful to keep his eyes darting around the field, looking out for any flying spears. Of a sudden, the group of enemy Hjor fell back into a defensive stance. Surprised, the Welcferian and friendly Hjor men paused briefly, some in mid-step, swords raised.

The ground rumbled, though Wrenflang's arms were at his sides. Zhy looked nervously around, searching for the source, though the battle continued to boil in its mass of red and white. The old mage was stuck—with such close fighting, his spells would kill both enemy and ally. Again the ground rumbled. Zhy took a step toward the battle, looking for the source.

On the northern horizon, a large and familiar shape could be seen, and it loped slowly toward the fray.

A bear! How does a bear...?

The animal trudged closer, and the soldiers of the "enemy" Hjor tribe stepped aside for it to pass, as if it were a pet. Zhy had seen a bear like this before, though it had been brown, and it did not fight. This monstrous, white-furred creature was anything but docile; huge paws swiped at the hair, gutting one of Hjor's soldiers. The men of the other tribe stood still, watching as Hjor Hjor's men panicked.

"Retreat!" Drunplug and Hjor Hjor bellowed at once. The men wasted no time in scrambling back, racing away from the huge attacker. One of the Hjor stumbled, fell, and the bear fell upon the poor man with a heavy thump; a muffled scream preceded the sound of gnawing flesh.

The Hjor and Welcferians clumsily fell into a line several paces away from the other Hjor. Suddenly the field went quiet except for the occasional scrape of a boot and the bear's heavy huffing.

"Have you ever seen them use one of those before?" Wrenflang whispered to Drunplug.

The soldier shook his head. "They are getting more and more clever, though I wonder how you would feed such a creature to keep it as your—never mind, he's on us!"

Wrenflang cursed himself a fool for not acting when the lines of men were separated; for in only a matter of seconds, the lines again collided, with the bear ripping and shredding. The field boiled into a murky fog of snow, blood, the flash of weapons and the crisscrossing arcs of light from Wrenflang's hands. Though he was limited in his range as the soldiers again were too close together for him to unleash anything too powerful.

Zhy stumbled, and fell in the snow, knees soaking quickly with the cold. He tried desperately to focus on a single point of the battle, if there was one.

There was a very brief pause, and Drunplug acted; he raced for the bear, but a shout from Wrenflang turned his attention to the massive homemade sledge that was descending rapidly toward his head—as Drunplug swung his sword, Wrenflang let loose with a familiar green webbing of light, trapping the bear as it raised its large paw. Its growl of frustration was deafening.

Finished with the Hjor, Drunplug turned, arcing his sword toward the bear. This time Zhy yelled, but too late as an arrow lodged itself in the back of the Welcferian soldier's leg. The warrior yowled, stumbled, spinning to find the assailant, but Wrenflang had already shot a bolt of fire across the distance and ignited the man.

For now the bear remained in its magical cage as Drunplug ripped the arrow from his leg, the barb shredding flesh and garment alike. The soldier limped slightly as he raced to continue the fight—his sword sliced a Hjor head clean, in time to spare Wrenflang from impalement.

Through the fog of the battle, Zhy could not tell the difference between the friendly Hjor and the attackers. Shapes moved wildly, slicing, cutting, firing, or falling disjointedly to the snow-covered earth. Soon, even the familiar forms of Wrenflang and Drunplug were lost in the fray, though the bear still howled—this time with a roar of satisfaction; he had slipped his netting and stomped toward Zhy.

Zhy scrambled to his feet, croaked a plea for help. The bear trudged a few feet closer to him.

"Wrenflang!" he finally cried, but his voice was lost in the tumult.

The bear sniffed the air, stopped and stared at Zhy. Dismissing him as an inferior foe, or perhaps discounting him as a worthy enemy, the creature huffed and turned to seek out others. When his attention landed upon Drunplug and Wrenflang, the bear bounded forward.

"Look out!" Zhy screamed.

Slowly, painfully, Drunplug turned at the sound of Zhy's voice, in time only to gape in a scant second of terror. The bear leapt, paws up, mouth wide. Its heavy bulk smashed into Drunplug and Wrenflang with a spray of snow and blood; the men soared through the air, landing on the hard ground. Again the bear roared and approached their prone and motionless bodies.

Zhy found it in him to sprint forward, screaming, screaming. Meaningless words and babble poured out of his mouth in a cry of frustration and anger—if he could somehow distract the bear. *My knife, I have a knife*, he thought blindly, extracting the small instrument and charging.

The bear continued to charge, ignoring Zhy.

Of a sudden, a familiar cry went up, and a dozen primitive arrows suddenly stuck from the hide of the large animal. It reared on its hind legs, teeth wide to the frozen air. Anger roared louder than pain and it charged again.

The brief respite was enough for Wrenflang to collect himself and attempt the discharge of another magical bolt. This time Zhy recognized it immediately and shielded his eyes—

As *Bolt of Sacuan* exploded and the bear vanished.

Wrenflang collapsed in the snow. Drunplug pushed himself into a sitting position and stared... bear tracks and a thin wisp of purple smoke were all that remained of the animal. "What?" he whispered.

Hjor men stood equally dumfounded, though the leader of the friendly warriors wasted no time in ordering an attack on their enemy—with their own swords lowered briefly, and without their strong animal, they were an easy slaughter. Zhy forced himself to focus on Drunplug and Wrenflang's barely heaving chest as the sounds of screaming and ripping flesh filled his ears.

"What was that?" Drunplug repeated.

Zhy cocked a half smile. "It's called *Bolt of Sacuan*. I've seen it used once and the mage that did it was laid up for several hours."

"Is he—?"

"He's very much alive, but surely very tired," Zhy replied.

"I am," the mage croaked. He remained still. "It was the only choice."

"I remember hearing that before," Zhy answered.

Drunplug snorted and stood. "Well, whatever it was, I thank you. Would you like me to fetch some blankets for you, so you don't freeze?"

"No, that will not be necessary."

Zhy thought he heard light snoring.

Hjor Hjor appeared, stared down at the mage. "Is he all right?"

"Aye."

The leader nodded and indicated the field of carnage. "We have won this battle, but if we don't start moving west, we will encounter more of these tribes, I'm afraid."

"Where did they get a beast like that?" Drunplug wondered.

Hjor Hjor scratched his head. "I don't know, but it was a very stupid thing for them to do. How do you feed an animal like that? Rather, who decides which of your villagers is going to get eaten...?"

"You don't mean they would—"

"Yes, Zhyfrael," Hjor Hjor answered. "The frozen seas are a thousand miles away to the east and west—where would this ice creature find its seals and frost birds to eat? No, the only option is a sad one."

"I had no idea, Hjor," Drunplug said softly. "I must apologize again for misunderstanding your people."

The man waved him off. "You can lament your crimes later, perhaps over a drink." He chuckled mirthlessly. "Right now we need to move west. I'll find men to carry the mage. Let's just go—there's no time to try to bring them to our side." The leader scowled. "No time."

Quickly Drunplug and Hjor set to marshaling and organizing the remaining Hjor. Tents were collapsed, rolled tightly and loaded onto sleds. Men strapped on skis and the entire army was moving westward within an hour—though even as the day had only passed its midpoint, the sun was already starting to dim.

φ

Wrenflang soldiered through the remainder of the day, and through the next, setting his ancient jaw in a hard line and focusing on his feet as the miles slowly passed by. The battle had sapped him of more energy than he wanted to betray; each tiny muscle felt stretched beyond its limits, his head pounded, and even his veins felt as if they were bound in knots.

"Wrenflang, you don't look well," Zhy said suddenly.

The mage startled, cleared his throat, and scanned the far horizon with pinched eyes. His heart fell rapidly—the Spires were still only murky lines on the western skyline. True, the vast mountain range was closer than it had ever been, but it still seemed too far.

"Wrenflang?"

"Er..." he cleared his throat again. "Honestly, Zhy, no, I am not all right. But we need to keep moving, or we will never get there... we're too late as it is."

"You look like you are going to collapse any minute, I think we should stop at least for a little—"

"No, Zhy."

Zhy started to protest, but he'd dealt with determined companions before. It was hopeless. The Hjor leader looked back and noticed that Wrenflang had started dragging one leg behind him... it would not be long before the old man collapsed. Wisely, he called a stop to the caravan and they set up tents for the night.

Wrenflang protested softly about the existence of daylight, but after he was ushered to a pallet, he collapsed upon it with a sigh; his soft and ancient snores filled the tent.

φ

"We need another mage. Perhaps even one of these Hjor, those who can start fires without timber, can help."

"Sir?" The young Hjor fidgeted. The old man had been speaking nonsense for the better part of an hour, but it was the first time that Wrenflang had addressed him directly.

Wrenflang pushed himself up to his elbows. The Hjor mats were made of ancient and moldy straw and each movement sent a fetid aroma through the tent. "You need to take a group of Hjor soldiers through to the Tunnels of Woe... it is vitally important that we seal as much as we can within those walls."

"Sir?"

"Yes?" he coughed.

"The preparations are already made for that. Please, you must rest."

"And Huyen, where is he?"

Zhy had just stepped into the tent and waved the Hjor boy away with a smile. The young soldier was grateful to leave—he was nervous and out of sorts in front of the old mage. "He's... gone, Wrenflang. Don't you remember?"

"Oh, Zhy, is that you?" Wrenflang asked, lying down again. He covered his eyes with a wrinkled arm. "I had a dream about Huyen, that he was lost and in trouble."

"He's dead."

"I-I know that, Zhy. Just a dream. I am very tired, so very tired. We need to move west, west through the Spires."

"We are already headed west. Fanlas, Drunplug, and Hjor Hjor talked and assigned a group of men to go to the Tunnels of Woe." He looked at the reclined form of the old man, his drawn features, his chest rising and falling. For second, he thought he saw his father's face superimposed on Wrenflang's—the dead face, staring up from a field of dead grass, a knife in his heart. Zhy shook the image away and thought of giant overflowing glasses of ale.

"But—"

He reached out and laid a hand on the mage's shoulder. "It is arranged. Rest. We will need your strength again, soon."

That you will, Wrenflang thought. He tried to speak the words, but fell back to sleep.

Chapter 22

The Fat Man Cometh

Do not underestimate the strength of a weak-looking man, or the power of a child. Those of us who may be physically inferior sometimes can be pushed into action—steel yourself against the onslaught.

Seer Zer'Wen

A fleshy fist slammed the pile books, scattering them to the dirty and dusty floor. The timid messenger held a piece of paper in his trembling hands and the boy leapt backwards at the violent outburst; the paper flittered to the floor and he left it there. Dran'Za spat and sent the messenger away. "It has gone too far."

The headquarters that housed the Knights of the Black Dawn was empty save for Dran'Za and the messenger, who had now ducked back into the kitchens. Every knight was out fighting, being recalled, or dead. The fat man cursed again as he scanned the hollow chamber—he had lost nearly half of his men, and could lose perhaps several dozen more.

"Slaughter. It's a Sacuan-blessed slaughter!"

With effort, he pushed his massive frame away from the table and called for the boy. The serving lad emerged timidly from the kitchens, and the smell of roasting poultry wafted out; for the first time in many years, the smell of food turned Dran'Za's stomach and he scowled.

"Sir?"

"Find me a pair of long skis and poles."

"Excuse me, sir?"

"I said—"

Someone threw open the front door, and left it open as they bounded down the stairs. Snow swirled in the empty hall, tufts of wind scattered the papers.

Dran'Za tried to make himself taller. *Damn Gorand!*

But his face lit up with unexpected joy when Narand strode into view. The knight was beat-red, his cloak white with snow. But, beneath the snow, the deep red stains were visible.

"Narand!" *So all is... lost?* Dran'Za assumed the news would be dire, but the look on Narand's face was hopeful.

"Dran'Za... I have some rather helpful news. There is a..." His exuberance slipped as his eyes worked around the room. Where was everybody?

"All are in the field," Dran'Za said softly. *And I will be, soon.* "It's bad. But I *am* glad to see you." It was hard for him to give a compliment, but his solitude had grown into loneliness here.

Narand smiled and brushed an inch of snow from his coat. "There's a trick, Dran'Za, a simple, easy trick to killing the gherwza!"

"And what about the mulargh?" he snapped, regretting his reaction. He unclenched his fists and forced a grin. "I-I'm sorry. Tell me. Tell me about the gherwza."

The knight shifted his weight. "It probably works on the mulargh, too," he muttered to the snow-covered floorboards. Then he looked up: "All you have to do is get them on their back!"

At that Dran'Za burst out laughing. The look on Narand's face was priceless—he'd seen that look before, years ago, in a dingy tavern somewhere near Darvein. They had been talking about women, then.

Narand scratched his nose, scowled. Then his lips cracked open and he laughed. "If only it was that easy with girls, eh!"

"Tell me about it," Dran'Za chuckled. "And stick to the bats!"

The knight told him in detail what Horesh had done, and Dran'Za watched him with a stern face, his mind working through the massive sea change that this brought. When Narand had finished, Dran'Za leaned his large butt against the table. Books fell to the floor.

"My friend, go spread this word. You are my best fighter, but you alone know this. I will send the boy—boy!" He called out; the messenger appeared silently. "Dance well, Narand. "Dance well and beat these demons."

"Will *you* dance?" Narand inquired.

The boy had returned with skis and a small tin of wax.

"Yes, yes I will. This doesn't change my plans fully, it only strengthens them. I'm going to see Gorand."

Narand sucked in air. "I see." He turned to leave. "I hope we meet again, Dran'Za."

"Aye," the fat man clipped, then turned to the boy. "One more note for you to send out to whatever network you have left living."

Dran'Za scribbled a furious letter, handed it to the boy. His attention shifted to the skis lying on the floor.

I'm fat but I can still use these things!

"Will you be partaking, of, of—of lunch?" the boy asked, his voice trembling. He had seen Dran'Za and all of his moods, but this attitude of determination and zeal was completely new to him. The fat man had a look on his face that was dark and dangerous, his jaw was set as solid as it could be, given his multiple chins, and his eyes appeared to consume objects with the voraciousness his appetite previously possessed.

"No," the leader of the Knights said softly. "No, there is no time. I've already eaten today."

The boy stared at him. *What? Go, go be useful!* "Go!" he barked. "Go deliver this note. Take a sword with you. Spread the word of this new revelation!"

"Sir!" he chirped and darted away.

Dran'Za's skis clanked against the staircase and any other object within a yard. With another curse, he tossed them to the cold ground and fumbled into them, then cursed himself again and pulled them back up, applied the wax. Finally he leaned a bulky shoulder against the building and strapped himself in. Once on the snow, his instincts took over and he was flying across the landscape. South. Towards Belden City.

Fat and out of shape, he pushed onward, driven by his decision and the new information. What he lacked in stamina and endurance he would have to overcome by sheer force of will.

"It has gone too far," he kept repeating as the snowy miles inched by.

He pushed himself beyond the limits of any normal man, but his mind only saw red, a red cloud over everything. Villages that he passed were either burning or being attacked—as much as it pained him, he did not stop; it would do no good for him to be lost before he got his message across to the higher authorities. If they still lived. And so, as he neared Vronga, his oversized and overstuffed heart filled with a new emotion: Despair.

Everything seemed lost, every small town, village, hamlet or farmhouse was lost. And with it those precious, innocent lives inside. How could something like this happen? How had the Protectors let the Temple of M'Hzrut fall? Where was the help from the Guard?

Could Narand and his new trick help turn this bloody tied?

To his amazement, Vronga stood, though the horse merchant had several harrowing stories to tell him.

Demons everywhere, from dripping bats to old men with appendages far too long and affixed with scythe-like fingernails. Blood, screaming, smoke, and the cries of battle sting rung in the merchant's head; each time he looked skyward he feared the onslaught of a thousand gherwza.

Somehow, though, the demons had abandoned the city almost as one entity, scattering in a multitude of directions, but not before leaving a terrible, slushy, bloody mess in the streets. Even now, Dran'Za could see the odd lumps of corpses, and the fastidious Healers and other citizens as they slowly picked up what they could... though snow had started to fall again.

Dran'Za thanked him for the horse and bid him farewell, even as the poor man sank to a chair, staring blankly at the ceiling, eyes glazed.

"May Sacuan keep you," Dran'Za whispered and walked out.

He never bothered to change out of his ski boots.

The leader of the Knights of the Black Dawn pulled himself onto the horse, grunted as his large bottom slapped the saddle, and started the animal off with a slow, steady walk. It was going to be a long ride to Belden City, and he intended to push the horse as hard as he could, though his enormous backside would be screaming in agony after only several miles. Such pain would need to be endured.

His horse was fast, and in excellent condition, even for the winter. Dran'Za had been cooped up for so long at headquarters, he feared he would no longer be able to judge horseflesh accurately; given the dire state of the world, who knew how long even a good looking animal could last? He feared that the animal would suddenly fall over and vomit blood, or sprout horns, or some other fantastical transformation only seen in children's stories.

"Call yourself a fool, Dran'Za, but look around you," he breathed as the animal raced southward, passing smoking ruins, gutted houses, and corpses hanging from leafless branches.

He finally put his head down and stared at the pommel of the saddle, letting the animal lead, while he repeated a prayer to Sacuan. The litany became a chant which he droned over and over until it grew into a dull roar in his ears. Anything to distract from the horror he was riding through.

Chapter 23

Blizzard

Snow is both friend and enemy. From it you can build a home and shelter for your family. The same snow can crash down a mountain and drown a village.

Seer Zer'Wen

Winter had turned into nightmare for most of Belden, and Bimb's manipulation of the weather wasn't doing any good.

A hundred miles southeast of Reldan, tiny villages languished under the vengeful wrath of a winter blizzard. The snow fell with a raging, relentless fury. Wind howled, tearing roofs of buildings, and the subsequent dumping of snow filled rooms. Citizens panicked, tried to find shelter, but the snow fell with such power that no one could move—horses whinnied in the streets, buried to their chests. Children were trapped and frantic parents dug through the thick powder with their bare hands in efforts to save them. And the wind howled.

It roared toward the eastern coast of Belden, and out to sea, creating waves taller than most mountains. Ships along the coast were flung into the air and shattered against the pounding surf. The screams of sailors were quickly drowned in the unending howl of wind.

φ

I had only a brief glimpse of what I had done and my heart sank. No, this would not do, if I could not get a handle on this, the world was going to have two serious problems. Lessons learned from the hurricane were worthless when it came to snow—instead of a controlled wind, only raging snow and ice ensued.

"Zhy, Zhy, Zhy. What have you done to me?"

A deep sadness filled my heart. Could I cause nothing but pain and suffering? Mother blamed herself fully for my condition and though it was not my direct fault, my *being* was enough for her misery. Fa risked his life in the wastelands near the Spires, most likely making up for his guilt over leaving me at the farm. And now a blizzard wreaked havoc on Belden, a blizzard that I had driven. There had to be a better way to do this.

My emotions had taken too much control. If I couldn't fully bury them, then I needed to get down to another level:

"The spaces between!"

Wind, rain, snow, and ice were merely larger objects made up of small particles. And small bricks can be used to build a large wall. I had been harnessing the finite particles of the universe, but that was not doing any good—I needed to be able to use the bigger pieces.

Wind, I needed wind most of all.

But I had to get out of here, away from people, far away so that I would no longer hurt them. With effort, I pushed up and out, away from the lower level currents of air, and pushed higher into the atmosphere. While I did so, I felt a tugging at my sides, the tugging of the dead space, the other side. Time was evaporating.

A great river of flowing air caught my eye—this must have been that stream that had caught me earlier, a stream I struggled to control. Now that I felt a little more confident, I floated down to it. Where it started, I was unsure, but it looped in a southerly direction, swooping over the northern edge of Belden, skirted Gray Gorge's southern entrance, and eventually bent directly south and to the east.

Riding it was like trying to shoot the rapids of a real river on a stick; it thrashed and bounced and shook me violently. There was no opportunity to control it, though its power was enviable. With a great deal of effort, I was able to push myself up and away from the raging torrent, where I could see how it brought with it the greater weather patterns of Belden. Huge banks of snow-laden clouds moved slowly along the sky as the river dragged them along with its undercurrents.

Farther back from the edge of the flow, I tried to pull on it.

How does one pull air?

I had to abandon the idea of the spaces between, but I did wonder at the multitude of particles that must be involved in such a raging current of air. Too many to deal with.

Diving below the river, the air warmed, and warmed even more as I dove even closer to the ground.

To boil water you needed heat. Heat was just energy.

Maybe I *could* use the spaces between! Perhaps it wasn't just a cliché and a concept for... well, whatever it was. I needed different air temperatures to move the river, it seemed, so to do that, I needed more of the little particles.

I was able to redirect the flow, but the consequences were again horrific. With the new warm air rushing up, thunderclouds the size of Welcfer boiled up into the sky, generating a constant flash of lighting, and hundreds of twisting, swirling black clouds in the shape of funnels. Only one village lay in the path of the massive storm I had created, but once one of those swirling clouds touched it, everything vanished in a cloud of dust.

With a cry of frustration I let go and floated back to my dead space. The final death started to seem a little more appealing and it took a powerful tug on my willpower to keep me rooted here. How easily I could float away, to the next plane, gone from the struggles of mankind forever.

But I'd caused this, Sacuan bless us!

No, no, no! There had to be something... and the weather was only causing destruction—it was something I was not going to have any sway over. I had seen how violent currents of air could be—nearly moving whole mountains with their fury. Nearly moving whole—

Mountains!

Could I move a mountain? Was it possible to go *beneath* the surface?

No, the thought was silly and childish. Well...

What *was* beneath the crust of the earth? Was there anything that could be used, twisted, changed, manipulated? Above ground, the weather patterns were too fluid and far too dangerous to move; but could I get my cold, dead hands (I laughed inwardly at the ancient cliché) on something beneath?

I'm not sure how I did it, but I looked to the ground, and willed myself *underneath* it, flowing and pushing downward through grass, dirt, and the bedrock beneath. And as I pushed myself downward, I wondered for a moment if the solution to the weather were really that simple. If I could flow through solid granite with a thought, why was it so hard to move the hurricane, or control the raging stream of wind?

Perhaps it was something I could attempt later—right now my attention was drawn to the world below.

φ

Beneath the rock, sand, and soil were huge slabs of thick stone, joined like strange puzzle pieces. It was even more complicated, and fascinating, than the world above. Except that there were spaces between (there's that cliché again!) each of them and with a little mental effort I found I could slide the slabs around. When I did so, however, I noticed that an entire mountain face had come loose and crumbled to the ground in a powder of crushed rock and debris. Thankfully the mountain was near the very top of the world, unreachable by any sane human.

"At least I hope nobody is there," I said aloud. My dead space was so silent, so stuffy, it helped to talk even if nobody was left to listen.

With a sudden thought I pushed myself forward, upward, and then to the south, where I thought Fa could be as he traveled with Zhy and Ugly Nose—er, I mean, Wrenflang. Wrenflang. I wasn't sure if I liked his real name or Ugly Nose better... I guess it didn't matter anymore; they needed help.

With my new perspective on the underworld, and the ease by which I could enter it, I tried again to push clouds around. Even the light, thin clouds in the extreme upper reaches of the atmosphere seemed to deride me, chastise me. They hung there, like scowling old men. How dare they!

I muttered something untoward and dove back down to a level at which I could see movement on the ground. The shape of a moose resolved itself into a mountain and I dove further, until I did see life, crawling inexorably along the deserted wasteland below.

I did not expect an entire army! I could see the snaking line of men and equipment—there was Ugly Nose—Wrenflang—with his white beard, and Zhy, and—

Fa.

A swell of emotion surged within my soul and my hand reached down to clasp him, but I pulled it back quickly. Too often such action had resulted in violent winds or storms—though Sacuan help me, I could do nothing to control them! Destroying their efforts would be beyond the worst clichés I could think of.

But, as I watched them approach the mountain, my stomach roiled—or whatever would be roiling in a dead man's soul. They were several hundred miles north of the pass that Lyn had showed me! They seemed of a purpose, heading directly west toward the Spires of Solitude, intently marching along, focused, dedicated.

Each of them walking toward a blank wall.

No passes were visible through the terrain—not here. The only way was beneath the ground... Could I make the mountain move? With the plates beneath the surface, the pliable yet enormous quantities of rock, could I get enough of a pull (or push, as it were), and knock down the mountain? Or would my efforts level everything around them and kill them?

Fa!

My heart ached...

I dove back beneath the surface, directly beneath the mountain that blocked their path.

There were plates, here, too!

I checked quickly to see how far Fa and the others had traveled—they were still some miles away. Hopefully that was a safe enough distance. If not, I was going to kill my own Fa, Zhy, and Ugly Nose. The chance would have to be taken; there was no path through, no other option. Our world was going to be devoured, devoured by a horde which I had let loose, left unguarded.

Back underneath the mountain, I found the plates and shifted them together, at first moving only a few feet of the rock, then finally spreading them apart, exposing a gap that seemed to have no bottom. Quickly, molten rock from beneath the surface bubbled from the fissure I had created, and I darted back instinctively. Round balls—a dozen of them—darted up from the endless bowels beneath.

"Demons!" I screamed, then slammed the slabs of rock back together, crushing the creatures between the blocks. Such a motion was already moving the ground above, hopefully not enough to cause too much worry— there was little time to check now; I had to get these slabs to move much more violently.

Instead of pulling them apart, this time I shoved them sideways, one along the other, like two tables sliding together in an inn. Nothing seemed to happen. I pulled again.

"That's it," I said with a smile. The entire world shook.

Chapter 24

A Flaming Glass

*Liquor can fortify men, can make them feel
more powerful than they are. It also stifles,
weakens, and breaks them, removes their
common sense and melts away all reason and
pure thought. Beware the fiery spirits of
drink!*

High Cleric Bertrand

The Welcferian and the Hjor soldiers were getting
along far better than they should have been.
Drunplug marked the change with a shrug: "They
have seen the gherwza and the mulargh... and
they are soldiers, above all. Just following orders."
But *had* they all seen such creatures? The past days had
turned blurry and he wasn't sure why the change had
come so sudden. "Just following orders," he muttered
with bitterness, looked up at Zhy and Wrenflang. They
held their bowls of steaming food.

Zhy opened his mouth to speak, but Hjor Hjor
appeared behind Drunplug and cleared his throat.
"Friends," he said simply. "Friends, you are each
welcomed into my tent, where we will share a drink.
Come." And he turned and walked away.

"All right then," Drunplug sighed, standing.

Wrenflang followed, but Zhy was slow to rise.

A drink? Great, a drink... I get to ... no, I'll just pour it out. That's it. Just pour it out. They won't notice—Hjor looks a little under the influence as it is.

"Coming, Zhy?"

"On my way," he said, following.

The tent was dark—almost utterly. Flaps moved to reveal tiny slices of moonlight, and in those brief snatches of light, Zhy could see that the Hjor soldiers sat in two small rows inside their leader's tent. Not all men were present, Zhy noted.

"Sit, please," Hjor Hjor announced. "My most trusted leaders are here, and now our trusted friends from Belden."

Zhy wondered where he should sit, not being able to see apart from the odd flicker of light, when someone finally lit a lantern and the place burst into life. Indeed, there were only twelve or so men inside, including Zhy's companions. A small retinue of haggard-looking Hjor—the men returned nods with waves and raised chins with perhaps a muted "Hello" before gazes returned to Hjor Hjor, who stood at the front of the tent, holding a bottle.

Zhy groaned inwardly. *Oh no...*

"Friends," Hjor Hjor repeated. "This is a very special drink—" he turned quickly and muttered some words to a man in front of him, who sprung to his feet. "While Qured retrieves the glasses—yes, perfect, thank you. These mugs and glasses have survived much... oh, that one is broken," he said softly. "I'll just take that. Thanks, right there." He looked up again, focusing on Zhy and then his men. Zhy noted that he spoke more for the benefit of himself and Wrenflang: "*Ghostdreams* can be made only once every three years, when the winterberries grow on the Icedown Plains, and when we—when we are not otherwise engaged." He glanced at Drunplug with a look of apology, but the Welcferian simply nodded. "In any case, it is a very potent, powerful drink, only shared among the leaders of the village, before a battle. We now share it with our friends, for we battle the true enemy!"

A dull cheer went up from the men but the room fell silent as the lamp went very dim. The sound of pouring liquid filled the tent, a sound that set Zhy's stomach to churning—he did not look forward to this. Unless... unless it remained dark.

Someone laughed in the dim light and the lamp finally went black. Zhy heard the sound of flint being struck and suddenly a dozen small blue flickers of light danced off of the canvas walls of the tent.

Did he just light the—

"And we light this drink, so that we are filled with two fires—one for the belly and one for the heart. Now, my friends, be not concerned, you do not have to drink the fire—though Qured surely will!" At that the gruff man chuckled. "We pass around these small deckels, we call them, which you use to douse the flame... and then you must drink!"

A muted hum of agreement passed among the Hjor.

Qured carefully passed out the flaming mugs and soon each man's face was limned in a soft blue glow; the alcohol flames flickered peacefully from the containers, sending a false warmth through the tent. *There is nothing warm about any of this,* Zhy reminded himself. *It is a cold, cold death that lies at the bottom of that bottle.*

Surprised at his own sudden burst of philosophy, he took a mug from Qured and smiled. The Hjor soldier nodded respectfully and handed Wrenflang a drink.

"I can't drink this!" Zhy whispered as he stared into the flames.

"Just douse the flame and give me the mug, then," the mage whispered.

Zhy nodded. Looking into the flames, he could see the clear liquid below, swirling, bending, swooping as fire kissed its bobbing surface. The smell of wintergreen was strong, overpowering, cloying as the heat ignited the sugars within the potent liquor. And flames that bore the

shapes of gherwza, mulargh and other hideous
monstrosities glared back at Zhy with dripping fangs. He
almost dropped the mug, but froze when the face of his
father floated up from the depths of the drink… it floated,
wobbled, scowled deeply, and was replaced by a demonic
visage.

Someone handed him the "deckel" and he slapped the
square piece of wood atop the glass with a thud, handed
it to Wrenflang. The mage drank his in one gulp, tapped
Zhy's knee with the foot of his mug. Carefully, Zhy
handed him his warm glass and took the empty, raised it
to his lips, and pretended to drink. Nobody seemed to
notice.

He sighed heavily.

"We are now strengthened by the power of
Winterdreams, and we will fight the demons and we will
win!"

Another cheer went up.

Am I any stronger, or weaker? Zhy wondered. He
could not shake the face of his father as it chastised him
in the fire of alcohol. Though the Hjor had said he would
be strengthened by the drink, he knew that at least his
strength would have to come from something that was
not fermented. And while the men in the tent chatted with
the reinforcement of the drink, he felt warmer somehow,
warmer and stronger.

"Maybe I'm not a complete failure," he muttered to
himself.

He turned to speak to Wrenflang, but the mage was
already singing a lewd song with one of the Hjor soldiers.

Zhy could only laugh.

Chapter 25

Loose Threads

Our minds can only conceive so much misery and so much exertion. Eventually we collapse in our struggles, our body quits us, our thoughts are removed and we wander those last moments before death.

Prophet Zher'wen

It was cold, so cold it was nearly hot.

He wiped away sweat from his eyes, though the liquid was sticky, clammy.

Blood. I'm bleeding.

"My box!"

Sorchal wiped more blood from his eyes, tried to look out over the horizon, find another box, another landmark. But he was blind. Blind. Bloody eyes were wide open, staring everywhere and nowhere. He stumbled forward a few steps and fell face first in the snow. The icy powder felt soothing on his raw and ragged eyes, cooled the searing, and staunched flow of blood—but he still could not see.

"My box!" he cried again, now crawling along the snow-covered rock. "My beloved box, why did you take it, why?"

Eventually, he rolled on his back, sightless eyes wide, frozen open.

His last words floated in a small puff of steam. "My... box."

Sorchal was not possessed. Nor was he alone in his plight. Over the course of the past months, men and women in both nations found themselves staring at a black wall, seeking comfort and release from even the most mundane objects. It could have been called madness, which in a way it was. But it was not demonic possession.

Unable to cope anymore with the stress of battle, the loss of loved ones, or the harsh and unforgiving elements, people simply let go of their grasp on reality and wandered off in the wilderness to die. In Sorchal's case, the guiding box was the last straw for a man who had endured so much.

He had witnessed a brutal slaughter at the Temple of M'Hzrut, had travelled solo through the Tunnels of Woe, gone back to the Temple, and accompanied Zhy and his companions through the most remote region in the world. Demons, the Welcferian army, and the searing cold had frayed his brain past its usable state; when he saw the box with the needle, he completely unhinged.

It should not be considered an indictment on their character or strength, those who could no longer maintain their connection to reality; for they had faced the worst in the world, the worst in their history, and a situation that was not survivable for many. Rather, for those who still remained, those like Wrenflang, the ever-strong Fanlas, and even Zhy, their very survival was testament to their strength.

$$\phi$$

Zhy would rather have been cast in the role of tag-along, an aimless drunk with little to lose, and nothing to gain. But his so-called "fragile" mind never let go, even though the struggles and trials that he had faced were a thousand times more horrific than he could ever have imagined—he would bitterly deny that he was strong or heroic, but his actions were speaking much louder than his feeble protestations.

"It was my fault."

"What—your fault?" Fanlas asked.

"Sorchal. It was my fault. I know Wrenflang decided that we were to move the Temple, but all of it was really my fault. We should have left him back there... he wasn't quite right."

"He *never* was quite right, but he was a good Protector," Wrenflang said.

"Do you—" Zhy coughed. "Do you know what he was doing before we left the Temple of M'Hzrut? Looking for wintergreen and singing. Singing."

Fanlas gave him a sad look, but no one else said anything. They continued in silence. What was to be said? Did they agree with Zhy, or were they ignoring another of his self-deprecating proclamations?

Sorchal's loss, on the other hand, was sadly a small fragment of a much larger avalanche. If the majority of Welcferians or Beldeners were to survive this ordeal, Zhy and his companions would have to succeed in their endeavor.

Chapter 26

Crossroads

If you meet a man in the barren lands, offer him all that you possess. For it will not be long before that man is you.

Ancient Hjor saying

The green lights bobbed and flickered, adding their rare crackling to the bitter night air. Zhy sat huddled around a meager fire with Hjor Hjor, Drunplug, and Wrenflang. Fanlas had long since retired. When Zhy saw the strange lights to the west he stood and let his mouth hang open.

"Ah, the lights!" Hjor Hjor exclaimed, ignoring Zhy's statement. "What words do you have for them in Belden?"

Wrenflang sighed. "We rarely see them in Vronga, but I have heard it called magic. People say the lights are the work of dangerous warlocks, as they summon up demonic minions from the great beyond."

"It's not magic," Hjor Hjor said flatly.

"What is it, then?" Zhy wondered.

"Spirits of the dead," the Hjor leader replied. "The spirits of the dead." His voice was husky. "They call us to work together, mend our tribal struggles, and remember those who have gone before—that they are not gone forever, but watch over us." As he talked, his gaze never left the swirling lights in the sky.

There was a long silence before Drunplug's voice softly broke the stillness. "I have seen the green lights many times, each time after a successful battle against—well—" he coughed. "I thought them blessings from above. Blessings of victory."

Slowly, the two men moved their focus away from the sky and looked at each other. Their expressions were stern, determined, but yet resigned to their current state. A thousand years of battle and strife had been set aside in the span of a few days, a feat not even possible in lurid stories—and yet the two men had stared at the selfsame lights that, for each man, indicated a completely opposite state of the world. For several long moments, the two battle leaders stared, then slowly pulled their gazes back up to the lights; which slowly began to swirl and blend from green to gold, to red, and back to green. The low crackle was a constant background hum.

No words were said the rest of the night.

φ

As they set up camp the following night, the green lights were no longer visible, but by now the forbidding craggy peaks of the Spires had loomed closer into view. Zhy looked at them while the sun dipped behind their gray peaks. There were no breaks, trails, crevices, or passes through the mass of rock, snow, and ice.

They were running into a wall.

Wrenflang sidled up beside him and swore. "Sacuan be damned," he muttered and turned away.

"What is the matter?" Drunplug asked.

"Take a look," Wrenflang said over his shoulder.

Zhy had expected the Welcferian commander to curse, spit, or stomp off, but instead his face went blank.

Drunplug scanned the landscape slowly; his eyes changed for piercing and bitter to defeated and somber. He turned and saw the same expression walk its way across the soldiers.

Men in the caravan grumbled at the sight of the mountain, and Drunplug ordered them to keep working on the camp setup. Light was fading quickly this close to the mountains. Since there was no visible path through the Spires, he wanted time to discuss their options—having come this far, it would be devastating to have to scour the mountains for a path, or, even worse, to retreat.

"Well, what are we going to do, Zhyfrael?"

Zhy jumped at the voice. Hjor Hjor stood in front of him, arms crossed.

"W-what?"

"If you are she, reborn, then your word will get us through."

Zhy stared. The man was serious. The Hjor's face was serene but determined, his lips set in a flat line.

"Get us through," Hjor Hjor said, then crunched away to the tents.

Get us through? How?

Chapter 27

To Move a Mountain

*Man thinks himself much more than he is—
with is arrogant pride and lustful ambitions,
he believes that he can move mountains with
his hands, stop the rain with a shout, or bring
snows to bay. How sad. How very, very sad.*

Prophet Vron'Za

The ground heaved, buckled, rippled, and bent.

Their balance gave way as the ground slid like river scum beneath them; men tumbled to the snow-covered ground with a rattle and clank of weapons and armor, and the air filled with curses.

Zhy stumbled, but kept his balance, staring to the west in wonder: The ground actually had *rippled*, he noticed. Like a flag flapping in the wind, the snow-covered rock bowed upward, flowed to the west in a ribbon of earth, then slammed back down.

"What was that?" Drunplug demanded, his entire body covered in snow.

The soldiers stared at the ground, waiting for another ripple, another shift in the earth.

"What was that?" he repeated.

Wrenflang was still staring at the ground, but his lips moved quietly before uttering any sound. "A quake."

"Here?"

The mage raised an eyebrow.

"Why?" Drunplug demanded. Before Wrenflang could answer, the Welcferian swore and muttered something about demons.

"I don't know," Wrenflang replied instead, pointedly ignoring the reference to the underworld.

How tired Zhy had become of the constant lack of knowledge! He had been complaining for months about not knowing anything, not gaining knowledge—what he had gained so far had been vast, but still not enough. Yet, so irritated was he at the phrase "I don't understand," that he bristled greatly at the old mage. How could he not know? He knew everything!

"What do you mean?" Fanlas asked in his quiet, solid voice.

"Quakes don't happen here," Drunplug answered, scowling at Wrenflang. "They are not supposed to—they belong further to the south and east, more near to Belden's border, where nobody lives."

"Nobody lives here, either."

"True, Wrenflang, but my men have been here and have never experienced this. Never."

"First time for everything, I guess."

The Welcferian commander growled. "Men!" he snapped, turning away from Wrenflang in irritation. "Scour the area, look for whatever warlock, mage, or wicked creature caused this." He turned to face Zhy and his companions. "If this is the work of demons under the ground, you will have to answer to me, do you understand?"

Has he gone mad? Zhy wondered.

Wrenflang shook his head. "What type of answer would you want me to provide? I told you, I don't know what caused it—perhaps there are quakes in this part and we felt the first of many years. If demons caused this, then we will deal with it. If we can. But there is nothing that I know about this that will help you."

Drunplug scowled and balled his fists.

"Bimb," Fanlas whispered.

"What?" Drunplug barked.

"My—my son, perhaps he—"

"Ach!" Drunplug spat and stomped away. But even as he growled, he wondered if what the big Beldener had said could be true. What could a man's dead son do? The Welcferian shot a look at Zhy and thought again. Fanlas's own wife had supposedly led him and Huyen back up to see the warlock—what was his name? Ar'Zoth...? Why could not the son do the same?

The same son who had caused this! Drunplug reminded himself with a deeper scowl. He swore again and opened his mouth to unleash a pointless tirade when the ground wobbled again, then heaved as if pushed upward from underneath.

Men screamed in terror. Out of the corner of his eye, before he landed face first in the snow, Zhy saw two Hjor sprinting away.

For a second, the earth was still, but then the ground surged, ice and rock wrenched up and out into the brittle air. Zhy and his companions were tossed to the ground like toys; they covered heads in anticipation of being struck by flying rock. But the trembling seemed to have ceased where they cowered, and moved west, rending and rocking the earth as it moved along the arctic landscape. The men slowly worked themselves into standing positions, and though the ground trembled slightly, the majority of the rending seemed to have moved further to the west.

He brushed off snow and looked at the men. All Hjor eyes were on him, waiting, expecting. Zhy grimaced, then looked at the mountain.

"Get us through," he whispered.

φ

"Fa?" I cried out. He was awake. Unreachable.

They were there, huddled in front of the mountain, at least a hubdred miles from the trail that Lyn had guided me over. Too far, much too far.

I could see Zhy's face down there. An instant rage boiled inside of me, a wish to kill him where he stood, and let the others through. No.

"The calm within."

I remembered Fa's voice in the dream: "You put yourself there."

Zhy had only done what was asked. If they had sent anyone else, I would still be alive, killing everything and everyone. Instead, a dead man appeared and put an end to the slaughter.

A temporary end.

"The calm within." Calm within a raging storm.

Again I pictured Zhy's face, and looked at him in the field below. The hatred was there, but it seemed a little duller; was it dull enough for me to have success with my attempt?

"Calm." *Fa, I love you.* "Calm... within."

I steeled myself and ducked back down beneath the earth.

It was time to move a mountain.

φ

The earth rumbled again.

"Get us through!" one of the Hjor shouted.

Zhy mumbled, then let his mouth fall open.

It appeared as if something beneath the ground was holding a carving knife and slowly tearing the rock apart—ever closer to the looming Spires and their sheer rock faces. Earth and stone belched forth from the cleaving scar that shredded its way across the landscape, and as Zhy watched, it finally reached an ice-covered slope of a mountain, and stopped.

But the quiet rumbling beneath their feet did not. Though the ground did not shake where they stood, it vibrated, pulsing slowly. Zhy's feet began to tickle and finally itched as the humming, violent quivering raged in intensity. The mountain in the distance shimmered, and Zhy swore he saw it sway slightly.

"No," he whispered, rubbing frozen eyes with equally frozen hands.

It *was* swaying!

Each man ducked as the mile-high mountain lolled back and forth, and finally exploded! Rock, snow and soil erupted in a city-wide cloud of debris. The travelers fell to the earth again, covering heads, sure that the enormous amount of rubble would crush them, each praying silently in the cold. Zhy tried to open his mouth to say something, but a wind like no other suddenly roared down from the east. The men hunkered deeper as the wind tore across the sky—and while it seemed strong enough to lift whole houses from their foundations, they were untouched as they lay on the cold ground. Instead, the wind ripped across the landscape, toward the rising cloud of earth and rock.

It blew the remains of the mountain westward, ever westward, though swirling winds picked up a small cloud of debris and flung it back in their faces. The men waited out the brief hurricane with heads bowed and hands raised; when at last a deep silence descended over the plain, the men looked up.

"Sacuan be damned..." someone whispered.

"Get us through!" the Hjor shouted.

Where a looming, towering, spire of rock and ice had stood, now a broad path of gravel and crushed rock extended before them. The ground, though rough, was flat and even as it stretched through the mountain.

"It looks like the moon!" Zhy exclaimed.

"And how would you know what the moon looks like?"

Zhy looked at the mage, his head cocked, eyes wide. "Wrenflang, I—I remember staring at it, on a very cold and clear night. It could have been many years ago, but I looked up and saw many pits and mountains and craters... this is how I thought it would look!"

If Zhy could have seen the moon, he would have been exonerated, for the scene now resembled the moon more than Welcfer. A wide flat path, perhaps a hundred paces wide, pushed its way between the remnant of the mountain, now cleaved into two parts. The channel itself looked like a network of a hundred thousand craggy stepping stones, whose mortar was the snow and dust that had settled down into the crevices. At the far end of the path, a low, snow-covered boulder poked a meager summit into the blue air—low and edged with easy hand holds it would provide little challenge for the men to cross.

"I can imagine," Wrenflang said, staring at the newly-opened fissure.

"How...?" Zhy wondered, staring. To the east and west, the Spires still clung to the Welcferian landscape in cloud-piercing, rugged, unforgiving peaks. The ground had heaved, bent, and shredded, but only where they stood.

"There was a word for that, that we learned at the University," Wrenflang said, his eyes glued to the rubble.

"What is that?" Zhy wondered absently.

"It was an ancient word who's roots were unknown, it was *duxelle el marchino.*"

"What kind of language is *that?*"

Wrenflang chuckled. "I have no idea."

"What—what does it mean?"

"Fanlas, in old stories it means a trick used to fix everything at the very end. Maybe a character who shows up that was never introduced, or a tree falling on the villain. Something wonderful, amazing, and almost impossible almost at once."

"But surely... surely that did not solve our problems?" Fanlas said sadly.

"No, it didn't. But it just saved us weeks of mountain climbing. It gave us time! Time!"

"What... how..?"

At that moment a single streak of lightning struck the ground not a few thousand paces beyond, and with it came a deafening crack of thunder. "Magic!" Zhy wheezed.

"No... no, that was real."

"Bimb," Fanlas whispered.

Bimb's dead, Zhy wanted to say, but caught himself. Perhaps Bimb was now talking to Fanlas, in the same way that Cerease had talked to Zhy. Instead, he asked quietly, "Is he talking—?"

"No, he's not," Fanlas said sadly. His voice seemed to be frozen and his words sounded thick and muddled. "No, but I don't doubt if he had something to do with this."

Zhy looked at the Hjor, and whispered: "But they think *I* did this."

ϕ

I had done it.

If a dead man could be exhausted from exertion, I was surely spent, though I floated back to my dead space to view the world below. Of the mountain there was nothing except a cleared path to Ar'Zoth's keep. In the past I had destroyed an entire mountain with magic, but such destruction would have been too much here—instead, creativity was called for. The earthquake and subsequent jet stream were the tools I used.

Fa and his companions could get back to the Keep, and back to the work that needed to be done. I could not help with that, for time was surely running out on my space.

But I had done it! I had moved a mountain!

The men below looked blurry—if only I could have learned how Lyn and Ma had seen so clearly into this world below—but I could see enough. They moved... they moved through the pass that I had created. And through the murk, there was the brief flash of white teeth as he smiled, his face turned upward.

I love you Fa, I sent down to the world of the living. There was no reply, but I did not expect one. I'm sure he knew, in his own way, that I had done something—after all I was able to tell him in his sleep of the things I had done. Perhaps I could see him again in his—no, time was short. Fa needed more strength now; it would be unfair to sap him while he slept, for talking to the dead took much of a person. Zhy would likely sleep for weeks after this ordeal.

My work was done.

Wait! I paused. No, it was not done. There was one more thing.

With a force of will I pushed the wind farther to the west, toward to the great courtyard that locked in the demons, even now who were dangerously close to the surface. A gust of wind heaved westward, clearing every last snowflake from the courtyard of the great castle.

There. That should give them a better sense of what to look for. The large cylinder with its intricately carved stone cap would be obvious to a child. My time was ending too quickly, and the world would have to rest on Fa, Zhy, and their companions. I was confident they could succeed... my struggle was now at an end.

Theirs was only beginning. Fighting the demons would be hard and I was not sure that Ugly Nose—what was his real name anyway?—could do what Ar'Zoth had done. But he would have to try.

I had moved a mountain. Only to provide them a straight path to their own.

$$\phi$$

"Zhy, what do we do?"

"And why do you ask me?"

"Only because you have been here before..."

He shook his head fiercely. "Sadly that is no help to you. This slab—I've never seen it!"

They had proceeded quickly through the pass and toward the large keep, quickening their pace as soon as the stone ramparts were within sight. After refreshing themselves in the castle proper, the man assembled out in the courtyard—their eyes and feet drawn to the large exposed slab of stone in the middle.

Wrenflang opened his wrinkled mouth to speak, but at that moment the great stone, with its demonic engraves, groaned under the collective weight of several thousand demons. It started to *bubble* upward, as if a huge fist were pushing upward from beneath it.

Then it blew completely off and landed in the snow with a hiss.

There was a horrifying pause as the group stared into a black hole, behind which could be heard a muffled roar of evil flesh sliding and rubbing. Zhy expected a multitude to boil out onto the snow and he stepped back cautiously, but it seemed the demons were cautious as well, and only a few of the horrible entities rolled out of the hole.

As the first demon slithered through the opening, Zhy lurched. These creatures bore no resemblance to the gherwza or mulargh. They had no discernible faces, apart from an unholy dripping "eye" in the center of their perfectly round faces... which were nothing more than a single row of teeth. Their forms were impossible to define, for a smoke-like substance dripped from their bodies in thick wisps. It was no wonder they took on the forms of old men, gherwza and mulargh, Zhy thought. These creatures were the size of medium boulders, as tall as Zhy's mid-thigh, and nearly to Drunplug's shoulders...

Zhy didn't get a chance for further inspection. Wrenflang fired two quick bolts at the demons and they boiled to char in the snow.

A few more slithered out, each as detestable as the last. A slight breeze blew, and Zhy could see, that beneath the smoky tendrils, the demons were covered in a thick gray scaly substance. No sooner had he began his inspection of the creatures, did Wrenflang fire again.

"This invasion is going to take some time!" the old mage joked. "I expected them all to come at once."

"It's cold here," Fanlas said carefully, his eyes locked on the hole in the ground. The fetid heat wafted across the courtyard. "And it's hot down there..."

Wrenflang thought a moment, then burned another demon with fire.

"Can you seal that again?" Zhy asked. What was the point of standing there, picking of demons one by one. There had to be another way.

"I'll need help."

They were able to muscle the covering back toward the opening. Wrenflang sent bolt after bolt after bold down into the hole while Fanlas pushed on the stone tablet—Zhy had never seen a man so strong.

Wrenflang used magic to heat the slab until it glowed.

"You're melting it!"

Indeed, the stone flexed under the tremendous heat that was being applied; small rivulets of molten rock dripped along the sides and hissed violently as they touched the cold snow.

"Only a little bit—this will help fuse it here until we can figure out what your plan was." He sighed. "But soon it will cool and be movable again."

"I don't have a plan!" Zhy blurted.

"You said something about cold, Zhy," Wrenflang snapped. "Cold. Snow. Think... we can't possibly freeze that pit down there, can we?"

Fanlas laughed. "You are talking about freezing... *freezing*... it's too funny. So funny it makes me want to cry. Zhy, you don't think it can be done, do you?"

"Who said I thought anything could be done? I only mentioned that they could not adjust to the cold. Which doesn't make sense, if they are escaping from the Tunnels into the cold air."

Wrenflang thought on that. "Didn't you say that Ar'Zoth and Bimb were both planning on releasing the demons?"

Zhy nodded.

"Well, there was no trace of anything here, any type of ward. A ward like that against demons would be obvious to an apprentice, surely."

"Maybe it was removed a long time ago," Fanlas offered.

"Then the demons would already be out in force! I don't understand... there was nothing holding them back before... nothing."

Zhy's eyes watered and froze to his lids. He wiped away the tiny ice crystals. "Except for one thing," he said, partially envisioning a solution, partially seeing his own violent death. "The snow."

Chapter 28

Battle!

Between war and hell, there is no difference.

Unknown

It was the sound of a million bees, the roar inside a hornets nest, and the whine of a coastal hurricane. All commotion stopped within the courtyard as several dozen pairs of eyes turned southward.

"Gherwza, and mulargh," Wrenflang hissed. He pointed at the first small black shape that appeared between the Spires and Ar'Zoth's castle. Hundreds more joined. The roar intensified, and nearly a thousand more demonic bats gathered behind the black veil.

Welcfer and Hjor troops crouched, spears, swords, and lances extended.

But the shapes remained stationary; a small black wedge in the sky, slowly growing darker until it hung in the sky, a thousand wings flapping.

What are they waiting for? Zhy wondered.

Drunplug's voice bellowed over the buzzing and screeching. The Welcferian commander sprinted through the snow, shouting orders at his men, then he clasped Hjor Hjor on the shoulder and barked orders. The Hjor men bounded away. *Where are they going?*

"Run to the Keep!" the Welcferian shouted, pointing at Zhy. "Unless you're going to fight with your knife, get out of the way!"

Zhy offered no protest and sprinted to the rampart, bounding up the stairs two at a time; he fingered his fruit knife and stood helpless, watching the battle. He turned to retreat into the castle, when his foot bumped against a man—looking down he saw several of the Hjor hunkered in the rampart, stretching strings on bows and nocking arrows.

"Tell us when to attack, Zhyfrael," one of them said. He tied off the string of his bow, flicked it with his finger. It sounded like an off-key sutan.

"Me? You want me...?"

The man was perhaps nineteen, face pocked with acne and frostbite. "Yes. Lead us."

Zhy stared. What? Lead them? How? He knew nothing of warfare, and he wasn't filled with the memories of Zhyfrael, as this man believed. He looked out at the courtyard: Wrenflang leaned against the cap; Drunplug had lined his men up in a square, each man facing outward; some Hjor had taken defensive positions behind rocks. What was he to do?

Just start talking... "D-do you have arrows?" *Idiot, of course they have arrows*—"I mean, how many of you—of them, arrows, are here?"

He cringed, expecting one of them to haul him up and toss him from the ledge for sounding like such a fool.

The Hjor bowman didn't blink. "Ten men, two hundred arrows, maybe a little more."

Ten men and two thousand demonic bats! Zhy looked up at the black cloud—it undulated, dipped, flapped, and screeched. It would not be long before that horde attacked. What were they waiting for?

"How good is your aim?"

The young man bristled.

"I never miss," he said, without a hint of arrogance.

Zhy's mind raced. Done with the questions, now it was time to give these men orders—ha! Zhy, giving orders? But the ragged face stared at him, mouth open.

He looked at the gathering squadron of gherwza, smashed his earlobe between thumb and forefinger, and spat out a bunch of words he thought made sense.

Sacuan help us all...

φ

Drunplug arranged his forces to the west of Zhy's position. The Welcferian commander arranged his men in a box pattern, each man facing outward. Since he was dealing with a flying enemy that would swoop and attack, he could not devise any traditional methods of war—his men would have to hold firm and not break into separate groups.

That was the Hjor's job.

Hjor Hjor's men had spread out, some in nooks and crannies to the northeast, others with Zhy in the castle, and a few behind Drunplug's men. Drunplug looked once, twice, and the Hjor were gone. *Clever bastards,* he thought.

Even Zhy was hidden, though every few seconds he could see the young man's stringy hair whip out over the ledge. It looked like the boy was running back and forth along the rampart. *What is that idiot doing?*

A thousand leathery wings flapped, the sound echoing across the courtyard. Drunplug's ears rang with the strange sound—like wet flags flapping in a gale; but accompanied by ear-splitting shrieks and howls.

The gherwza descended.

"Arms ready!" he screamed. Drunplug took another glance at the rampart and saw Zhy's hair, then his face. *Idiot, he's going to—*

But a dozen Hjor archers popped from their positions, arms drawn back. Zhy yelled something unintelligent and their dark shafts arced upward, toward the gherwza and mulargh.

Very few hit their mark the first time, but the men were already drawing again.

"He's setting the range," Drunplug whispered. He didn't wait for the second volley of arrows, but he could hear it whoosh across the sky; a few high-pitched squeals and the slap of flesh against icy stone set his lips to a half-smile.

He had work to do.

Drunplug gestured to his men and sprinted to the strange lid in the middle of the field. Wrenflang waited for him. It was their job to protect it as much as possible, for they believed the birds would attack this opening.

Wrenflang crouched and waved Drunplug over.

"Listen, mage, you better—"

The scaled limb of a mulargh slammed into Drunplug's shoulder, the claw tearing through his armor. He sprawled forward, tried to catch his balance by gripping the cap, but slipped on the ice and fell face first in the snow.

Wrenflang muttered something and Drunplug heard a crackle. The smell of burning flesh followed.

"Did you get it?" Drunplug asked, wiping the snow from his face. He held his sword in his hand.

"I only burned him. He's coming back."

Him? These all look like horrible bitches to me! He chanced a look at his men. They fought well, as well as an army can fight a flying demon.

One of his men went down and he cringed. *He had a little boy, too...*

Wrenflang shouted and he heard the crackling sound. The mulargh was approaching from the north, screaming at them, its razor teeth bared. Drunplug tightened the grip on his sword and fell into a defensive position, while Wrenflang let loose with a blinding flash of light.

Bolt of Sacuan struck the beast's left wing, completely erasing it from existence. The forward momentum of the creature carried it toward Drunplug; he let it come at him, stepped lithely to the side, and sliced its head.

Wrenflang muttered something and collapsed in the snow.

The mulargh, headless, still thrashed. Drunplug sliced it into several pieces and crouched next to the cap. Wrenflang breathed, but was spent—what had the demon done to him?

Drunplug resisted the temptation to help his men, though they were struggling at fighting these creatures; a slash of a sword would cut off a wing, but the damned bat continued to gnaw and slash. Surprisingly, the Hjor attack was quite effective: Attack and retreat, attack and retreat.

He had to remind himself that it was because of the combined effort that it worked. Without his men to hold their position, the chaos would be worse.

"How can it get any worse?" he pleaded, as another mulargh screamed down from the sky.

It's beady eyes were locked on Drunplug.

φ

Fanlas was a blur on the battlefield. He did not stick to one group or the other, but darted where needed; he filled the hole left by a fallen Welcferian soldier, giving them enough time to fend off two gherwza before he darted away to hack the head off a monster that chewed on a Hjor warrior's leg.

Taking a lesson from the Hjor, he ducked behind a rock no bigger than an oversized pumpkin, pressing his muscular body against the rock and snow. He cocked an ear to listen for louder sound of chaos—sounds near to his hiding place.

Fanlas's ears picked up the sound of leathery wings flapping. Above the shrieks, cries, and howls of agony, he struggled to focus on the single sound. *Bimb taught me how to hear the other instruments within the music.* In less than a second, the memory returned:

> *They sat in an inn, eating chicken. There were two sutan players, a drummer, and a flutist. Bimb closed his eyes, smiling.*
> *"What are you doing, son?"*
> *"Listening to the rhythm of the other sutan."*
> *Fanlas couldn't hear it—only the main instrument.*
> *"Don't listen to others, Fa. Only three notes— strum, strum-strum, strum. Listen. Listen."*
> *Fanlas listened. And heard it. It took two more songs before the strained notes beneath the main melody could be heard. They were loud, clear; all other noise drowned.*

As now the bat screeched overhead and Fanlas leapt up, sword swinging.

The gherwza caromed and of end as it tumbled to the snow, headless. Fanlas ducked back beneath his cover and waited for more, listening for the notes beneath the notes in the terrible song of battle.

$$\phi$$

"What are you doing?" Zhy demanded.

The young boy had the nerve to drop his bow? They were low on arrows, but not completely out—a few of the Hjor even braved the chaos below to retrieve arrows. Zhy's mind still whirled with images of a gherwza tearing the head clean from one of them.

"Demon!" the boy replied simply, pointing toward Drunplug's position.

Zhy saw the mulargh, moving impossibly fast. "Mulargh! Then pick up your damned bow!"

"No."

I've lost control. Of course. They've finally figured out I'm a fake.

Zhy's eyes widened when the young man raised his hands, light dancing between his fingers. A ragged, dripping ball of light formed, the boy screamed a Hjor curse, leaned on his haunches and threw his arms out. The tendril of lightning cracked outward, shot across space and struck the mulargh in the back.

Zhy saw the flash of Drunplug's sword as he swung, but it only whispered through thin air; the momentum of the attack spun the Welcferian down and he landed face first in the snow. Zhy repressed a chuckle.

The Welcferian commander fumbled in the snow, then stood, staring first at his sword, then up at the rampart. Zhy waved at him, and pointed to the boy—

Who promptly collapsed to the stone, eyes wide.

"Sacuan's scrotum! No. No..."

He'd seen so much blood and death today that he felt numb. Absently he watched as the Hjor carefully released more arrows down into the swirling battlefield. One of Drunplug's soldiers took a stray one in the neck, while a Hjor in the field was gutted by a gherwza. Blood and brain matter turned the snow pink.

Zhy could no longer tell the difference between human or demonic screams. This was not battle, it was slaughter. His eyes went blank, and a thought kept churning in his mind:

This is the fate of the world. It can't be. But it is. This is a story, I'm in a story. I have to be...

A Hjor next to him cursed as another pulsating, writhing mass darkened the eastern pathway.

φ

The new cloud of demonic creatures appeared over the eastern mountains, then swooped low through the cut passageway. The last of the Hjor arrows fell upon the gherwza in the field, and the men tossed their bows aside, drawing spears and racing to the melee.

Drunplug's forces were dwindling; he had lost a dozen men. The pink snow churned as his remaining soldiers continued to slash and hack at the flying creatures.

There was no way this battle could be won.

Wrenflang still lay motionless in the field.

Zhy's archers were now dead, all of them.

And why am I allowed to live?

φ

Drunplug took a glance at the bats coming over the pass and spat in the snow. His men barely held against this group—his attempt at a unified defense, with the men holding a box pattern, had failed miserably and the battle had descended into an unorganized fray. Soldiers slashed seemingly randomly, screaming, crying as talons shredded muscle and punctured flesh.

The screaming, whether it be from man or demonic beast, had blended together as a dull roar in his ears, a background noise to the whoosh of his own sword. It seemed to slice more through the brittle air than through bat.

And the Welcferian commander darted nervous glances to the squadron that waited from the pass that Bimb had created. *Come on then, come on... Darrell*—he thought with a sudden pang of sorrow. *We need you now!*

"Attack!" he screamed at the waiting squadron. "Come on, attack!"

Yet the pulsing squadron waited, thousands of wings flapping.

At their vanguard, a demonic bat waited. A bat that had been a man.

Yarel.

Chapter 29

Down in a Tunnel

∿
∿

From a tunnel of hollow earth, stone, and blood shall the demonic host arise; beware for you will not see them coming, because you do not know where to look.

Cleric Hyun, Order of the Knot

They had succeeded in sealing a few of the "holes", though Rhys still only saw solid rock. Felyar, however, seemed excited as he tried to explain the disturbances. Where the Welcferian had been shy and skittish inside the tunnel, he was now comfortable and even enthusiastic about finding and closing the holes. A great multitude had *not* been clawing or scratching to get out and attack them, and the vaunted Tunnels of Woe were now silent except for the constant dripping of water.

"Look over there," he said, pointing. "Do you see how the lights do not align with each other? For the past mile, each side of the tunnel has a light, one right across from the other. But not there!" He scratched his nose.

"That much I do see," Rhys nodded. "I've seen it each time, but I don't see where the holes are. Where are the demons coming from?"

"Have you even watched what I do? I-I'm sorry, I did not mean it like that," he said quickly, noting the brief look of hurt that crossed Rhys' face.

"Actually, I haven't... that blue light you send out is blinding."

"Well, I use blue and red," Felyar replied. "Not that the colors matter, but the energy does—I have to heat up the rock and melt it."

"Melt it!"

The warlock laughed. "I would say it is my favorite magical spell, but I don't like that we have to use it against demons."

"How does one..." Rhys trailed off. He had read something of the kind in his studies. Though he knew there was exacting science behind each spell, and use of the structures of the universe, its employ had always seemed foolish. So much potential for bettering the world was wasted on webs and bolts of energy. Now he thought himself a fool for not expanding his own horizons, and not learning more.

"You make it really hot."

At that Rhys burst out laughing. Felyar joined after a moment. The Tunnels echoed with their chortling for several moments. Felyar finally scratched his nose, cleared his throat, and thrust his arms into the air, aiming at a spot above the lights.

Two spirals of light danced on his fingers and this time Rhys watched in fascination as they curled up into the dark blackness above, illuminating the rock of the tunnel wall. He focused his attention, squinting against the dazzling light, and watched as a gaping black chasm opened. The rock wall looked slick, wet, like the back of hard-shelled river beasts he had read about in books.

Soon the water vapor sizzled from the rock in a fog of steam and the rock began to change from pitch-black to a slightly glowing red. As Felyar moved his beams upward past the opening, the glow of the rock grew angrier, redder; a pulsating slab. Finally the rock buckled and became viscous, eventually flowing down from the top of the opening.

"You are melting rock..."

"And the demons within, I hope." The warlock grunted. "I can feel them."

φ

Rhys and Felyar trudged through the tunnel, chatting absently and gazing at the lights, looking intently for any off-set lights. For Rhys, it seemed very strange that the differences in lights would clearly indicate an opening for the demons, but Felyar checked random intervals between "normal" lights, and found nothing.

They were having a discussion on birds when Felyar screeched to a halt and held up his hand.

Thud, thud-thud, thud.

"What in..."

The thudding grew louder by the second, and soon the tunnel was filled with the heavy padding of very large feet.

"Sacuan help us," Rhys whispered.

Felyar didn't wait for the creature to come into view. He launched an arc of red light from his hands, which dimmed in the murky tunnel briefly, then exploded against an invisible barrier.

Rhys gasped. The light only lasted a second, but the afterglow burned his eyes; a giant rodent, with the tail of a rat but the face of a bat.

Felyar tried another bolt of red light, this time splitting it into a dozen threads. Several small explosions rocked the tunnel and the stench of burning fur filled Rhys's nostrils.

The creature screamed, and pounced forward, coming into the circle of blue light.

Sacuan help us all! Rhys thought. He stumbled backward.

Felyar held his ground, firing bolt after bolt of energy at the huge creature, but he only succeeded in searing fur. The animal whined again and crashed forward, devastatingly fast. A hair-covered leg lashed out and struck the warlock in the chest.

As Felyar sprawled to the damp stonework, the creature lifted its leg to kick again. Stunned, Felyar was immobilized. His breathing crackled, and Rhys assumed he had crushed his ribs.

The massive foot raised up, ready to crash down. Rhys screamed at the beast. Though unarmed, it was a last chance to free Felyar.

Stay smart, stay strong. "Come here! Come here and take me!"

The giant rat snorted as it turned, thankfully setting its foot back on the ground instead of Felyar's face.

Rhys gagged as the creature snorted again, breathing out a rotting, fetid cloud.

Behind the creature, Felyar moved slowly. Red, orange, and yellow strands flickered between his fingers, then went out.

No... no... Rhys thought about running. *Stay smart, stay strong.*

Again, the warlock tried a spell, but it fizzled.

The bat-rat monstrosity stepped closer, bared its teeth. Four rows of long, needle fangs reflected the blue light. *Things:* beetles, roaches, small rats, and even human-like body parts dropped from the yellowed fangs. Again the air washed over Rhys in a sickening plume.

Stay smart, stay—

Felyar tried another spell.

Nothing.

Rhys cracked his back against the wall of the tunnel. The creature stepped forward, cocked its head; then closed its maw for a second before baring it wide in front of Rhys's face.

The blue lights went dim and Rhys felt a warmth run down his leg. Felyar moaned in the background; even the creature noticed the change and cocked its left ear.

"Jump out of the way!" Felyar barked.

Rhys barely moved in time. The last word had not left the warlock's mouth before a coal-fire orange flame enveloped the creature.

It thrashed, screaming as it was immolated. But it never lost its balance. Instead, it turned and darted for Rhys, who sprinted back up the tunnel.

"Stop!"

No, Sacuan damn you no! But Rhys slowed his pace all the same. *Stay smart—*

A hot, red light blinded Rhys and he covered his eyes. *I wasn't even looking back...* he turned, slowly, as the glare faded. The creature had shrunk.

"One... more..." Felyar gasped.

Yellow lightning skittered across the floor of the tunnel and struck the demon, now half of its size. With the stench of roasted animal and the sound of meat sizzling, the bat-rat kept shrinking in size until it resembled a simple rat—

At which point Rhys' boot crushed it into the stones.

"What—what was that?" he panted. "And.. How—how many more of *those* are there?"

Felyar's eyes were glazed, but his chest moved. He knelt on the hard ground. "I don't know."

Rhys looked up at down the tunnel, eyes seeing bats and rats and deformed demons in every unlighted corner. *Sacuan help us, I pray we are not the only ones doing anything!*

Chapter 30

Victory or Chaos?

How does one win a game? By collecting the most pieces? By losing the least? By grinding his opponent into the dirt... or by simply surviving?

Prophet Haran

Yarel flew to the side and perched on an outcrop, attempting to blend in to the slate-gray rock. From there he could see the carnage below; the humans battling the gherwza and mulargh, a force of a handful battling the worst of the demonic underworld.

His trailing squadron of gherwza screeched, anxious to attack, anxious for human blood.

They would not dine on human blood today.

He had gained control of the bat, and brought with him as many beasts as he could enlist. His visions of the world below had showed him that the worst of humanity did not compare to the terror that demonic beasts (such as himself) could unleash. Now converted to a gherwza, however, he could not go back, could not apologize.

His only choice had been a suicide mission. Flying his horde northward, he noticed the congregation of mulargh and gherwza, and thereby saw his chance to do something halfway worthwhile.

It wasn't a change of heart so much as an admission that he had failed in every aspect of his life. Destroying these lying, conniving, scheming creatures would be a pleasure.

He could then destroy his own life.

The humans are on our side, he sent. *Attack the bats— attack the mulargh. Attack everything that is* not *human!*

His bats attacked with fury, eager to draw blood from their own kind.

ϕ

Something else appeared in the mountain pass. Zhy groaned out of frustration. Yarel's bats were busy attacking the other gherwza—even two mulargh lay dead in the snow. Drunplug, Fanlas, and Hjor fought smoothly and fluidly. The distraction was enough that they had a golden opportunity to gain an upper hand.

But Yarel's creatures were losing. More and more dropped, leaving the original demonic beasts an open pathway to the soldiers.

And now *this.*

The creature shambled forward. It had been a man once. Now it's too-long arms dragged on the ground, the elongated claws scraped at the snow behind it. Zhy could hear it chanting:

"Gozath, ruler of the swirling depths! Gozath! Gozath, ruler—" the recital built to a roaring crescendo, the creature known as Untrel shuffled forward a few steps.

Untrel.

He had been a Counsel Guardsman once, sent to the north. Bruce, Zhy, and Darrell had been attacked by a Wildman wearing a necklace of skulls. After Untrel had killed the man, he took the necklace, and thought it fashionable to don the necklace. But something demonic had slept within the necklace, and when he had placed it around his neck, Untrel transformed. He had since been roving the northern wastes, killing anything that stood in his path. Protectors, random citizens, small animals: He had even attacked a balsam tree near Gray Gorge.

His nose had long since gone missing. His clothes were torn open to reveal diseased and frost-bitten flesh, flesh that had fallen away from slabs of fat; now it dangled like torn pieces of fabric from his bones. Black, dead, oozing pus. "I am Gozath!" the creature gurgled. It took one step forward, then with one quick, fluid motion, he moved forward several paces, inserting himself into the fray.

Wrenflang rolled over in the snow, eyes open. The old mage brought himself to his knees, scanning the scene with a look of a man dropped into the ocean. Seeing the bats, the soldiers, and now Untrel... his arms started to move, light dancing.

"NO!" Zhy screamed at Wrenflang. The old mage did not seem to hear. He screamed again and Wrenflang paused.

Untrel's target wasn't the men.

"Another duex et matche, or whatever he called it," Zhy whispered to himself. The man calling himself Gozath was a blur as his arms wind milled through the collection of demonic bats.

One gherwza attempted to take off, but Untrel's arm extended, his claws reached under the belly of the creature and he flung it far across the field where it landed on its back atop a tiny outcrop.

Simultaneously his left arm ripped the head off of a mulargh that was screeching toward him, its mouth open wide. "Gozath!" Untrel screamed, turning to slice another bat; when he turned, Zhy saw his face, or what remained of it.

The Counsel Guard! Zhy realized with wide-eyed wonder. His eyes misted and he blinked rapidly against the cold.

Untrel ripped into the remaining demons, losing an arm in a spray of blood at one point. But yet he shuffled forward, killing until no more demons remained. The bulk of soldiers turned to stare at this husk of a man, one arm dangling in the snow, frost-burned face smeared with blood.

Zhy jumped back from the edge of the rampart and began to descend the stairs. His boots had cleared a few of the icy steps before the crackle of magic raised the hair on his neck.

When he looked up, Untrel was engulfed in flames, his deformed mouth open in a wide smile.

"Sacuan be damned, Wrenflang, why?" Zhy screamed turning to face the mage. The old man dropped his hands to his sides. "I—he..."

"Why would I save him, Zhy? He was already dead." Wrenflang turned and hurled a bolt of lightning at a stray gherwza.

A bloody bat's wing landed in the snow next to Zhy and he darted back to the meager cover of the stairs. Turning back, he only watched as Untrel's corpse burned to nothing. *He saved us, once, twice.* Zhy inhaled the cold air and blew it out his nostrils. "War is hell."

φ

Yarel watched this last, then forced his demonic bat on a flight further west. Most of his bats were dead, which was what he had wanted; they had at least disrupted the other squadrons. Now these humans could do what they wished here—curse them all. *It's time to die,* he reminded himself: upward, upward he rose. A few cursory lightning bolts zipped past him, but he kept flying.

Higher, higher, he climbed. And ever eastward until the rocky shoreline of Welcfer vanished behind him.

Yarel drove the creature into a cold that was nearly absolute, that would freeze even the hottest liquid in a fraction of a second; until his own demon froze solid and fell slowly down to the icy water below.

Chapter 31

The Fat Man Taketh

We shall forever protect those most in need. What is done for the lowliest impacts the highborn and the holy.

Cleric Bertrand

ran'Za arrived at the Counsel Guard headquarters only to find the place in complete disarray. Men scurried in a thousand different, disparate directions, sending missives this way and that. Whatever remained of Belden's army had to be directed in the struggle against the demons, but yet it seemed as if the apparatus only spun in conflicting directions.

No one seemed to be in charge, and news of Jafren and Gheren came as a shock to him. Not a single person was in charge.

He grabbed a messenger by the scruff of the neck. The poor boy's eyes were wide in terror as they took in Dran'Za's frost-bitten face and raging eyes.

"Boy! Do you know who the Knights of the Black Dawn are?" he barked.

"N-no, sir, no, I have not—"

"Gah!' he spat, flinging the young man down. The messenger scurried off to wherever he was going.

Dran'Za stalked down hallway after hallway. He asked the same question a dozen times and nearly gave up. A man with a sword at his hip breezed by him. Dran'Za would have ignored the soldier expect for the fact that he wore a necklace that bore a cork shaped like a knot.

"Excuse me, but are you a Protector?" he asked, for the first time asking instead of barking.

"I—yes, I, well—"

"You are or you are not."

"Sir, I am, and you are..?" he looked ashamed. Ashamed? Why would a Protector be ashamed?

"Dran'Za...I am the commander of the Knights of the Black Dawn, have you—"

There was an audible gasp and the man stepped back.

"I—yes, excuse me, I must—"

His fleshy hand clapped the Protector on the shoulder. "There is nothing to be afraid of. We are fighting the demons as much as you are."

"We are not fighting. That is why I am here."

"You are not fighting?"

"No, we have been recalled. I came here to ask for help, but cannot find anybody in charge."

"I have the same problem," Dran'Za started, then caught himself. "What? Recalled!"

"Sir—the High Cleric, he has recalled all of us, he claims the demonic threat is not real, or that it is because of the sins of mankind."

Dran'Za's face turned a deep shade of purple and a vein on his neck throbbed in his rage. He did not realize he was gripping the poor Protector's arm so tight that he nearly broke it—the man finally squealed and Dran'Za muttered an apology.

"Sir?"

"Sacuan curse him forever!" he screamed. A few serving men who were in the area scurried off, and sound of slamming doors filled the hallway. "Curse him! Did you know that his ancestors *created* the Knights of the Black—" he broke off, his throat choked with fury. He swore again and he stomped out the front door.

The Protector caught it before it slammed, but Dran'Za was already halfway down the steps.

"Sir?"

"What?" he replied, turning, his face still purple.

"What can I do?"

"Join us."

"Wh—?"

"Join us," he repeated. "Gather your men and meet in the courtyard in front of the High Cleric's. Gather everyone you can."

"Why, what are you—"

"I'm putting an end to tyranny," Dran'Za said, his voice ice. "An eye has gone blind." With that, he turned and stalked down the path.

The Protector clenched his fists and nodded curtly to the doorframe, mouthing the strange phrase. "An eye is blind... *what?*"

φ

"Your Grace, very few are responding to our call. Only a few Protectors have returned to the City. And reports have stopped coming from other cities."

High Cleric Gorand turned to scowl at the messenger.

"Then we are going to send a new order. This cannot be tolerated. Go—" he waved the man off as he reached for a sheet of parchment and his quill.

Gorand scratched intently on the paper, head bowed, eyes blazing; he was so focused he did not see the secretary standing there, watching. At last he scratched out his name violently and tore the paper away from the desk. "Here, send this out."

The boy stepped forward and his face went ashen as he scanned the paper. "Your Grace, this—"

"I know. Send it."

"But..." he stammered. "You are ordering the execution of all Protectors, Counsel Guards, *and* the Knights of the Black Dawn. Sir, they do not even—"

"Not any more they don't. Go!"

The boy stumbled from the room and Gorand fumed in silence.

It was real. It was here. The purging of mankind had started. A slight flicker of sadness wafted through him but he buried it with a hard swallow and a prayer.

Outside, the secretary had not gone two steps before Dran'Za slammed bodily into him. "Move aside, boy," he growled. Loose, frostbitten skin hung from his face, slicked with pus.

"Sir, you cannot—"

Dran'Za shoved the boy aside, then put his entire weight behind the door, crushing it in a hundred splinters and fragments of cherry. A large ragged chunk met the thick toe of his ski boot and sailed across the room, clattering in a corner.

High Cleric Gorand leapt to his feet, face awash with terror. The name "Gheren" was partway across his thin lips, but died in a tremble as he took in the hulking frame of Dran'Za.

"Dran...." he mouthed. His back thudded into the edge of the window casement.

"High Cleric Gorand, I'm going to—Sacuan be damned, man, what have you done!" Dran'Za barked. Behind him, he heard the scuffling feet of Gorand's secretary, but did not turn. *Let them come... let them come.*

Gorand stared dumbly. He had barely recovered from Gheren's treason, and now the leader of the Knights of the Black Dawn stood before him, sword drawn. How?

How had the fat man arrived in Belden City? And why had he disobeyed his orders?

"You've nothing to say?" Dran'Za hissed.

"I..."

"Then—"

"Yes," the High Cleric clipped, venom dripping from his so-called holy tongue. "Yes, you fat slob." A brief glance at the sharpened steel. "You are not the only one to come here claiming that my authority is no longer valid... the first man lies in the basement of this building, waiting for a burial that he does not deserve. Your presence, while a surprise, is irritating, and will be dealt with the same way."

What have you become, Gorand? "The Knights were founded by your elders, by those of your own blood! How dare you call my actions treason!"

"Are you mad, Dran'Za?" He spat the name. "I gave the orders for you to disband nearly a year ago."

With that the sword tip faltered. What? How? No, the man lied, the holy man had gone mad with his power and was merely talking to keep his own head attached to his useless shoulders. How dare he call Dran'Za a fat slob! Obese, and obscenely so, still he had covered a tremendous amount of ground on skis—there was still a flicker of youth left in him. To say that he'd send orders to disband the Knights was an outright lie. Wasn't it?

But as he thought back through the fog, smoke, and food of his past years of service, Gorand's forced words echoed in his mind, finally finding purchase on a strange event...

His forehead lay pressed against an old tome, dreams of sun-splashed beaches filled his vision. Suddenly someone· was tearing down the trees and ripping them into pieces... no, no, that was the sound of paper. He came awake slowly, his eyes only seeing the yellowed hardback of the book, but the sound of tearing paper was clear; lifting his head, he heard the sound of scuffling feet. But a fresh pile of correspondence had been splayed next to his book. Sighing, he dropped his head back to the book.

Sacuan bless his men! Bless them all! Such an order could only come from a madman... a man obsessed with the sins of the innocent. Disband the Knights of the Black Dawn? Never! Not even with a direct order from the reigning High Cleric, the same cleric whose ancestors had formed the elite group of demon hunters! Surely his men would have seen the order as a hoax, farce, or forgery and discard it outright. Sacuan bless them all!

Gorand reached a robed hand over to his desk and hefted a leaded cup to his lips. A thin read stream trickled down the corner of his mouth and he wiped it absently. "Ah, so I see you do remember... the order was given, was it not?"

"I never received such an order," he replied. *For it is the truth, Gorand... it never reached my desk.*

Gorand peered at him through thin slits, his nose screwed into a detestable, bulbous mass. The order had been sent; perhaps not received by Dran'Za, but it had been sent.

"Half of my men are dead, the other half unaccounted for. They battle alongside as many Beldeners as will fight, they battle a horde of demons. Though the Temple of M'Hzrut may stand, it is on shaking ground, and until we can contain the threat, we will need even more people to fight the cause. That includes Protectors. That includes you."

"Point that filthy sword somewhere else, preferably at your own throat," Gorand rasped. He darted a furtive glance behind Dran'Za, no doubt seeking the reinforcements his secretary had gone to retrieve.

"Gorand, what has become of you?" Dran'Za wondered aloud. The cleric took another drink from the leaded cup and snickered. The leader of the Knights of the Black Dawn continued, his voice now sad and worn. "I remember a young man, a man who visited us in the north, who gave us blessings, and bestowed upon us the grace of Sacuan—to fight demons. That man even brought us a basket of pastries from a bakery in Reldan. But most of all, I remember a man who would have fought for the innocents of this land!"

"And I remember a skinny man who followed orders!"

"Entire villages are being destroyed, women and children are dying... even if I received such orders, yes, I would destroy those orders. And I would have the backing of nearly all citizens in this land; the word of the High Cleric would mean nothing."

"You are an apostate and have disobeyed the orders from those who created you. No one would deny that."

Dran'Za bit his lip. "Then you can kill me after the demons are dead. If the letter of the law must be followed, follow it. But follow it only after we have come out of this slaughter!"

"This slaughter is necessary!" the Cleric spat, eyes wild, wine-tinged spittle dribbling from his quivering lips.

"Never, it is never necessary."

Gorand reached for the goblet, but his fingers only came within an inch of the leaded handle.

Exhausted, heavier than he should be, Dran'Za was still fast. He leapt forward six feet and swung the sword in a sweeping motion, letting the full weight of his fleshy arm push it across the small space between himself and the High Cleric. The weapon paused only as it cut through the spinal column at the base of the man's neck, and then swung into empty air. Gorand's head rolled toward Dran'Za, he kicked it away, and sheathed his bloody sword. He whispered a prayer to Sacuan for both of their souls, though his lip quivered. Hands and arms still tingled with the force of the attack, exhaustion rippled through his wide legs, and he leaned briefly on the edge of the cleric's desk.

With another brief prayer, the leader of the Knights of the Black Dawn exited the room and stepped into the small antechamber, where he abruptly stopped.

The secretary had summoned men. Twenty or so armed men stood in the antechamber, swords drawn. Dran'Za tried to hold his sword steady with trembling hands. Blood ran down the thin runnels and dripped to the floor in great drops. "An eye was blind, and now an eye has been removed," he stated matter-of-factly. "The High Cleric would rather that the world be destroyed by demons than we as Knights of the Black Dawn, or as Protectors, should fight them. The sins of mankind, he said, had led to this. No sin can be so great as to cause the death of children."

"You have committed treason and murder," the secretary said dryly, stepping forward. He stood slightly to the side of the armed men. He had apparently been brainwashed by Gorand, for he continued as if Dran'Za had not spoken: "For this, you are under arrest for such crimes, and you will be tried and executed. Men!"

A floorboard squeaked as a man shifted his weight.

"Men!"

Silence.

Dran'Za held his sword steady, others likewise remained upright. Yet not a muscle moved in the group.

"I said, arrest this man."

"Do not arrest that man," came a disembodied voice from behind the group.

"Who are you?" the secretary snapped.

"My name is Salnur, I am now a Knight of the Black Dawn, and I fight for Dran'Za."

Dran'Za craned to see the man in the back, and when his eyes locked on the familiar face, he suppressed a smile. It was the Protector he had met in Belden City. How many men had this Salnur found? Or was he alone? He heard feet scuffling behind the throng, but could not see anything.

"Let him step forward," someone muttered to the loud protests of the secretary.

Gorand's pet bounced up and down, barking his repeated orders, squealing in frustration.

"Is this true?" asked one of the soldiers.

"I have seen corpses no bigger than a—" Salnur broke off, his voice catching. "Children are dying, I have seen it. Children!"

The sound of swords sliding into sheaths filled the room. Gorand's secretary had gone silent; if only because he lay on the ground. Dran'Za sheathed his own sword and grimaced.

"Salnur, how many men do you have?"

"Two thousand, sir."

At that he whistled. "Two *thousand?*"

"Make that five," the leader of the soldiers said. "Five thousand strong... we fight the Dark. We fight with the Dawn!"

Dran'Za held up a hand to quell the chanting that was inevitable. This was not a cheap adventure story; he didn't need the name being shouted about, and he didn't need any silly antics. It was time for action.

"With that many men, we are an army," he said instead. "We will stop calling ourselves the Knights of the Black Dawn—we no longer need to hide. We will fight in the open and we will defeat the demons."

Again, he had to staunch a brewing roar from the soldiers. "When it is over we will merge with the Counsel Guard. If they ever find a leader."

"Sir, whom do we follow?"

"We follow good, and we follow Sacuan."

"No, I mean, you, Sir, who are you?"

Dran'Za opened his mouth, then closed it. *And it is past time in which I shed this arrogant name...* "Drana. You can call me Drana. Not Sir, never Sir... come, let's fight."

As they exited the building, he smiled as the shouts went up. They could shout now, but soon they would be knee-deep in blood. Drana smiled as he stepped into the chilly air. The smell of the sea stung his nostrils, but he knew that smell would be replaced by a different smell.

Too easy, he thought. Too easy. He had defeated the very Order that had given him his work, and done so with ease.

He'd also effectively dismantled his own Order.

Gorand was dead. An old friend, a man he had held dear. A leaded goblet and a perverted mind had erased everything that Drana remembered—he had to remind himself of that.

Today was the first victory.

"An eye was blind," he muttered.

Chapter 32

A Tired, Old Cliché

I shall stop my fight against demons when the very underworld lies frozen

High Cleric Bertrand

It took several hours to assess the damage, bury the dead in shallow graves of snow, and either help the wounded or finish those beyond help.

The men returned to the Keep and refreshed themselves as best as possible. Much work was still to be done. Wrenflang, Zhy and Fanlas chatted as they stared out the windows at the churned-up snow in the courtyard.

"Zhy, the ice is the thing." He sighed. "It is something you said earlier: Can we freeze them out? Maybe. We can't freeze the underworld, but these things may be stopped by cold. I'm not sure of the details, but if we can..." Wrenflang trailed off, watching the courtyard. The slab appeared to ripple, as if demons below were driving into it from underneath. "The only thing that could hold them is the proper magical ward, but that won't solve our problem. Not the full problem... not in the least. Listen, we *are* going to cool this thing, freeze part of it, so we can deal with it forever. We need lots of snow and ice. Drunplug!" he barked, a bit too harshly.

The Welcferian commander ambled over to him, his jaw set. "What are we going to do?"

"I need ice and snow. We need your men and the Hjor to fill their sleds with snow and ice—I can help cut the ice blocks with magic, but I'm afraid we'll have to manually bring them over. I can't expend too much energy now."

"And just what are we going to do with all the ice and snow?"

Zhy looked at him, then the other soldiers. Each man was past exhaustion. How much more of this could they take?

"We are going to freeze Hell," Wrenflang replied flatly.

A week ago Drunplug would have laughed in the man's face. He'd heard all the clichés about the underworld freezing, not having a frozen hell's chance, and so forth. A grizzled mage stared in his eyes and told him that was exactly what he was going to do. He choked back his guffaw and forced a flat expression upon his face.

There was nothing funny about any of this. He'd seen the old mage succeed several times so far, each time against odds that were high. Could he freeze Hell? Drunplug doubted even the most highly skilled warlock could muster enough strength to even *cool* the pit of the underworld, let alone freeze it. Who was this man, anyway? And if he was stronger than even the mad Ar'Zoth of which he spoke, how long would his service be beneficial to mankind?

Drunplug shook off his dark thoughts and nodded imperceptibly. "All right, then that is how it goes." He took a deep breath. "If you can do it."

"In all honesty, Drunplug," Wrenflang said, "I'm not sure that I can. But we have to try. We have to try. Zhy," he snapped. "I need your help, but between you and Fanlas, keep an eye on that Sacuan-blasted cap."

Zhy looked to the west, where the sun's last rays struggled to clear the higher mountain peaks. "Um... Wrenflang, it is going to be dark soon."

"Sacuan blast it!" The mage scowled at the far mountains. "Well, fine, we work until dark... then we can sleep in the Keep, with at least a two-man guard on this— on this thing—at all times. Understood?"

The men around him nodded.

"Then let's get to work."

Torches were found within the Keep that could at least guide a path from the mountain from which they gathered the blocks of ice and snow. Ar'Zoth had left behind a few tools as well, the odd shovel, a strange pole with a hook on it, and a saw. These were gathered as well, for they could be used to cut the snow into blocks.

With Wrenflang giving orders, the men set to work. Day was fading to a cold arctic night, but a huge moon was rising from beyond the Spires, its brilliant light reflecting off of the snow, basking the workers in its glow. The grizzled mage grunted and kept them working.

After several hours, Zhy looked up at their work and his eyes went wide with amazement. A huge hole had been punched out the north end of the courtyard in order to provide access to the snow-covered mountain beyond. The entirety of the Hjor clan, along with Drunplug's men and Fanlas, stretched across the frozen landscape, from the center of the portal and nearly a third of the way up a mountainside. Men at the fore were cutting massive blocks of snow and setting them gingerly onto sleds, then hauling them carefully down the mountainside. When the lead man would take his block, the next in line stepped forward and began cutting; in the meantime one of two sleds had made it back up the line.

When Zhy looked to the courtyard, he remarked that it had started to take on the appearance of an oversized decorative paving stone, with the huge circular lid surrounded by an ever-growing rim of ice. Deep blue veins were painted on bright white slabs, with streaks of brown dirt adding a strange pattern to the developing structure.

Wrenflang bounded out to the farthest man and soon the snake started coiling back toward the courtyard as the weary soldiers returned.

"Now what?" Zhy asked absently.

"Get some rest." Wrenflang's voice was thin and reedy; the day's exertion had strained his aging body, but his mind had kept him running and digging, and shouting orders.

Zhy wondered if the man would awake in the morning.

φ

Cold sunlight streaked over the eastern Spires, the icicles of wan yellow-orange light casting long spear-like shadows over the ring of ice and snow. Zhy arose with a start as the morning sun splashed his face. Many of the soldiers were starting to move about, while others still lay on the floor with eyes closed.

"Has anyone seen Wrenflang?" he inquired softly, trying not to wake those sleeping, and keeping his voice quiet for those who were emerging from their slumber.

Someone grumbled about the "old bird" being outside, but he thought he heard "wizard" from one of the Hjor. He nodded respectfully. Another soldier called him Zhyfrael again—all he could do was bow and smile a grim smile.

How had he sewn up a feud that had lasted centuries? Had he? Was it his name? *Too simple, too Sacuan-blasted simple!* He thought, and stumbled and ran his foot against a sleeping soldier. The man was so exhausted from the previous day, however, he merely grunted and rolled over. With a whispered apology, Zhy shrugged into his coat and stepped outside.

The air froze in his lungs and the morning's sleep in his eyes turned immediately to a horrid green icicle. Zhy cleared his throat loudly and rubbed the crust from his face, cursed, and stomped forward.

When he arrived, Wrenflang was staring at the large slab in the courtyard, face set and arms crossed. He cocked an eyebrow as Zhy approached, then returned to his assessment of the strange contraption.

"What is the plan?" The words were slow and sluggish. How quickly one adapts to the warmth of a building, Zhy noticed, and how harsh the cold and ice can be.

"Good morning, Zhy," the mage replied. "The plan remains the same."

What plan? Had he told me the plan? His head was still full of the previous nights' dream—a warm, impossibly-beautiful girl, smiling, laughing. *With* him, not at him. Every feature popped vividly in place of the white, stark snow: The perfect up-turned nose, soft blue eyes, rounded chin, and long brown hair. Her lips were full and inviting, and she laughed softly; white teeth exposed against the lush mouth. She reached up and pulled his head toward hers, fingers buried in his long mane. Closer, closer, her face and his—ever closer, their lips nearly touching, before meeting in a softly crushing, wet heat of infinite pleasure. He felt like a river of melting snow, cascading into a puddle of water. Eyes closed as the kiss went on and on, hands began to move, move to places he only imagined and the night exploded in a red fire of ecstasy, his heart nearly stopped with pleasure, and his—

"Zhy!" Wrenflang barked.

"Sacuan's scrotum!" he snapped as the image collapsed into tiny fragments. He tried to finish the thought, complete the dream sequence, but Wrenflang's nose filled his vision. "What?" he snapped. *Am I lying on the ground? What happened?*

"Get up, fool. What is the matter with you?"

"I—um..." he grumbled as he hauled himself to his feet.

"Never mind, never mind. Yes, yes, there is a plan," he repeated, bristling at the strange interruption. "Zhy, we are going to remove the thing, this lid. But as soon as that lid is off, demons will pour out. We've left a gap in the ring for a purpose—Hjor and Welcferian soldiers will guard the gap as they pour out... so far these have been easy to defeat. I shouldn't need much time as I move snow down into the pit."

"I see." The man had a reason for his madness, surely. After all, he'd sent Huyen off with the guiding box, deliberately sought out the Hjor, and now he was nonchalantly declaring that he was going to let demons out. The reasons made sense in a way, fighting fire with fire, but it was... it was cliché. And saying that word over and over was starting to turn the very word into one. Zhy groaned.

"Now what? Are you going to say this is all—"

"Yes I am. Because it is. Prime the pump, fight fire with fire, open the pit of demons so you can save the world. Breaking the—"

"I know, Zhy, I know." His voice was sad, worn, his age on display. With a grimace, he stretched his back. "But Ar'Zoth, Bimb, whoever he was, was trying to open this to let out a million more. Tens of millions! We need to open this so we can get something down there to kill the rest of them—and I'm not sure..." he trailed off, sighed heavily, and frowned. "I'm not sure anymore what is going to work. My plans have been successful so far, but this would make a third time: The box, the Hjor, and this. Can I do it?"

The last question was to himself, but Zhy had been thinking the same thing about his own abilities. How much farther could a man go, especially in this climate? True, they had the relative shelter of the castle, but it now marked months in this weather, the snow, the ice, and the devastating winds. What if Wrenflang's plan did not work? What if more demons escaped out through the hole? The men among them, Hjor and Welcferian soldier alike, were hardened, strong men; but they could not survive five minutes against a million—did he say *million?*—demons, and have any hope at success. The numbers were too strong against them.

Zhy's father had taught him a thing or two about numbers, chance, and luck. Luck, he had said, was simply the tumbling of the right numbers at the right time. Or it was skill guised as luck. *Now why hadn't I thought of that before? Am I really skilled?* The sudden thought was devastating and humbling. Had Zhy truly had skill, or had his enemies been utterly worthless? Though brutal, perhaps the weather had not been all that bad, or the—

No, no, no, he reminded himself. His success against Bimb was due to the cold, hard numbers his father had raved about. The madman had *believed* Zhy to be dead, because he had been. But there had been other, more specific instances which he had attributed to luck... were those outcomes based on skill, or—

"Zhy, what are you mumbling about?"

He stumbled. "You can hear me? Oh, of course you can!" He smiled, this time genuinely. "So I'm not crazy, or dead."

"You're not dead, that's for sure."

Zhy paled, but the old mage could not repress his smile and burst into laughter. He found himself returning the laugh, forced at first, but then the severity of the situation pushed his worry far beyond its rational concern; and Zhy was soon sobbing jovially.

Fanlas ambled over, grinning, sharing their mirth. "It's good to be able to laugh in a time like this," he said, his voice booming.

Wrenflang smiled in return. "It is, Fanlas, indeed it is. If you don't laugh, you'll cry."

Zhy stopped laughing, bit his lip and turned away. *I think that is what I'm going to do,* he thought, but Fanlas's hand was already on him.

"Son, trust in yourself, and all will be well."

"Thank you."

The burly man walked away to attend to some other task.

"Well, Zhy, are we ready?"

"No," he said, but the smile he tried to force fell flat.

"I understand." Wrenflang glanced at the ring of ice around the cover, hoping that it would be enough to do what it was supposed to do. "Fanlas!" he called out, and the strong man ambled over.

"Ready?" Bimb's father asked.

"I think so. Bring the two Hjor men over then."

Fanlas did so, and with very little apparent effort, were able to lift the heavy lid from the opening, revealing the gaping, black pit. Steam from the heat below billowed into the air, and Wrenflang quickly assigned a Hjor to fan the area with a folded-up canvas tarp. Zhy watched intently, waiting for the ensuing horde to escape from the steaming abyss, but so far only a sulphurous-laden stench reached his nostrils.

Wrenflang scowled, rubbed his wrinkled hands together, then created a white-hot beam of light between his fingers. He stretched the light outward and toward the ring of solid ice, first testing a small section to see if it would melt. The block of blue and white collapsed into a tiny rivulet. The mage smiled and directed his full attention on the ring of frozen water and snow, making sure to route it down into the pit.

Is he not going to watch for demons? Zhy wondered.

The water hissed and steamed as it hit the blasphemous opening.

Even as he was able to channel the melted snow into the water, he spat in frustration. The heat from the depths was evaporating the liquid; super-cooled or not, made little difference. That there could be so much heat just beneath an arctic landscape seemed utterly bizarre.

"Huyen, come here... can you freeze this as soon as it reaches the edge?"

The Knight of the Black Dawn was nowhere in sight. "Where is he?"

He was never here. Zhy shrugged as casually as he could, then started walking toward the Keep. "Maybe he's inside, I'll get him."

Wrenflang looked up, eyes wild. "No, of course not Zhy, I—I forgot. Momentary lapse."

A single demon popped from the hole. Before the mage could work any magic, three Hjor arrows struck the steaming creature and it tumbled back to the darkness.

"Sacuan blast it!" Wrenflang screamed, letting go of his hold on the magical energy. "Fanlas! Quick, get this cover back on!"

As soon as the cover fell into place, Wrenflang collapsed atop it. He still cursed and muttered under his breath. "Stupid, I was so stupid... I need to wait. Where has my patience gone, Sacuan damn everything!" when he looked up, his eyes were mattery, then turned cold as they locked on Zhy.

"Let's go back into the Keep for a moment. I need to think."

φ

After a quarter of an hour, Wrenflang stormed from the Keep, muttering and cursing at the cap in the center of the courtyard. He beckoned the men to follow, scowling at the laggards.

"Sacuan damn it all!"

He's losing it, Zhy thought. *He said ice was the key, why isn't it working... what is colder than ice?*

"Can we get this colder? Even colder than snow...?" Zhy heard himself ask. The idea seemed so foreign, so beyond what he knew what was possible in the world, but his journey so far had showed him much that was beyond his wildest imaginations. If magical spells could wipe out living creatures, though stifling the caster, could there be a way to make things colder than ice?

Most disturbing of all, could they really freeze Hell?

Wrenflang was on his knees, tears of frustration freezing on his cheeks. He pounded the snow with an angry fist, then stood slowly. His head hung in exhaustion. "Colder than snow? I'm sorry, Zhy, there is nothing colder than—" His jaw fell open, but he was staring only at the blank snow.

Fanlas put a hand on the old mage.

Wrenflang remained silent, mouth working as if he were giving a silent lecture. He even shrugged once for effect. "Toular."

"What?"

"Teacher Toular, Zhy. A grumpy old instructor at the university in Vronga. I took one class from him, but he was so far beyond anybody's ability, we thought him crazy. He *was* crazy; he left the school to raise tomatoes in a fish pond."

Fanlas chuckled.

The mage continued. "He was difficult. The most difficult of all! Men!" he suddenly stood, grimacing against the protest of his aging joints. Hjor and Welcferian soldiers snapped to attention. "Men! I need ten to stay here—" he indicated a few men. "The others, continue to bring ice down. Make a big pile of snow and ice on the northern side of this ring." He breathed out a cloud of steam, looking at the already high ring. "Yes, more. I know, I know..."

Someone had thoughtfully cut an arch through the ring, else they'd be fully enclosed. A man stood guard in front of it constantly, Zhy noticed, a Hjor man with a permanent grimace on his face.

"Toular," the mage said after he had given another set of orders. "Toular was an impossible man. But he often talked of the ability to freeze the very gasses in the air. All magic is really just pulling particles from the air, in the spaces between everything, but super-cooling was something he had been experimenting with. There were rumors he had made his house disappear, but others said there were tiny pieces of it all over..."

"How...?"

"I'm not sure, but it had to do with gasses. In the finer spaces, somehow... you could get it to cool down below what would seem possible."

"The spaces between things, you say?" Fanlas wondered. "Bimb always said that—I didn't realize he was hiding his other side." He stepped out of the circle again.

They were interrupted as the lid to the pit buckled once, tipped open a half a foot and slammed shut. In that split second, a single-eyed, dripping, drooling demon slithered out and skittered across the courtyard.

Men drew their weapons and slashed futilely at the creature—but it darted quickly across the ground, looking like a water beetle skimming across the surface of a river. The Hjor and Welcferian soldiers alike jumped out of its path. The horrid creature leapt sidewise, its mouth open, snapping at the air, each time missing flesh. A sword slashed downward, clanging loudly as it struck the stone, and the demon leapt sidewise, at last finding purchase.

A Hjor soldier cried in agony as the teeth dug into his leg. Blood poured from his wound and the demon's teeth crunched down on bone; the soldier grimaced as he tried to reach around with his sword and strike the demon. A Welcferian slashed at the demon once, twice, and dispersed it into two dripping, slimy halves.

"Don't cleave them!" Wrenflang barked, ignoring the writhing man on the courtyard. "Keep them whole, I have an idea! Zhy... go collect corpses."

"What?"

"You heard me, go collect corpses!"

Zhy lurched. "I'm afraid I—"

"Go!" the mage barked. "If you want to save the world—ach, I hate that cliché! Just go, get them and bring them back. But make sure they are dead!"

Chapter 33

Collecting Corpses

Who will bury our dead? Who will collect the bodies and bury them in the temple?

Unknown

Zhy tightened his gloves and set out, Fanlas following. "Son, I'll help you, you look a shade paler." He smiled wanly.

"Thank you," Zhy muttered.

"I had to collect at least a hundred dead sheep once, from a neighbor," the bulky man said.

"Yes?" Whatever Fanlas was trying, Zhy wasn't sure it would help in any way. They were not collecting sheep, they were gathering dead demons. Well, demons they *thought* were dead... who knew what these deviate creatures were capable of?

"It isn't the same, I know, Zhy. The task was not easy, then either."

"Why is that?"

"Well," Fanlas began, scratching his huge chin. "Something had killed all of the sheep, and it wasn't disease."

"They were killed on purpose? Who would do such a thing?"

"Not who, Zhy, what. Something awful killed them."

Now he is making things up to appease me. He never mentioned a word about having dealt with demons in the past. And suddenly he claims a field of sheep was killed by one?

Fanlas coughed. "I know what you're thinking. We never saw the creature, never heard it. We only saw what was left behind. The poor creatures looked to have been shredded or torn, as if pulled apart in several different directions. These—" he looked up to the sky. "These mulargh and gherwza, they attack like bats or large birds of prey. But this ... this Gozath creature? What he did to the demons? He tore them apart? Why? Was he a demon, or not? I—sorry, Zhy, it's all so confusing."

"It is. What about the sheep?" he asked with a grimace.

"I think a demon did it." Fanlas set his lips in a line and remembered. He thought of Bimb, his throat thick with phlegm; he cleared it loudly.

"Tearing people apart? When did you hear that demons did such a thing?"

"Oh, one of the Hjor told me. He was scouting in the Icedown Plains, close to the Temple of M'Hzrut, when he saw three men torn apart."

The men were silent for a moment.

They found a dozen or so corpses that were not completely shredded by swords or punctured with arrows. Fanlas gingerly kicked each dead demon with his boot, then instructed Zhy to carry it back to Wrenflang.

Zhy's throat felt two sizes too big as he placed a gloved hand on the dead skin of the demon. Even through the glove, he could feel the sliminess of their outer shell, the miniscule scales that lay beneath the shiny red and pale blue surface. They had no hair to grasp, no fins, or other easy handles—and he surely did not want to grip them by their teeth, fearing the mouths would clamp shut in reflex. Instead, to his horror, he had to carry each one with two hands, cradling the beast like a bundle of firewood—though he kept his arms outstretched as far as possible.

By the time he had carried several of the creatures back, his arms were exhausted and his nose was filled with their awful, urine-soaked-in-sulfur odor. Fanlas clapped him on the shoulder.

"Now what?" Zhy asked.

"Hmm..." Wrenflang began. "This does not appear to be enough. No, wait, it can work, it can work. I thought—" he scratched his white beard. "I counted fourteen before, now there are only twelve, what happened. No matter, no matter. In any case—"

A deafening screech and a disturbingly loud flap of wings filed the air—a mulargh swooped down, and rocketed into Wrenflang, huge claws digging into the old man's back. He howled in pain as his delicate frame was smashed against the courtyard.

Fanlas drew steel, struck at the hard shell, but his sword could have struck solid stone. He cursed, raised it again, then thought better.

Creatures with hard shells, he figured, also had something soft that the hardened coating was intended to protect. There were turtles down in a little creek behind his farm, and he'd even taken Bimb with him once or twice when he hunted them—though Bimb was easily distracted by the number of bulrushes swaying in the breeze. When found, a turtle could be flipped onto its back and easily slain—but these weren't turtles.

Quickly, he flipped the sword around, gripping the blade edge firmly but carefully; he used the hilt to reach under the shell of the mulargh. Fanlas flipped it as he had so many turtles. The demonic creature released itself from Wrenflang with a sickening pop of suction; and as soon as the beast rolled forward, Fanlas tossed the sword up and gripped the hilt. He had just begun to thrust the weapon forward when he stopped.

The underside of the mulargh was alive with motion, a slithering, hissing bulbous of flesh and various body parts: eyes, ears, noses, teeth, and tufts of hair covered the pale, moist flesh.

Wrenflang barely finished screaming the word "Kill!" when a mouth on the mulargh opened and spat something at Fanlas.

Turtles had never squirted liquid, but a pig could, if the jugular was cut poorly. As soon as the liquid left the dying creature, Fanlas had a flashback to the farm; strangely enough, the sound of the mouth opening on the mulargh was similar to that of a sow's throat being cut. He ducked immediately. A purple glob of—something— whooshed past his right ear and dropped into the snow behind him. When it landed, the snow boiled furiously, and from the charred patch, a giant rat emerged.

As soon as Fanlas was clear of the mulargh, Hjor arrows riddled the creature and Fanlas jerked his attention back to the mulargh. Though still on its back, it spun on the shell, mouths and eyes opening, closing, hissing, releasing more purple blobs as it tried to flip itself over. Fanlas closed his eyes and thrust with the sword—again, again, a dozen times. Blood and purple liquid splashed and squirted, some drops finding purchase on the ground, and each time rats emerged from the pits.

Fanlas relentlessly attacked the creature, never turning his back on the screeching and scrabbling in the snow. Both Hjor and Welcferian alike attacked the demonic offspring with as much fervor as Fanlas showed. His massive shoulders were numb by the time the creature stopped moving and the sounds of rending flesh and grunting warriors abated; and at last, Bimb's father dipped his sword to the ice and stretched his frame.

The time for reflection was a millionth of a second—as soon as the mulargh lay dead, Wrenflang was on his feet, grimacing against the pain, and barking orders.

φ

Zhy groaned inwardly, but put his head down and trudged out to collect even the corpses of the demonic rats. Many had been slashed so many times that they looked like birch bark, rippled and peeling. These were left behind—others sported no more than a few arrows, and these were candidates for Wrenflang.

The old mage knelt in the snow, grimacing from his wounds. If it weren't so brutally cold in the courtyard, he may have bled out, but the chill kept the wounds closed and free of infection. Wrenflang worked tirelessly, methodically, conjuring a strange mixture of spells. Strange filaments were woven into the wounds of the corpses, into their eye sockets, and up their tiny rectums. A pile of intestines and tendons lay in the snow at his side, and, after finishing his magic, Wrenflang sewed up the holes with the various parts.

"No! No! Back away, back *away!*" he barked suddenly at a Hjor soldier who dared step too close to his growing pile of bloated carcasses.

"May—may I ask what you are doing?" came the gruff reply of Drunplug.

Wrenflang grumbled and kept working. The Welcferian opened his mouth to ask again, when the mage barked out a reply. "Filling these bodies... with *what* I really can't explain very well, but it's gas that's colder than snow and ice." He waved his hand briefly and furiously, then returned to his work. "Don't bother. Zhy gave me the idea. In any case, if we can get this thing colder than we ever thought possible, we will be able to—"

"Freeze Hell, right," the commander mumbled and walked away.

Fanlas watched him go, his chest still heavy from the exertion; breath came out in large heavy plumes as he breathed. "Zhy... Zhy, come here," he motioned his companion to him.

"What is it?"

"Zhy... Zhy, is he all right?" Bimb's father wondered, darting brief glances at Wrenflang, who continued to fill the corpses with his magic, tie them off, and set them gently into an organized pile.

"I'm sure he's—well, I don't know," Zhy stammered. "He knows what he's doing."

"I hope so, Zhy." Fanlas slowly took off his gloves, held them between his knees, and rubbed his large hands together. "Zhy, did you notice it?" he asked slowly, donning his gloves.

"Notice what?"

"You can't see the whites of his eyes," Fanlas whispered, walking away.

A frozen finger shot up to rub furiously at a red earlobe.

φ

Drunplug called his men to him for a brief rest, sharing a few bites with the Hjor, and the two sides chatted idly, though many watched Wrenflang nervously. Those who had looked into his determined black eyes stumbled a step—he seemed a man possessed, driven by some unseen force, focused to the point of madness on his gruesome task.

"It's time, Zhy and Fanlas, it is time!" Wrenflang yelled. He stood suddenly, too suddenly. He had been hunched over for so long that his head filled with blood when he straightened his aging frame. Coupled with the loss of blood, the combination was enough to create a dizzying sensation of vertigo. His black eyes rolled in the back of his head and he stumbled, falling sideways. As he did so, a bolt of green fire flew from his left hand, arced into the sky, and exploded against the side of the mountain they had just cleared. Instead of snow cascading upon the men, dirt, pebbles and ice pellets rained down. As one, the line of Hjor and Welcferian men stepped back a pace.

Not a man moved to help.

Wrenflang growled and eventually righted himself. He glared at the motionless men.

"You must help us!" he screamed at the soldiers. Spears slammed into the snow, swords disappeared into scabbard. Drunplug returned his stare coldly and shook his head.

$$\phi$$

"Men," Drunplug announced quietly. "If he attacks again, you are free to carry out an assault." He looked over at Hjor and noticed the man addressing his own soldiers in a similar fashion. "You will most likely be joined by the Hjor—after this mage is taken care of, you will be free to—" there he stopped, as a look of horror walked its way across the faces of his men. He had been about to say *Do with the Hjor whatever you please,* but thought better.

The instinct was so ingrained in him still, and their time with the strange natives so limited, that he quickly reverted to his old frame of mind. But the faces of his men had told him in awful clarity that thousands of years had been collectively erased—perhaps not entirely, but wiped clean enough that now his men thought the Hjor as comrades. Did the Hjor reciprocate? Drunplug wondered.

He looked over, and Hjor Hjor nodded at him, then tipped his scruffy head toward Wrenflang. That was answer enough. Drunplug bit his lower lip and shakily repeated his order against Wrenflang. The mage had possibly gone mad—with the power he had already shown, the small collection of Welcferian and Hjor soldiers were overmatched. At least they understood each other and were ready to act.

Drunplug grudgingly accepted their marriage.

A thousand years or more... a thousand years... his mind kept churning this phrase over and over.

φ

"Unbelievable," Wrenflang muttered. He balled his fists, stared once more at the motionless line of soldiers, then spun to face Zhy and Fanlas. "Fine, then. Fine. All right, men, it's just us... these so-called soldiers have decided to go dumb in the last minute."

He has lost it, Zhy thought.

"No I have not, Zhyfrael," the mage snapped. "Fanlas! Please come here and remove this cover... I hope it is the last time you will need to do so."

Bimb's father stared.

"Is something the matter?" he barked. Zhy looked at his eyes. They were pure black. No white left.

At least they are not red... Zhy thought. But a growing horror crawled up his spine. Another man had had black eyes.

But Wrenflang continued his tirade: "Do I need to blow this off myself? Fanlas, you saw what I can do with a tiny little lock. Now come over here."

Mad as Ar'Zoth.

Wrenflang was on the cusp of berating Fanlas again, when he turned to face Zhy. His voice was calm, soft, refined—thankfully free of any malice. He sounded nothing like Ar'Zoth... he sounded like himself. Even his pupils shrank to a normal size. "I am tired, Zhy, and cold, and I'm not sure this is going to work. I may be acting the madman, but I am not mad. Ar'Zoth would have blown up this entire pile of corpses, even if it killed him, he would have done it just for a laugh." He sucked in air, turned to Fanlas, and the whites of his eyes disappeared again. "Now, Fanlas, it is time."

φ

Wrenflang created a familiar green net of light and with it gently lifted the pile of corpses into the air. "Move the lid," he said softly.

Fanlas was able to pull the lid to the side, and with Zhy's help he slid it from the opening. As soon as the cover cleared enough space, Wrenflang hefted the horrible burden up and over the dark opening. *If any demons get out, we're dead,* Zhy thought.

"When I give the word, Fanlas, you have to put the lid back. We won't have any help from these soldiers, so it is up to us." This last was nearly shouted.

Zhy glanced quickly at the Hjor and Welcferians. Each man seemed more intent on inspecting his boots.

Fanlas let out a bestial roar as he hefted the stone in his arms, hoisting it above his head. Veins the size of small branches popped out along his neck and forehead and he took a single, wobbling step forward. Zhy thought the ground beneath trembled, and he wasn't sure if it was from the weight Fanlas carried or the horde of demons below.

One of the Hjor soldiers watched in awe as Bimb's father carried the huge weight by himself. No, all of the Hjor, and all of the Welcferians watched a single man heave the heavy weight by himself—on orders from Drunplug they remained still. However, there was something disturbingly wrong with one young Hjor—his eyes were too wide and never blinking, and he bounced on his heels as if he would spring—

Which he did, straight at Fanlas!

The deranged Hjor leapt the hundred paces between the line and Fanlas in nearly a single bound. The Hjor was upon Fanlas before any of the other soldiers could nock an arrow.

"Gozath! Ruler! Evil! Die! Love of the spirits!" the man screamed as he launched at Fanlas's leg. Teeth dug into his calf.

The strong man grimaced but never faltered with his load. Instead, he snapped an epitaph through clenched teeth, then muttered, "Can—someone—please—get—it—"

It's time to act again, a voice echoed in Zhy's head. He ran after the man and kicked him in the stomach, but the deranged man clung to Bimb's father. Zhy cursed, then lashed out once more. His boot connected with the stomach, but with little success. The man was like a rabid dog locked on its prey.

Wrenflang watched out of the corner of his eyes, not daring to take his focus off the task at hand. Fanlas kicked out violently with his own foot, trying not to lose his heavy load, yet also knock loose his attacker. With one more thrust of his powerful legs, Fanlas thrashed outward, and the demented soldier ripped free with a tearing of clothing and flesh. Bimb's father stumbled, but held the heavy lid steady and plodded forward.

Free from his host, the Hjor faltered in the courtyard, righted himself, then launched himself once more at Fanlas—

Only to be riddled with a Hjor arrow.

The demon recoiled slightly, giving Fanlas a sliver of an opening from which to stumble forward, dragging his shredded leg and hefting the lid.

Hjor Hjor ambled over to the corpse and unceremoniously sliced its head. He grunted something at Wrenflang, then returned to his men.

Fanlas stepped forward. Wrenflang released his bundle and Bimb's father immediately dropped the heavy lid atop the opening.

Hjor looked into Wrenflang's eyes and noticed that his whites had returned, if only small speckles—the leader of the native Welcferians nodded, then looked back at Drunplug. The commander stood perfectly still, watching.

"I believe it would be wise to retreat," Drunplug said, loud enough for all to hear.

"We are safe," Wrenflang said softly.

The ground rippled and men panicked. But the tremor was slight and did not repeat itself. Drunplug shouted at his troops and they calmed themselves, mostly; many still shifted nervously, exchanging looks between the cap and the frozen ground.

Wrenflang spoke again. "Stay strong, maybe one more—"

The ground buckled again and loud murmurs went up from the Hjor and Welcferians, but again Wrenflang attempted a calming reply. None listened. It took coaching from both Drunplug and Hjor Hjor to settle them down, and even then the soldiers stared at Wrenflang.

"What now, mage?" Drunplug asked.

Wrenflang gave him a curious look, then nodded at the Hjor soldiers. He turned to Zhy, a half smile on his lips. Zhy started: The mage's eyes were now blue! A sparkling, stunning blue.

"It is over."

With that, he turned and walked back toward the castle.

Chapter 34

How it All Goes Down

*The powers that Man possesses can easily be
its salvation or its damnation*

Seer Zher'Wen

A dozen frozen corpses.

That was enough to nearly destroy the demonic underworld. If the men had been able to watch the events unfold beneath the surface, they would have stared in bewilderment at the power that a few dead demons could unleash. Wrenflang's tactic had worked nearly perfectly; and, as Zhy would try to deny, the question from Zhy was the spark to the idea.

The entire chain of events needed precision and flawless timing and spacing. Demonic scales were impervious to the blistering heat, mostly; while the outer shell protected their bodies, heat still penetrated to their core, even as it would a man seeking shelter from a fire in a metallic structure: the flames may not touch him, but he would surely feel the heat.

Wrenflang's masterwork was to create a thin shell of magic around the main "explosive," a shell that would eventually fail against the rising temperatures in the hellish underworld. That failure was part of the plan, designed to occur only after the bundle had dropped several hundred feet below the surface. Wrenflang counted on a tunnel system that descended rapidly downward, and he had gambled correctly.

Once the outer shell failed from the heat, it would expose that heat to the frozen particles within the strange balloon. These particles were the very pieces of air that had been cooled far beyond freezing.

In the spaces between matter, Wrenflang had untied the very components of air and super-cooled them with Toular's technique... getting that substance into the bubble was the hardest challenge in the already cold air.

After Wrenflang dropped the bundle down the shaft, it bounced off a rock—very nearly striking a jagged outcropping nearby, which would have ended the entire process. However, the package rolled smoothly down the hill, the demons that approached the top avoided the strange load of corpses that bounced down the terrible cavern. As it dropped deeper into the earth, the shells of the balloons warmed, eventually heating the thin ward that Wrenflang had set around the frozen gasses.

When at last the film burst, the resulting explosion was greater than the rending of the mountain that Bimb had accomplished. The super-frozen gasses, when exposed to the heat of the underworld, expanded from the small bubble into a sheet of liquid ice in under a second—in the confined space of the tunnels, this ever-expanding mass had nowhere to go but down, down, ever downward, to fill nooks and corners of the depths. After two seconds, the flowing gasses had heated beyond their point of containment and *pushed* against the rock sides of the tunnels, but most the rock was solid enough that it gave no more than a thousandth of an inch. Most. In the resulting explosion, softer rock shattered under the violence of the event, collapsing the tunnels down, one upon the other, nearly infinitely into the very pit of Hell itself. Since the tunnels didn't start to honeycomb until several hundred feet lower than the surface, the solid rock above held firm, though the explosion was still enough to cause small ripples above ground.

Though heat would return to the underworld, the super-cooled explosion dropped the temperature to literally thousands of degrees below zero. Coupled with the shockwave of the denotation, this abrupt change in climate was enough to end the lives of *billions* of demons.

Wrenflang had done it....

He had frozen Hell.

φ

Zhy and Fanlas followed Wrenflang, thinking he was going straight to the castle; however, the mage turned abruptly around and walked back toward the sealed portal. He scowled and directed his attention to the ring of ice and snow that he had had the men place around it— by now, the solid blocks had been trampled by feet, demons, and was stained red with blood.

"Is something wrong?" Fanlas asked quietly.

"No, we've done it, Fanlas, but I think I'd like some insurance."

"How so?" Zhy wondered.

The mage scanned the courtyard and the mountain beyond. They had taken most of the snow and ice from the mountain, and the bare rock and dirt that was exposed could be a good material to bury the cover... but working with frozen dirt would take months, since they had no means of transporting it.

"Well, I can do some later. Anyway," he said quickly, drowning the growing question from Zhy, "we can at least move this ice and snow atop of it."

The Hjor and Welcferian men had quit milling around and were now in the process of packing up gear and weapons. While a few nodded respectfully at Wrenflang, many avoided his gaze, and his person, by several paces, instead only paying attention to his respective leader.

Wrenflang grumbled and called Drunplug and Hjor Hjor to him—they reluctantly obeyed.

"Are you both done with your childish behavior?"

"Listen, there is no need to—"

"Drunplug, what you and the Hjor did borders on treason. No, it *is* treason, though right now, you belong to no authority, your treason was against the world. What was the reasoning behind that pathetic charade?"

Hjor Hjor cleared his throat and stammered. "You had gone—we believed that you had gone crazy and we were prepared to... er, well—"

Drunplug stiffened. "We thought you had been taken by the animal that bit you. So far any man who is taken by a mulargh is dead or possessed himself."

"I'm not any man!" Wrenflang snapped, then scowled, regretting his words.

"We realize that. Now." Drunplug tried to will the embarrassment from his face, but could feel the red blotches growing. Perhaps the overgrowth of whiskers could cover it up.

"You are very lucky," Zhy heard himself say.

"Are we done?" Wrenflang asked, not allowing any more response. "Good, then I need your help once more—they are free to finish their packing. We'll all leave through the pass, but first we need to move all of this snow back atop this—thing."

Drunplug and Hjor Hjor nodded and returned to their men.

"What are you doing?" Fanlas asked.

"Doing something that should have been done a long time ago, apart from reversing the existence of this thing in the first place. While that is impossible, we can put a ward on this portal that will prevent any further encroachment from here."

"But..." Zhy wondered, thumbing his earlobe. "Didn't you solve the problem already?"

Wrenflang nodded. "I think I have, but this barrier needs to be here, before we bury the thing."

Fanlas and Zhy watched as Wrenflang strung together a complex array of threads. The resulting knot of light looked like a child's game gone awry, but organized in some strange fashion; each beginning and ending seemed to be a reverse of the other, but still locked into the pattern. Deftly, he stretched the web out and around the cover of the pit, pulling it down like a cloth covering on a jar.

Zhy's eyes reflected the myriad array of colors, and he watched in awe as each thread slowly turned to a bright, pulsating red.

φ

Drunplug and Hjor Hjor let most of their men start through the pass ahead of them, while each turned back to Fanlas, Zhy, and Wrenflang.

"Farewell." The old mage sucked in air then blew it out. "May we never meet here again."

The men walked slowly away from the castle, toward the rift in the mountain that Bimb had created. A few chattered idly, and even more cast glances back at the old man who had saved the world.

Zhy and Fanlas watched the soldiers leave. Hjor Hjor had gone a few paces, then turned, and walked back to Fanlas. He beamed at Bimb's father.

"Well, what about you, Hjor Hjor?" Fanlas asked. "Are you going to go back to the Icedown Plains?"

"No," the big man said in his flat voice. "We'll be heading back to Foltrag. Drunplug has decided to escort us there, so we can explain our history. Maybe they have seen the demons, and maybe they will understand that we helped. And," he added, looking long at Zhy. "We will declare that a new Zhyfrael has redeemed us, a Zhyfrael in a man's body."

Zhy nodded absently, not hearing. Then it crashed into him. *A new Zhyfrael...?* "No, I. *No!*" he repeated.

"Oh yes, Zhyfrael... oh yes," Hjor Hjor replied with a smile.

"I hope you are successful," Fanlas said softly, waving off another protest from Zhy. It was time the boy realized how important he truly was. "You are welcome to travel with us until we head south for M'Hzrut."

"Thank you."

Drunplug had paused, watching. He waited for the others to catch up. Wrenflang lagged behind them all, head down.

φ

They had just entered the mouth of the large canyon that Bimb had created when Wrenflang called a stop. He motioned the Hjor and Welcferians to continue, and they trudged on gratefully.

"It isn't finished, my friends," the mage said, his voice hoarse. "An old university saying is 'the learning never ceases.' The greater battle does not end, though we have won here today."

"I imagine there are more demons in the world that need to be killed?" Zhy offered.

The mage nodded. "I hope others are engaged in that task. It's not that, Zhy, but something else. Remember I told you that simply sealing this would not be the solution? This was the major source, but not the only one. Others may be working to seal those other points." He blew out steam again, and cocked his ear, facing southeast. "I understand this place. Finally. And why I was supposed to come here."

"I thought your plans..." Zhy trailed off, shaking his head. "What *were* your plans anyway?"

"I wish I knew them all," he chuckled. "When Fanlas found me at that inn in Vronga, I could tell something big was happening. I didn't realize how big." He cocked an ear. "I can still hear a buzz, Zhy. Far, far in the back of my mind, I hear it."

"What are you getting at, Wrenflang?" Zhy asked. "Do you mean to stay here?"

"I have to."

Fanlas stared at the two men.

Zhy scowled. "Wrenflang, I have one question—*who* put the huge slab down? Who opened the portal in the first place?"

The mage bit his lip, then grimaced as the cold bit through the small cut that had developed. "That is something many of us would like to know... the question has an answer, far back in history, you could find something in the Archives perhaps, but..." he trailed off.

"It has bothered me," Fanlas put in, grimacing. "We spent our energy on ending things, on closing this up. I thought about it many times—how did this get here in the first place?"

"What madman would put it here?" Zhy asked as soon as Fanlas had finished.

"My friends, anyone who knows the answer to that question is long dead. And if anything remains in the Archives, which I doubt, the paper has long faded, or it's written in some long-dead variation of our language. No, you'll never find the answer to that question—we simply have to react to the actions of a madman. Perhaps actions taken a thousand years ago."

Such an answer was infuriating. As a child, Zhy had often questioned his father, posing him riddles that did not have answers. Each time Zhy would work himself into a rage of frustration—why were there not answers to *everything?* Especially to the largest question of all: Who had opened a portal to the demonic underworld, and why? Why?

"Zhy, you are muttering to yourself again."

"I-I'm sorry, Wrenflang. I wish we had answers to it."

"Son, sometimes questions have no answers." Zhy's throat caught—with those words, Fanlas suddenly sounded like Zhy's own father.

Zhy stopped. "Wait, something is wrong."

The grizzled mage turned back, a look of irritation on his face. "Yes, Zhy?"

"Through all of this, through the battles, not a single person has turned on us."

"What do you mean?" Wrenflang asked, the start of a scowl forming on his frozen lips.

"Bimb, Yulchar, even Ar'Zoth in his own way—they have all turned on me or my companions... We had one Hjor go insane, but who will turn now?"

"Ha! Zhy, don't you get it?"

"No." A confused shake of the head.

"This is the last chapter—well, not the last, but at least we are mostly near the end. There is no time for that. The story must close, it must be untied!" he barked a laugh and turned away, his white hair flowing, small pieces of frozen sweat clinking together as he trotted away.

"But—" Zhy called after him. Then he smiled. "Untied."

Wrenflang's only reply was a wave of his right hand.

Zhy turned to Fanlas. "Well, what do you think?"

"Me?" the burly man shrugged. "I didn't understand a word you two just said." And he turned and trudged toward the Temple of M'Hzrut.

Zhy made to leave, but stopped short. There was still an unanswered question—a thousand of them, of course, but at least one nagging doubt that needed an answer before he left the man here in the north. Zhy thought about the power that the mage had displayed, the ability to freeze the underworld itself, and his black, dark eyes. Eyes that were now blue. And then he though on the net of lights, the web of *red*, deep, scarlet filaments of light, knotted impossibly. Red!

"Wrenflang, wait!" The mage stopped and turned, still smiling. "Are you...?" Zhy wondered. He took a few steps toward Wrenflang, and the old mage likewise walked closer to Zhy.

Wrenflang could see the calculating behind Zhy's face, his processing of the past events. He nodded slowly, his gray head suddenly appearing younger and fuller. "Am I what?"

"I've thought a lot about what you have done. The spells you knew, the red net of light... working with the demons that way. Even though they were corpses. You aren't really a—"

"You could say that is what I am," he answered.

"Thank you," was all Zhy could manage.

"No, Zhyfrael, thank you. You can deny yourself until you die, but this world is safe because of your actions. We worked together, but you provided the key. Don't ever forget that."

He was beyond protesting, his lower lip shook violently. "I won't."

The others were a good quarter of a mile away, but yet Zhy and Wrenflang still stood among a swirling cloud of snowflakes, staring at one another, each trying to capture the others' face for their permanent memory. Months of travel, tribulation, battles, and a final unbelievable encounter were now at an end.

"So this is farewell, then?"

Wrenflang trudged closer. "Well, Zhy, I suppose it could be. But I'll get to work on fixing those stairs... somehow." He chuckled. "Maybe let some folks know, back in Foltrag, the Temple, or even back in Belden, won't you? Everyone needs to know, as much as they don't want to." His eyes misted and he cleared his throat. "Farwell, Zhy," he said at last.

Zhy pulled the old man toward him in a sudden show of emotion. Tears froze on Zhy's cheeks. Tears that he was glad to let freeze, and not fall to the bottom of a canyon, honest tears of joy and the pain of goodbye—not tears of death or madness. His throat felt oversized with the lump blossoming inside it, and he turned quickly to walk eastward, head down, face slicked with salty frozen ice.

Chapter 35

Death of a Horde

When the pillars fall and the Temple crumbles, demons will spill out upon the earth, devouring all creatures, all men, all living things. The world will cease.

High Cleric Gorand

The larger battle turned with an audible snap of silence. When not burning from a mage's fire, or pierced by an archer's arrow, demons were crashing into trees or jumping from heights. Old men would simply collapse in heaps of dead flesh and shattered bones.

Warlocks' spells against the feared mulargh were nearly useless, for the animals careened from the sky seemingly of their own accord. Above one small village near Moult, a giant hawk lifted from the marsh and rocketed skyward toward a swooping mulargh. Onlookers stared open-mouthed as the smaller bird attacked the much larger prey and rendered it senseless—by digging its talons into its soft underbelly and flipping it over on its back in the air, the hawk incapacitated the demonic beast and it hung limply in the air, its appendages flapping. A brief, short screech burst from the mulargh's jaws, then silence. The hawk flew over a rise with the dead creature in its teeth.

With Wrenflang's occasional control of the demons, coupled with the closing of the small portals, the demonic threat was eroding quickly from Belden's landscape. But Wrenflang also knew that his vigilance would be tested and that his skill would not be lost in the cold north—madness could overtake him if he was not careful. Yet, the hushed silence that hovered wonderfully over the country felt much different and much more manageable; if Ar'Zoth still lived, he would have breathed a heavy sigh of relief. Still, the threat was never completely eliminated.

$$\phi$$

Rhys and Felyar had reached the first exit in the Tunnels when the blue lights dimmed, flickered, and went black. Red light danced on Felyar's fingers but faded—there was nothing left, no energy for casting spells.

"Great Sacuan's..."

Rhys opened his mouth to reply, but found even that too difficult. *Best to die here, I guess.*

There was energy, however, to fling hands over eyes when the lights burst back to life. The blue light was blinding, as if staring at the sun's reflection off of a well-polished mirror. "What!" Rhys screamed.

Felyar slouched, then slipped down to the damp ground. "It's over," he breathed.

"Over? How do you know?"

"I can feel the demons, now. Or the lack of them. They are—I don't hear the buzzing as loud. It's as if someone is controlling them. It's... *quiet*," he added with a sigh.

Rhys stared, then shook his head.

"No wonder warlocks go mad."

Felyar shot him a glance, scratched his nose, then burst out laughing.

φ

As long as a skilled warlock held the castle in the Spires, the bulk of the demonic horde was kept in check. Though demons could still spill out into the world, knights of the Black Dawn were able and ready to handle any minor disturbances, although Drana would soon change their name, hoping dearly to simply merge them within the Counsel Guard.

Villagers slowly picked themselves from the carpet of devastation and began to put their lives together again. What could be replaced or fixed was done so with care, while the loss of life was marked with gravestones or simple epitaphs. In the south, flowers adorned the tombs of the deceased, while such foliage would have to wait until spring in the north.

φ

Heayar—the last living person still at the Temple of M'Hzrut—still waited by the fire, which had now dwindled to coals. He had quickly burned through the large stack of wood and was reluctant to fetch more, fearing that a swath of demons would burst through the door—or worse, that nothing would happen and he would be stuck here, alone.

When the knock came at the door, he leapt, readying his spells. "Come in!" he barked.

His arms fell heavy to his sides and he nearly collapsed as three fresh Protectors entered the temple, faces flush from the cold and eyes wide with—hope? *Hope?*

"Thank Sacuan you are alive!" one exclaimed.

"I'm... yes, I guess I am." *The lights, what about the lights? Why are these men still alive?*

"Can I tell him?" One of the Protectors asked excitedly of his companions, who nodded.

"Tell me what?"

"The demons, they are dead."

"Dead?"

"All of them!"

"What? Not all? Surely... what madness—"

"Yes, yes, have you not heard! As one they began to die, and the ones we didn't flip over (a long story, you will have to hear soon), were easily killed. It's over! It's *over!*"

Heayar finally collapsed.

Chapter 36

After

Our work must never end. We may allow ourselves only little rest before returning to our tasks.

High Cleric Bertrand

Wrenflang scoured the massive castle, looking for a teapot that wasn't shattered or bent beyond recognition. "Was it you, Ar'Zoth, or Bimb who did all this?" he wondered, staring at the chaotic mess that both men had left behind. The shattered chandelier still clogged the entry way, though he had swept away the small shards. No point in having that if the stairs were gone, however; well at least until he could fix them. Maybe in a few years. The grizzled mage gave up and retrieved the battered pewter set from in front of the fireplace, and set to hammering out the dents with a kitchen ladle.

"This will take some time," he thought as he worked. As he did so, he thought back on Ar'Zoth, and what little he knew of him. The master warlock was always a little unstable, but in a way of a prodigy, not a psychotic who was bent on unleashing total destruction. Had Wrenflang had any information on Ar'Zoth's exile, he would have done something—but it was too late now.

"Ar'Zoth, old man," he said staring into the fire, "I'm sorry it has come to this. I should be able to keep things in order." His thoughts went out to the courtyard. Soon his aged feet followed, and he looked at their handiwork. The ice and snow still lay atop the deadly portal, and strain as he might, he could hear nothing. No loud buzzing, hissing, crying for release. Only the whisper of snowflakes. The buzzing was there, to be sure, but so muted that it didn't matter anymore.

As he let go of himself and let his mind's eye travel out over the distance of Welcfer and Belden, he could feel the demons as they died, could taste the metallic blood in their mouths as they let go of their grip on life. A few hunters remained, most likely Knights of the Black Dawn, and Wrenflang felt the tips of their swords as they punched through the hearts of the remaining creatures. The mage sighed, rubbed his nose.

"He called me Ugly Nose," he whispered.

φ

A hot sun rose quickly in Belden City, baking the clay roof tiles, and driving the citizens to shade or cool buildings. A burly innkeeper arranged his tables and stools, pausing longingly at one well-polished stool. He shook his head sadly, wiped his brow, and continued with his work.

The sun's rays beat hotter on the western edge of town. In a crumbling house, a thin curtain rod gave way and a ragged cloth fell to the ground, sending a sheet of sunlight into the room. Dust hung in a thick cloud, and the grimy window was thick with soil, but neither could match for the intensity of the light pouring in through the dirty window.

He awoke with a jolt.

"Not again," he groaned. His lips were cracked and his mouth a thick wad of cotton, but somehow the words seemed crisp and clean in his mouth.

Expecting a searing pain, he rose slowly, but was more than surprised to note that his muscles were loose and limber, and his head was clear and clean. But he was thirsty. A brief picture of an ale mug flashed across his eyes, but it was replaced quickly by an image of an overflowing cistern.

He nearly stuck his entire head in the bucket from the well, and he drank until his stomach felt like bursting. Zhy drank so much water, he needed to lay down in the brittle grass and let the sun bake his face while his body slowly digested the ice-cold liquid. *Cold... I never thought I'd enjoy cold again.* He was so focused on slaking his thirst, that his mind did not register the late autumn sun, the dry, barely-green grass.

A sun that should not be.

He had traveled—again—for thousands of miles, battled with the demonic underworld, faced the feared savages of Welcfer, and—his mind caught on that tired old cliché—he had frozen Hell. Now he was home? In the autumn?

"Have I died again?" he croaked.

Another glance at the trees eased his sudden fear: the leaves and stems that remained were green. They were *budding*, not falling. It was Spring! He rubbed his eyes, and remembered the long journey back through the Tunnels, through the burned-out husk that was Forshen, and back along a road littered with wagons, dead horses, and the bodies of men. But everyone he had encountered seemed joyous, free, and happy as they began rebuilding. A little voice in his head had wanted him to proclaim to them his victory, *their* victory over the demons, but the voice of Father would burst in and reproach him as an arrogant fool.

"I'm not dead this time," he muttered to himself. "And no gherwza brought me home, either!" he remarked with a sudden bright smile. Spring. Spring! "I'm not dead!" he barked.

Zhy chuckled again.

He remembered collapsing after the battle, or was that after the long haul to the Temple? His feet felt sore, as if he had walked on stone. Stone! Yes, stone, the Tunnels, again. Again, again, again. Why had everything happened at least three times? He shook his head and looked around again, double-checking to ensure it still was spring. The warmth, the color of the trees, and the slowly-greening weeds in his yard didn't lie. The hush of the surf was muted, but louder somehow, more awake.

"So what in Sacuan's name..." he trailed off, his gaze stuck on the well. With a start, he returned inside and gazed at his reflection in the dirty mirror.

"I haven't shaved in weeks, but that's all I have for a beard? What in—" Abruptly he stopped. His glance darted everywhere and nowhere, and he quickly knew where he had to go and what he had to do.

"Time," he muttered as he slammed the door behind him. "Good evening," he said to the small child playing sticks in the street. His mind raced faster as he ran through the events of the past few days, and then he stopped abruptly.

"This is so cliché. Beyond the pale," he groaned, holding his head in his hands. "No, no it can't be. I'm going to walk into that inn, yes, and..." he trailed off as he picked up his pace.

His hand paused in front of the door handle of the inn.

"Now, Zhy," he muttered to himself, uncaring if anyone saw him, "you will open that door. Kahl will greet you. Maybe get an—no, no, just a water, more water. And food. Lots of food. It was all a dream, a horrible, pathetic dream, that is so cliché I think I could vomit."

But what if he's there? A voice whispered.

"Then it's even worse," he spat. "You've pushed me too far. It can't end like this."

Oh, it can. And it will. But maybe you should stop thinking that this is some sort of contrived story and finally be the hero. You've had plenty of opportunity.

"I'm not a hero," he spat. A grizzled patron nearly bowled him over as he exited. Seeing Zhy talking to himself did not faze the man—he merely smiled briefly and went on his way as if he had seen Zhy only last week.

"Not a hero," Zhy repeated, opening the door—

—And he nearly fell over when he saw a familiar bulky shape in his seat.

This was a dream, a horrible...

But after he rubbed his eyes and looked again, the figure belonged to no person that he knew; the man was bulky, dressed for adventure, but not Bruce. With a heavy sigh of relief and a twinge of sadness, Zhy nodded to the man, and to Kahl, and sat down.

Kahl paled, his hand frozen in the act of pulling an ale. His mustache-covered mouth dropped open a few inches. Zhy swore he saw the moisture pool in his dark eyes. "Good afternoon, Kahl."

"I—" the big man cleared his throat. "I—I don't—Zhy? No, it can't—" He bellowed. "ZHY! *ZHY!*" Suddenly unfrozen, he shook himself, let the glass drop on the bar, and raced from behind the counter, trotted toward Zhy; and lifted him up off of his stool with a massive hug. Joints popped and creaked, and Kahl clapped him hard on the back with his meaty paws. "I am so relieved, Zhy," he said, his voice muffled in Zhy's shoulder. "You have no idea how you have been missed." Kahl held him like that, the only sound in the bar was the creak of joints and quiet sniffing from within the folds of Zhy's shirt.

The stranger regarded the scene with a look of bewilderment on his face. A face without scars.

Zhy couldn't help but smiling as the burly innkeeper let him go, his own tears slick on his face. Kahl took a step backward to regard him.

"Yes, Kahl, I survived. Well, no, not really. I died—I died at one point, but that's for another story. It is good to see you." He opened his mouth to say more, but again his throat caught and he fell silent.

"Here, here, let me get you an ale!" Kahl wrung his hands and turned clumsily to face the bar.

"No, Kahl, thank you," he said, holding up a hand. "I would only like some food, and water. But in a moment. How have you fared?"

The bulky form swung back to face Zhy, the smile still plastered on Kahl's rugged features. "Me? Oh, I have fared better... it has been quiet without you. But by Sacuan I am glad you are back." Suddenly his eyes darted to the stranger, and then back to Zhy. "But where is—"

"Bruce, he... he did not survive. Nor did Darrell, our companion, he—"

"I know Darrell," Kahl said, with a smirk and a twinkle in his eye. "I know them both well—I'm sorry it went poorly. But here, here, that is for another day... I was just trying to convince this man here not to go north, he seems to be on the same misguided adventure Bruce was." Kahl winked at Zhy's dumfounded expression—how could Kahl know about Darrell?

Still staring at Kahl, Zhy addressed the stranger. "No, don't bother, if you're going to find Ar'Zoth, whatever you have found out, it is not worth it."

"And why is that?" the man snapped, his voice thin and reedy. "You don't think he will teach me?" His eyes suddenly narrowed. "How do you know about—?"

"He would have killed you, as he did my companions."

"Your—"

"You best get to Vronga and study, that is your only option. Don't bother with Ar'Zoth, or Bimb, or whatever his name."

"Bimb...? I don't follow—"

Zhy let his gaze drop from a still-smiling Kahl and spun to face the man. "Ar'Zoth is dead."

"How do you—"

"Because I killed him."

He let the phrase float out into the inn and for a brief, sick moment, enjoyed the stares. *I'm not the hero!*

It wasn't the full truth—Bimb had killed Ar'Zoth, true, and it was Huyen who had killed Bimb, but without Zhy there, playing the role of the dead man that, Huyen never would have succeeded. His actions had saved the lives of so many... *And the archers, the freezing of the underworld...* With a sinking feeling, Zhy realized that he would not be standing here had it not been for his own actions—the world would be overrun by demons. Sure, they had had help from Bimb after he, had died, but Zhy had been the center of it all. He nearly hung his head in frustration: *All this time I did not want to be the hero... I am not the hero.*

And the voice... the scathing voice returned. *Do you honestly think I would not cast it that way? I could not resist!*

He reached out to try and reply, but something seemed to snap in his mind, and the voice was gone—for some reason he could not explain, the voice was gone forever; it had fulfilled its objective.

"You...? How?" At this Kahl nearly burst out laughing, his smile was wide across his face and the rivers that flowed from his eyes were those of pure joy.

"Does it matter? If you'd like, I can tell you the whole, bloody story. But first I need to eat."

The innkeeper coughed again and nodded to himself. He ducked back in the kitchen and addressed someone there.

"You have help now?" Zhy wondered.

"Aye, the daughter and her man have returned and play music at night. They also cook, and the food has never been better." His face was permanently etched in a satisfied smile.

Zhy shook his head. "I thought they tired of your greed." He regretted the words as soon as they left his mouth, but Kahl did not bat an eye.

"No, they—well, yes," he said, pausing. "But that greed was for a purpose, and now they have returned."

Zhy could only wonder at what that meant.

Kahl returned from the kitchen, and absently wiped a smudge from the bar. The stranger sipped his ale. Zhy looked around, glad that the place was not shrouded in a fog of alcoholic stupor and he smiled his own smile, comfortable at last in a place he thought he would never again see, in a town he thought he had lost. And he reflected on his long adventure and the precarious situation he, Bruce and Darrell had placed Belden into; had they not traveled north, what would the outcome have been? Or was the trip necessary in the long run? He stared blankly at the bar as the thoughts washed over him.

"What are ye thinking?" Kahl asked, a massive plate of steaming lamb and boiled potatoes in his hands. He set it down in front of Zhy.

"Oh..." he began. The meat smelled wonderful and his stomach rumbled. "About the whole journey... after this is gone I'll have to tell you."

"We'd enjoy hearing every detail, especially if you killed a dangerous warlock!" the stranger piped.

Zhy swallowed a lump of meat. By Sacuan, it was delicious! "It was really the journey of a drunk," he replied softly, but his former self-deprecation had faded. "A drunkard's journey." Zhy chuckled. "And now it's over."

The innkeeper smiled. "I wouldn't call you a drunk anymore, Zhy." He clenched his rag. "You're a man now, Zhy. You've grown."

"So tell us about this warlock," the stranger piped. "Did you really kill him?"

Zhy let his eyes fall away from Kahl's and nodded slowly. "In a way... it's a long story, like I said. He was a very, very dangerous warlock."

Kahl's next words sent a chill up Zhy's spine: "The most dangerous man in the world, he was. It was a great risk you took to save the world, Zhy, you and your friends—it seems you had many more companions along the way. I want to hear it all. You have saved the world, Zhy, and for that we owe you more than we can pay."

The fork clanged loudly as it fell to the plate. Zhy stared numbly at Kahl, who only grinned. "How...?" he began. "What do you know, Kahl, and when did you—"

The burly innkeeper chuckled, and then winked at Zhy, his bushy eyebrow dipping like a protective blanket. "I know everything. Zhyfrael."

Epilogue

Fa, my knot is going to be untied forever, now. I have to move to the final place...

"I thought you had gone."

Part of me is already there, I can feel it pulling. I have done much... you were able to go through the mountain because of me, because of what I was able to do. It took much effort, and I may have caused more problems learning my way, but I hope I have repaid the world for my sins.

"You have, son, you have. When I saw the mountain move of its own accord, I knew it was you, I could feel you and hear you, though you have gone. I love you. I look to the day when I can see you."

I love you Fa. Please, you must write this down, I don't have much time... write it all down. Perhaps someday you can share this, maybe as a story, though we all know it is the final truth of what happened. The world had almost ended at the hands of an idiot child, and had been saved at the hands of a wandering drunk. The story must be told.

Fanlas awoke and began writing. His eyes were glazed and the light was dim, but his hand was a blur as he wrote and wrote and wrote. When finally his head sank to the desk and sleep took him over, Bimb ducked back for one brief second before vanishing forever.

One thousand, four-hundred and seventy six turnips. I counted, Fa. I can count real good. I'm going to play the Sutan now—

φ

"*Ma?*"

"*Bimb, I am here...*"

He sighed... this world was different than the others. It was vivid and clear, and stunning! The final death was one of peace and contentment.

Bimb was home.

"*Bimb, Lyn is here.*"

"*Hello, Bimb, I am sorry for everything.*"

"*I am sorry Lyn. I wanted to be strong and smart. And play the sutan. I killed your son. He killed me.*"

"*Yes, Bimb,*" *Lyn replied. "You have done things right. You have fixed much... and in his own way, my son has also done good to help the world.*"

At that he smiled. "Your son saved the world."

"*It is good to know that." He said this as if there were never a doubt.*

And Lyn floated away.

Bimb turned to drift toward a stunning vista—a sun-splashed mountain range, a ring of clouds encircled the upper peaks, and magnificent birds that flew in high, arcing circles. He stood atop a rampart, breezes blowing past; behind him a dozen sutans were lined up, perfectly in tune. He bent to pick one up, when a voice stopped him—a voice he had never heard.

"*I wanted to thank you as well, and I will thank this Zhy whenever I should see him here. Bimb, I am glad you have done good by the world. And by my name.*"

At that, huge arms embraced his incorporeal form, the towering figure beamed at him with ageless features, and was gone.

φ

They had called him greedy, and thankfully accepted his apologies, after the ordeal. But he had had to be a little avaricious and overbearing. It took money to bribe away a Welcferian mage and place him dead in the path of Bruce and Zhy. It took plenty of money to pull Bruce away from a lucrative engagement on the down-west coast, and still convince him that the warlock was there. The note in the trunk was clever—thanks to a friend's uncle. But everyone wanted money to stay quiet or forget things. Everyone wanted money. Money, money, money.

Especially the Keeper.

When Kahl had heard a story a secret tunnel, and then another about warlocks in exile, he started to think. In his youth he'd read many tales about doomsday and the end of the world, and something about warlocks and demons struck a chord. Not fully convinced of the veracity of his strange obsession, he wanted more information; so he headed to the Archives. Turned away, he had to come up with a better plan, which involved money. Lots of it. As humble as he portrayed himself, the Keeper enjoyed the finer things in life (his tea set alone cost more than Kahl's first house.)

And once he discovered the truth of Ar'Zoth and the disastrous mix-up in paperwork, Kahl set wheels in motion. Like Jafren, he knew that the Counsel would never listen to the flimsy evidence, and that it was a lost cause to try with Gorand. So he started his own machine.

There were many moving parts, and it took years to get them going, but at last, when the mercenary sat down on the stool, Kahl's heart skipped a beat and he knew then that his plan had been invoked. In Zhy he had seen several things. Like everyone else, he saw the stumbling, pathetic drunk. But he could also see glimpses of the man's father—a hard-working, dedicated person who would gladly sacrifice himself for the good of others. There were many tough men who came and went—but they would be too eager for glory and fame. Zhy, on the other hand, would deny to the end that he was any type of hero, but would persevere and complete the task. Kahl hoped that the cold and unforgiving climate of the north would keep Zhy sober.

That had been his plan.

He did not count on Bimb, the Knights of the Black Dawn, or any of the twists and turns that Zhy had faced, but he had set the machine in motion and now he beamed at his accomplishment. So Zhy claimed he was not any type of hero? His father had been a hero in his own way—strong, clever, quick-witted; Zhy possessed those qualities, but he had kept them so buried in ale that he didn't know he had them. Kahl had seen flashes. His plan relied on Bruce keeping Zhy sober and a string of good luck.

The only kind of luck that comes in stories.

Kahl had drawn the plans, even if Zhy did not know there were plans. Zhy carried them out, but Kahl had laid them.

He smiled again and wiped the bar.

It was finished.

The End of A Drunkard's Journey

Some More Words

Well, there you have it. It's not the next Jane Eyre or Crime and Punishment. It's not even close to the Wheel of Time. But it was fun. This series was a joy to write, although this last installment gave me some fits, mainly because I just didn't want the story to end. But it had to be concluded and I am happy that everything (sort of) worked out in the end.

There are a billion people to thank for this entire story. A heaping ton of thanks goes to my fearless editor Amy Eye, who kept this ship upright and pulled be back from the dark abyss time and again. The very first incarnation of this entire story was a rambling, shambling, monstrous pile of goo that she helped me solidify and tighten up. For this story, I enlisted the help of Jodi Ralston, and she provided excellent critique of the plot, the threads, the direction of the story (or lack thereof).

A big thank-you also to the cover designer, Karri Klawiter, for creating one hell of a cool cover concept!

I need to thank my family for putting up with my use of the phrase "Great Sacuan's Scrotum!" and reminder that Antarctica looks like the Spires, not the reverse. Thank you to my co-workers at my "real" job—for those who have read this, or those who have passed it to others, I really appreciate the kindness! Thanks also to the readers of this story—the suggestions you have made have been considered, and many incorporated in the slight revisions to Part I... keep the ideas coming folks! I want to especially thank those who read this, don't like it, and tell the world. It means that it's not perfect. Nothing is. But that doesn't mean we can't continually improve ourselves and work to deliver our best.

In-Laws, out-laws, and to anyone who has read my work, or even thought of reading it, I am very thankful.